# Cool, Sweet Water
## Selected Stories

## PAKISTAN WRITERS SERIES

### SERIES EDITOR: MUHAMMAD UMAR MEMON

**Khadija Mastur** was born in 1927 in Lucknow and grew up in a family that valued learning, reading and political dialogue. Her father was an avid reader and her mother an active writer for sundry women's journals. With the death of her father in 1937, the family suffered unusual hardship but endured its ordeal with great dignity. Mastur and her younger sister, Hajira Masroor, worked actively for the Muslim League in 1946, and a year later, when Partition came along, her family migrated to Lahore, Pakistan. Here, in 1950, she became the secretary of the Lahore Branch of the Progressive Writers Association. Mastur married Zaheer Babar, a journalist and nephew of the well-known Pakistani poet and writer Ahmed Nadeem Qasmi. The couple had two children, a son, Parvez, and a daughter, Kiran. She spent the rest of her life in Lahore. She died in 1983 in a London clinic following a long and fatal illness.

Khadija Mastur wrote in a simple but eloquent style. She is the author of several collections of short stories and two novels, *Aangan* (The Courtyard), recipient of the Adamji Award, and *Zamin* (Earth). She was posthumously honoured with the Baba-e-Urdu, Dr. Abdul Haq Award for her collection of short stories *Thanda Meetha Pani* (Cold, Sweet Water).

**Tahira Naqvi**, who teaches English, has translated the works of Sa'adat Hasan Manto, Munshi Premchand, Hijab Ali, Ahmed Ali and, most recently, Ismat Chughtai. She also writes fiction in English. *Attar of Roses and Other Stories of Pakistan*, her first collection of short stories, was published in 1998 by Lynne Reinner Publishers and *Amreeka, Amreeka*, her second collection, will appear in the summer of 1999.

**Muhammad Umar Memon**, the Series Editor, is Professor at the University of Wisconsin. He is also a creative writer and critic and has translated widely from Urdu fiction, of which six volumes have appeared to date.

# Cool, Sweet Water
## Selected Stories

### Khadija Mastur

Translated by
TAHIRA NAQVI

Series Editor
MUHAMMAD UMAR MEMON

**OXFORD**
UNIVERSITY PRESS

# OXFORD
#### UNIVERSITY PRESS

Great Clarendon Street, Oxford OX2 6DP

Oxford University Press is a department of the University of Oxford.
It furthers the University's objective of excellence in research, scholarship,
and education by publishing worldwide in

Oxford  New York

Athens  Auckland  Bangkok  Bogotá  Buenos Aires  Calcutta
Cape Town  Chennai  Dar es Salaam  Delhi  Florence  Hong Kong  Istanbul
Karachi  Kuala Lumpur  Madrid  Melbourne  Mexico City  Mumbai
Nairobi  Paris  São Paulo  Singapore  Taipei  Tokyo  Toronto  Warsaw

with associated companies in Berlin  Ibadan

Oxford is a registered trade mark of Oxford University Press
in the UK and in certain other countries

© Oxford University Press 1999

The moral rights of the author have been asserted

First published 1999

All rights reserved. No part of this publication may be reproduced,
stored in a retrieval system, or transmitted, in any form or by any means,
without the prior permission in writing of Oxford University Press.
Enquiries concerning reproduction should be sent to
Oxford University Press at the address below.

This book is sold subject to the condition that it shall not, by way
of trade or otherwise, be lent, re-sold, hired out or otherwise circulated
without the publisher's prior consent in any form of binding or cover
other than that in which it is published and without a similar condition
including this condition being imposed on the subsequent purchaser.

ISBN 0 19 579053 7

Printed in Pakistan at
Al-Rehman Paper Craft, Karachi.
Published by
Ameena Saiyid, Oxford University Press
5-Bangalore Town, Sharae Faisal
PO Box 13033, Karachi-75350, Pakistan.

# Contents

Acknowledgements     vii

Introduction     ix

Glossary     xxxvii

They are Taking Me Away, Father, They are Taking Me Away!     1

The Miscreant     7

Excerpt from *Aangan*     24

Excerpt from *Zamin*—I     30

Excerpt from *Zamin*—II     37

Cool, Sweet Water     43

Suriya     49

Trust     57

Harvest     85

The Hand Pump     110

Springtime of Life     129

The Heart's Thirst     135

| | |
|---|---|
| In Stealth | 151 |
| Bhooray | 160 |
| Lost and Found | 175 |

*[handwritten annotation bracketing the three entries: "male point of view — women; social inequality"]*

# Acknowledgements

I am indebted to Professor Muhammad Umar Memon for his assistance and advice on matters of content and style, and for his patience. I would also like to thank OUP for giving me this opportunity to bring Khadija Mastur to those who may never read her in Urdu, and for their cooperation and patience when I was beset with time constraints. Finally, I would like to thank Ahmed Nadeem Qasmi Sahib for talking to me so graciously and with such ease about Khadija Mastur's life and works.

Tahira Naqvi

New York, December 1998

# INTRODUCTION

Khadija Mastur, one of the youngest members of the Progressive Writers' Movement, will be best remembered for her fictional portrayal of the unending anguish of ordinary people, scarred by poverty and denial; the frustration of women who have been left behind in the race for equal rights and social justice; and the tragedy of political upheavals that portend disaster for the common man. Like her predecessor, the well-known Indian writer Ismat Chughtai, she never deviated from what she considered important in her choice of subjects and steered clear of the temptation to explore issues which might be fashionable for the times, but with which she could not identify or for which she could not muster sufficient empathy; such writing would have smacked, inevitably, of insincerity and artifice, as some of the work produced by her contemporaries did.

Along with her sister Hajira Masroor, she is among the last of the class of writers who gave to Urdu fiction a sense of clarity of purpose and design, and in particular brought into focus the issues surrounding women's roles in the Muslim society of pre-Partition India and, later, Pakistan. Living and writing together and having a deep affinity for similar concerns, the two have been compared to the Brontë sisters. When asked about her preoccupation with women's lives, Mastur justified her position by saying that 'a woman in our society has many problems and a woman [writer] has to look at things from her own perspective.'[1]

Women writing about themselves and exploring personal, emotional and sexual issues was not common during the period when Chughtai and later Mastur took up the pen. In 'Alvida, Khadija Behan' (Goodbye! Sister Khadija), Mirza Adeeb, a noted writer, observes that 'when I saw Khadija I didn't want to believe that this was the same Khadija Mastur whose short stories had created such a stir in the literary world. I couldn't imagine that so much energy could be packed inside such a frail, weak girl.'[2]

Such observations were often made by male writers in those days, Ismat Chughtai's first published work, half a decade earlier, having been mistaken to be her brother Azim Beg Chughtai's when it first appeared in print. Adeeb continues by saying that he was astonished to discover that 'she [Mastur] was such a simple, homebody type of girl on the surface and such a rebel, a revolutionary in her work' (ibid.). She sat before him 'like a bundle, crouched in a chair, her eyes lowered bashfully, and both she and her sister Hajira were wearing burqas' (ibid.). Similar observations were often made about Chughtai as well and reveal what male writers and male readers perceived to be the 'proper' persona for women writers. Certainly these women were not expected to create a 'stir' and be 'rebels' or be 'revolutionary' in their work. Perhaps this attitude has continued to this day, through Partition and carried over into Pakistan's short literary history, and we have, sadly, only a few women writers of Urdu fiction today who can be viewed as rebels and revolutionaries.

Mastur's fiction is characterized by a stark, often disturbing realism that impresses the reader with its uncompromising tone, and owes a great deal to the fact that she wrote what she saw, what she knew. Her fiction grew out of her life, and her life provided her and her sister with firsthand experiences of privation and despair. Of all the women Progressive writers, she and Hajira Masroor were the only two who suffered extreme hardship. The vividly accurate descriptions of everyday life, the minute details of physical characteristics and personality traits, the keen observation of life in the streets, in the dark corners of penury and deprivation, all these have afforded her a special place in the annals of Urdu literature.

In his preface to Mastur's collection of short stories titled *Chand Roz Aur* (A Few More Days), Faiz Ahmed Faiz remarks that 'one of Mastur's characteristics is her specificity. She paints less and embroiders more.'[3] Here Faiz is referring to the economy of her style which, although not picturesque and prismatic, maintains a certain focused quality which helps her construct a lucid, perceptive, unaffected, and extremely powerful story. Unlike her predecessor Ismat Chughtai, she gives such primacy to plot and character that language is reduced to a secondary position. One tends to agree with Ahmed Nadeem Qasmi when he says in an essay about Mastur's style that 'no one realizes how difficult it is to create a simple sentence as opposed to a sentence that thunders, echoes, hisses, and screams.'[4] Unencumbered by the weight of a fanciful, complex writing style and by erudite scholarly references and literary allusions, her fiction flows as pure narrative, a river of events and emotions in which the reader is hurled along, without obstacles, to moments of grim realization about the harsh life of those who don't live in sprawling bungalows, are not privileged to attend English-medium schools—men and women who constitute the bulk of Pakistani society, people who are the pulse of a city or a nation, the masses whom many of us may never chance to know except perhaps in an *afsaana* by someone like Mastur. She belongs to the class of writers without whom the view of the world would become unredeemingly one-dimensional. Writers like her inform and move; sometimes, in fact, they may be our only link to the reality and diverse manifestations of life.

However, although her use of language does not function along the same lines as Chughtai's, Mastur, like Chughtai, never strays far from the harsh realities of the lives of men, women, and children who often survive in the underbelly of society. Again, like Chughtai, she focuses on women by writing about their pain and suffering in a candid and forthright manner. Much as other writers in the Progressive Movement, she endows her work with a brutal realism, one that compels the reader both to accept without question the pain and tragedy of her characters' lives as real and to question its unfairness. Avoiding oversentimentality and mawkishness, she lays bare the streak of anguish in the lives of characters like Suriya, the proud servant girl in the story 'Suriya'; Chunni Begum, the aging woman in

'The Hand Pump', who would not eat what she hadn't earned herself; Razia, in 'Trust', who struggles all her life to find fidelity in love; Kaneez of 'Harvest', who yearns in vain for a husband, a home, and respectability; and the young woman in 'The Heart's Thirst', who, stifled by poverty and the oppressive social mores of her society, seeks her heart's desire in the attentions of a lecherous, scheming shopkeeper, the beautiful suit he promises her becoming a metaphor for all that she is denied in life. But, as Muhammad Sadiq points out in his short and rather unsatisfactory discussion of Urdu fiction in *A History of Urdu Literature*, 'poor as her [Mastur's] people are, they are not passive and resigned ... [they] think that life is worth the struggle.'[5]

In addition to Mastur's powerful portrayals of women's lives, there are stories, a few included in the present selection also, that reflect her abiding interest—so commom among writers of her generation—in the consequences of Partition, especially in terms of its tragic destruction of human relationships, and of everything that was humane and civilized. Excerpts from Mastur's *Aangan* (Courtyard) and *Zamin* (Earth), her first and second novels respectively, have been placed in this selection to allow the reader a broader sense of Mastur's art and of her interest in exploring the devastating effects of socio-political strife on the lives of people. Where *Aangan*, written in Pakistan, examines the far-reaching consequences of Partition on the people who migrated to Pakistan in 1947, *Zamin* takes up the nation's futile attempts at regeneration and growth.

As with Ismat Chughtai, Sa'adat Hasan Manto, Qurratulain Hyder, Ahmed Nadeem Qasmi, Krishan Chander, Rajinder Singh Bedi, and other important Urdu fiction writers, Mastur's writer-self emerged at a time when India was evolving into a nation. In the midst of political and social turmoil and besieged by a heightened sense of identity, these writers brought to their fiction something unique: a creative engagement with the meaning and effects of independence from the British Raj, followed by the bewildering need to shift loyalties and deal with a brand-new sense of patriotism. Tormented by changes that seemed too overwhelming and charged with enthusiasm at the thought of new beginnings as free peoples, no wonder they wrote subversive and revolutionary prose that will be regarded without parallel in the literary history of the subcontinent.

Written in the fifties and the recipient of the prestigious Adamji Award, *Aangan* recounts a journey that commenced with Partition, bringing the narrative across the border to Pakistan. The journey ends in *Zamin*. Set against the declaration of martial law in Pakistan, *Zamin* clearly brings not only Mastur's literary self full-circle, but also becomes a symbolic point of closure for every Pakistani who remembers Partition.

In her short stories Khadija Mastur concentrates on women's lives, their roles in society, their complex relationships with their own psyches, with other women, with their husbands and other men, with the society of which they are a part and its mores. The Pakistani woman, she once remarked,

> has travelled a great distance, for example, in terms of education, socially as well, but women haven't been able to take full advantage of the strides they have made. The Pakistani woman has moved forward, but our society hasn't kept pace with her. Even now it's the man who has the upper hand in our world, [...] women still can't find jobs, and if they do find work, they're still given the status of women, not of a participant or a hard-working person. It's unfortunate that women don't insist on their rights, they don't employ the opportunities that are available to them, they don't make use of their education, their learning. If this continues, it's possible that they'll be pushed back.[6]

The stories in the present selection are representative of Mastur's dedication to writing about women's inner lives, each work being a tribute to the voices that are often lost in the clamour of a world where women are regarded to be at their best when least visible.

## II

Born in 1927 in a small town outside pre-Partition Lucknow in India, Khadija Mastur, in her own words, 'spent my childhood playing with children whom people referred to as low, [...] and my games were different from the games my sister and brothers played.'[7] It was perhaps this firsthand contact with people living on the edge of poverty and despair that prepared her for her future intensely perceptive and moving portrayals of their inner lives.

Around the age of eight, soon after she had finished reading the Koran, she decided she would start writing stories. Having heard the word 'plot' from her parents and having discovered what it meant, she began telling everyone that there were a thousand 'plots', in her head, the declaration was often greeted with laughter and derision. In 1936, she went with her sister and a family friend to see a company called Paristan Theatre perform in Lucknow. Here, as luck would have it, she ran into Shaukat Thanvi, a well-known Urdu fiction writer. She spoke to the older writer of her desire to write stories. Instead of taking her lightly, Thanvi Sahib encouraged her. His kindness made a deep impression on her, and whenever in future she talked about herself as a writer, she never failed to recount the incident with a special feeling. It is not surprising that she did so, since women, especially young women writers, were an oddity in those days, and an aspiring writer like Mastur needed all the encouragement she could get.

Khadija Mastur's father died in 1937, an event that changed the life of the entire family. With no steady source of income, she and her siblings lived through the darkest days of their lives. An eighteen-year-old maternal uncle came to their rescue at the cost of immense sacrifice to his own future, a loving wonderful man who died tragically of tuberculosis a year later. About that period she writes:

> How we spent our lives for a long time is a complicated story. Any recapitulation of those days will not be without considerable pain.

[...] We endured that period of sorrow and despair with forbearance and pride and even those who were constantly probing into our lives couldn't figure anything out. We were never embarrassed, we had become extremely sensitive in those days, we could recognize the tiniest ray of love and affection from a distance and trod cautiously under its canopy. We were betrayed once or twice, but despite the betrayals my faith in love and the greatness of human beings was not shaken.[8]

Even though Mastur could not attend college, her education does not appear to be deficient in any way. She uses language with maturity and confidence, and her knowledge of history and politics is impressive. She is, in the words of Ahmed Nadeem Qasmi, 'more interested in reading life and less in reading books.'[9]

But it was not until 1942, five years before Partition, that Khadija Mastur started writing seriously. She published her earlier stories in the journals *Khayal* and *Aalamgir*. In 1945, her story 'Hunh!' received a favourable review from Syed Ehtesham Husain, a respected and well-regarded critic. His praise motivated the young writer to begin taking herself more seriously.

When she published her collection of short stories *Bochaar* (Sprinkling), the well-known Progressive critic Akhtar Husain Raipuri wrote its preface. In it he pointed out that sexual awakenings and greater reliance on realism were becoming increasingly evident in Mastur's work. This new awareness eventually drew Mastur to the Progressive Writers' Movement. Later, in 1946, impelled by the political drama of independence fast unfolding around her, she, along with her sister Hajira Masroor, also joined the Muslim League as an active member. But, according to Ghulam Hussain Azhar, it was only after 1947 that her socio-political ideology developed fully and she began to deal substantively with social issues in her writing.

In 1950, as a result of her growing interest in the progressive aspects of Urdu fiction, she became the secretary of the Progressive Writers' Association, Lahore Branch. Draped in burqas, both she and Hajira Masroor attended every meeting and worked zealously to keep the organization afloat. Her mature and seasoned approach to social and political issues, along with her continued interest in women's lives, led to a further refinement of her ideas, most clearly evidenced in her third collection of short stories, *Chand Roz Aur*. The nascent realism in her collections *Khel* (Play) and *Bochaar* took on a definitive form in this work. But while her stories offer, in the words of Qasmi, 'tremendous insight into every aspect [of politics and history],' they do not 'pontificate' or 'lecture.'[10]

Mastur moved to Lahore after Partition and lived there for the rest of her life. Ahmed Nadeem Qasmi, the noted poet, journalist, and writer, was a close family friend and it was he who helped her and her siblings set up new lives in Pakistan. In 1950 she married Zaheer Babar, Qasmi's nephew and himself a well-known journalist. The couple had two children, a son Parvez and a daughter Kiran, both featured in the story 'Cold, Sweet Water'.

Because of their views and statements that were interpreted as subversive, Qasmi, Zaheer Babar and Hajira Masroor's husband Ahmed Ali Khan were subjected to frequent incarcerations, in 1951, during the government of Liaqat Ali Khan, and again in 1959, during Ayub Khan's martial law. Mastur draws upon their experiences in *Zamin* to portray vividly the despair of Pakistani intellectuals in those democratically bleak days. Her letters to Qasmi (who was like a brother to Mastur and whom she lovingly called *Bhayya*) during his incarceration in 1951, are highlighted by a sense of loss and a feeling of intense helplessness that might very well reflect the mood of the people in general during those repressive times. For instance, in one of them, she says:

> *Bhayya*! you have been away too long. Even though I'm in the same city I can't meet you, I can't see you. I've been to Jail Road many times and each time have wanted to turn the tonga in the direction of the jail, but what's the use? What's the use of striking one's head against frightening brick walls?

Speak *Bhayya*, what should I say? If it is greatness to tolerate everything then one should ignore this military government, this worst kind of military dictatorship. Why is everyone swearing at it? Is this a sign of greatness? I say, everyone should tolerate it. Why are people shouting protests? This is a very cowardly act, just as it is cowardly to cry when suffering great pain. *Bhayya*, you have done nothing and you became the target of oppression and cruelty. Sleeping on the floor, the cramped cell, and the worst kind of food—all this makes my soul tremble. I have no peace, how I have wept! Even Hazrat Yaqub became blind from crying for his son Hazrat Yusuf. What torture this is for me! I wish that injustice would die, for then I would live.[11]

Mastur's fiction was widely published in such literary journals as *Adab-e-Latif*, *Nuqoosh*, *Javed*, and *Adabi Duniya*. In his obituary essay, 'Yadoon ka Thanda Meetha Pani' (The Cool, Sweet Water of Memories), Mansur Qaisar talks about his meeting with Lui Chen Lin, a professor of Urdu at Peking University, whom he met at the Institute of Modern Languages in Islamabad. Lin informed Qaisar that the work of Progressive Writers was being studied extensively by scholars in his department, and that among the works translated into Chinese were the short stories of Khadija Mastur. He said that 'Mastur's stories have given Urdu fiction a new direction.'[12]

Mastur won the Adamji Award for *Aangan* and also received an award for her collection *Thanda Meetha Pani* (Cool, Sweet Water) posthumously. She had hoped to explore in greater depth the ideas and themes of *Zamin* in a new novel, now that she had become even more familiar with the political landscape of Pakistan, but her failing health did not afford her this opportunity. She had always been frail and, finally, the disease which had been following her insidiously for years, caught up with her. She became seriously ill. She fought her illness courageously. At the advice of her doctors, she was taken to England for treatment, but she did not recover and died on 26 July 1982 in a clinic in London. Her body was brought back to Pakistan and she was buried in Lahore. The following couplet by Mehshar Badayuni was engraved on her gravestone:

When the candle of life was about to be extinguished Khadija said, 'This world of the moon and the stars is very beautiful.'

### III

The present selection commences with stories and excerpts that reflect Khadija Mastur's interest in the sociopolitical issues of her time, especially as they relate to Partition, its aftermath and its ramifications for the newly founded state of Pakistan. The decision to begin Mastur's collection with these works is mine alone and has been motivated by the turbulent events India and Pakistan face fifty years after Partition. Fiftieth anniversary celebrations everywhere, in these countries and among expatriates in the diaspora, have been accompanied by troubled ruminations on what the implications of Partition have been and what nationhood means today, especially for those of us who have origins in Pakistan and especially when both countries have just detonated nuclear devices. It seemed fit, therefore, to review what a writer like Mastur had to say all those years ago about the very issues that continue to plague us to this day.

'Miscreant,' a brutally stark narrative revolving around the terrible side-effects of India's division into two countries and the inhuman behaviour that surfaced among Muslims, Hindus, and Sikhs in the first days of Partition, tells the tragic story of Fazlu, a young, simple-minded, loyal man whose friends include both Hindus and Sikhs and who cannot understand the palpable fear in their eyes when stories of rioting invade the tranquillity of his small village; he fails to make the connection between the idea of Pakistan and the fact that the Muslims are in majority here.

'When Pakistan is created, don't start thinking ill of us Fazlu Bhayya.' A strange kind of fear would flutter in Fazlu's Hindu friend's eyes.
'Come my friend, what are you saying? We grew up together—have you forgotten I was the one who was responsible for the

meeting between you and your sweetheart? And now you're talking like this? I'll think of you as one who is the very best.' Fazlu would place his arm around his friend's neck.

'I don't know why I'm scared.' Fazlu's Hindu friend would gaze into Fazlu's eyes as if he were about to leap into them.' (p. 9)

Fazlu's naïveté results in gruesome tragedy. The course taken by the ensuing events appears to signify the mood not of just one small village where the Hindus, Muslims, and Sikhs have been living in peace for centuries, but of the whole country. Fazlu's fate is a metaphor for Partition: very few could escape its harrowing aftermath without being scarred in some way.

In 'They are Taking Me Away Father, They are Taking Me Away' (the line from the Punjabi epic poem 'Heer Ranjha' and spoken by Heer as she is taken away to a husband she does not love, while her beloved Ranjha stands by helplessly), we encounter the helplessness of another young man during a communal riot, who like Fazlu, finds himself in a situation over which he seems to have no control. Unable to stand up to his bloodthirsty companions, the young man tries to wrench a young woman away from their vicious grasp and, failing, watches in horror as the young girl is carried off forcibly to be raped and brutalized.

'Have pity, don't touch her!' Coming between the girl and the man with the bloodshot eyes, he screamed like a madman.

'Why? Will her body be soiled? We do all the work and he wants to reap the benefit. I say, go your way now.'

'No, no!' He tried once again to put himself between the man with the bloodshot eyes and the girl, but the man with the bloodshot eyes placed his dagger on his chest. Then he lifted the girl and threw her over his shoulders as if she were a lamb. The girl did not make a sound, she did not resist, but when the man turned to leave she stretched out her limp hands toward him. He wished that the dagger had pierced his chest at that very moment. Agitated, he leapt toward her again, but was thrust back and the man with the bloodshot eyes wrapped the girl's arms around his neck. As if in extreme pain, the girl shut her eyes. (p. 4)

For a moment, both Fazlu and the protagonist in 'They are Taking Me Away Father, They are Taking Me Away' become the conscience of a people as they struggle to overcome hatred and the desire for retaliation.

The inability to comprehend this hatred that has suddenly surfaced between people who have been living as citizens of the same country for centuries bewilders everyone. It is echoed again in the excerpt from Mastur's novel *Aangan*.

> Kariman *Bua* sighed when she heard the reports of violence. 'How everything has changed. There was a time when the Hindus would give their lives if the Muslims in their village were threatened and the Muslims would sacrifice all to save the honour of the Hindus. Such was the spirit of brotherhood that it seemed the two had been born from the same mother.' (p. 24)

This is how Fazlu had felt before the monster of vengeance overwhelmd him. But as Kariman *Bua* puts it, 'nothing remains now.' Indeed 'both have daggers in their hands now.'

The Muslims achieve a separate homeland, which unleashes a new terror, as we see in excerpts from *Aangan* and *Zamin*. Division, not only of land, but also of loyalties, heightens the already overwhelming sense of confusion at the time of Pakistan's creation. Not all Muslims can migrate to the new country; not all want to. There are centuries of tradition, a culturally rich heritage, roots that go deep, and in being pulled out will not grow afresh. Families are torn apart, brother is separated from brother, sisters find themselves on opposite sides of the border, children leave behind parents; so many give up everything they possess because 'at least it will be our own people governing in Pakistan'. When *Bari Chachi* of *Aangan* decides to leave, her older brother, *Bare Chacha*, proclaims passionately, 'Why will you go to Pakistan? This is our country [i.e., India], we have sacrificed so much for it and now we should leave and go.' Aliya, his young niece and *Bari Chachi's* daughter, is saddened to see her loving uncle so tormented by her mother.

> 'Aliya's heart was breaking ... A turmoil raged inside her ...

May God bless you with peace, *Bare Chacha*, she prayed silently, may all your dreams be fulfiled.' She cannot tell him that 'in reality she too wanted to run from here.' There is the very tangible violence that has to do with the killing and other atrocities carried out during Partition and then there is the unseen but deeply felt violence that shredded people's hearts, shattered their confidence, and left them crippled emotionally and psychologically, perhaps never to be whole again.

In the first excerpt from *Zamin*, the narrative brings into focus the earliest setback that was to have lasting effects on Pakistan's sense of nationhood. The death of Quaid-i-Azam, the founder of Pakistan, leaves the new nation without a leader. Democracy is not a concept the first Pakistani politicians have grasped as yet and the stage is set for catastrophe.

> Sajida felt that the Quaid-i-Azam's body was lying next to her heart and she couldn't even cry.
> 'Oh my God, what will happen now!' *Khalabi* dashed out of the room ... *Arre*, we didn't even have a chance to settle down ...' (p. 34)

Nazim, the young man who has dreams of making it in the new country and whose idealism in the first part of the novel fills him with hope even at this, the bleakest hour for Pakistan, retorts caustically, 'How strange that with the Quaid-i-Azam's passing, many people see the death and destruction of their country.' He envisions a future rich with promise because the people will, he believes, rise to the occasion and take the new country to great heights. He laments that some have 'lost their sense of selfhood at the passing of just one leader', because his faith in the power of the people to evince change is still intact.

In the second excerpt from *Zamin* we meet the same Nazim, recuperating from torture received during incarceration in a Pakistani jail. His excitement and idealism have been dissipated already. He is embittered, cynical, and disillusioned. His spirit, like his body, is broken and he feels nothing but despair at the 'destruction' he sees around him. There are clashes with the Qadianis, who are suddenly being referred to as *kafirs* by non-

Qadianis who are suddenly being referred to as *kafirs* by non-Qadianis. There's looting and bloodshed in the streets. A bloody corpse arrives in the neighbouring compound and Nazim's wife Sajida hears the women wailing at the feet of the corpse and shouting, 'Go, go and kill ten to avenge the death of one and become martyrs.' Sajida is transported into another time, not so much in the past, the period of Partition. She feels 'her head swimming and images of blood, riots, the streets of Delhi, the refugee camps spin before her eyes. It is as if time has not moved at all.

When sectarian riots begin in Lahore, *Zamindar Sahib*, a friend and frequent visitor to Nazim's house, says that the 'looters should be allowed to do what they want, the Qadianis are not Muslims, they are people who are fated to go to hell.' In light of the increase in sectarian violence in Pakistan today, these are ominous words and Nazim's reaction to the words chillingly prophetic:

> I agree that these religious scholars should finish off all the *kafirs* in the world, but *Zamindar Sahib*, tell me something—how spacious will that hell be where all these people [non-Muslims/*kafirs*] are headed? Heaven is only for people like you, isn't it? (p. 38)

As far as I know, Mastur is the only writer who has dealt with the treatment of minorities, specifically the Qadianis. A dark period in the history of Pakistan, this was the time when, under pressure from the self-appointed guardians of faith, the then prime minister, Zulfiqar Ali Bhutto, declared the Qadianis non-Muslims. They were subsequently forbidden to have anything to do with the Koran, or enter mosques to offer prayers. The fate of Qadianis in Pakistan was a subject not openly written about in the ensuing years and it was indeed courageous of Mastur to have addressed it in such strong and no uncertain terms.

Following upon the heels of sectarian violence comes the first martial law, another nail in the coffin of nationhood. In the excerpt from *Zamin*, as the corpse next-door is taken out for burial, Nazim mutters again and again, 'I hope this martial law doesn't prove to be the black cloud of the future.' An awful sense of foreboding clamps down on the reader with vicious force as the novel proceeds to its end.

Mastur didn't live long enough to write her third novel, one she had been planning for a while, but one can guess what her themes might have been, where she would have gone with it, and the trilogy might have been an apt literary statement on the life and times of Pakistan.

A surprisingly refreshing change in outlook appears in the short story 'Cool, Sweet Water'. Largely autobiographical, the story is set during the 1965 war with India, one of the three clashes between the two countries. This period in the history of Pakistan is unusual and almost set apart from other periods that came before or after. One could say that beginning in the late fifties and all the way to the late sixties, Pakistan experienced something of a renaissance, a stabilization of all those institutions a country needs to function smoothly and effectively. One can only guess at the causes. Perhaps people had settled down and allowed themselves the luxury of accommodation, of coming to terms with their confusing, but inevitable, destiny. Writers, educationists, and artists who had migrated to Pakistan had had opportunity to affirm their identity in the new homeland and were now able to create a culturally rich and immensely productive atmosphere. Faiz Ahmed Faiz, Sufi Tabbasum, Ahmed Nadeem Qasmi, Ghulam Abbas, and so many others, poets, writers, critics, artists, nurtured the nascent institutions. We, who were growing up in those times, were conscious of a sense of nationhood, a sense that there was something to be proud of. There was so much dynamism and zeal with which our writers and artists and educationists filled the existing vacuums, we even ignored the fact that we were already servicing the first of many martial laws. Ayub Khan seemed a benevolent military dictator. And giddy with this budding and altogether exciting sense of accomplishment, we also developed and built up patriotism, a special pride in the army that was to protect us from all evils and threats. And so when the 1965 war with India came along, the army rose to the call and the nation rallied. Never before was such faith in the country and its armed forces so forcefully expressed. In 'Cool, Sweet Water', Mastur is drawn into this spirit as well. The humanist in her declares, 'I love peace, I hate war.' But she adds that she loves 'that war as much as she loves peace when that war is fought for freedom, for honour, for the survival of one's country'. The soldiers on their way to the front wrenched our hearts. I remember vividly that we rooted for them, spent long hours preparing care packages for them, knitted them sweaters, prayed for them, and wept for them. When Mastur sees a truckful of soldiers who are dancing the *bhangra* she is nonplussed. 'There was such fervour in their clapping,' she says and continues, 'Oh God! Are they really going to fight cannons and bullets?' She 'stares at them in disbelief,' and finds that 'their faces were illuminated with the bloom of flowers.' And a little later she realizes that she is no longer afraid of death. 'For the first time death was like the taste of honey,' she confesses. Unable to reconcile herself to the idea of loss of civilian life during a war, any war, she is troubled to see the people in the village where a bomb has fallen. Although she is relieved there is no loss of life, she feels as though she is isolated, and ends the narrative ambiguously. The bomb has left a small crater and sitting next to the crater is an old man asking for donations to build a well there 'out of which will come cool, sweet water.' Perhaps Mastur hopes for abiding peace and an end to war, even one that's being fought to preserve 'honour'. Unfortunately, the army was never again to command the same respect and love of the nation.

Next come Mastur's stories of women. In many reviews and critical evaluations of her work, these women have been referred to as 'Khadija Mastur's women', a qualifier not altogether inappropriate since the women in her narratives evolve and develop as characters in ways that one could ascribe to Mastur's style alone. These women are young and old, some of the younger ones burning with the fire of unfulfilled passions, some of the older ones proudly staking their claim to respectability despite the tragic and often calamitous conditions surrounding their lives, and all are courageous, fighting sometimes against unassailable odds, to maintain their selfhood.

In 'Suriya,' the narrator, a woman who has not had too much luck with sweeperesses, is charmed by her new sweeperess, a pretty young girl of ten or twelve, who has 'a strange kind of dignity reflected on her face'. It becomes apparent very quickly that Suriya is diligent and conscientious and so proud that she won't accept a penny more than what she earns from her work. The narrator, fond of the child and anxious to help her, offers her one rupee as a reward for her excellent work and is enraged when her money is politely turned down. 'I have enough in my house *Bibiji*, I'll take only my salary, nothing else', Suriya says, arousing in her mistress, who takes this gesture of generosity as an affront, a desire to 'slap her'.

Suriya is reminiscent of Chunni Begum in 'The Hand Pump,' the woman who, from the time she is rejected by her husband and her in-laws until the time that she is old, sick, and friendless, depends on no one but herself to stay alive. Like Suriya she toils ceaselessly and with pride, using her intelligence to better her lot. Like Suriya, she will eat only that which she has earned. In the end, old and infirm and beaten at her own game, Chunni Begum still hangs on tenaciously to her pride so that when she does accept tea and a piece of bread from a solicitous neighbour after starving for two days, her tone is neither obsequious nor humble. She has done her poor neighbours a favour by putting in a hand pump for them and since they had stopped paying her for the water after the first few times they used the pump, she tells herself that the tea and bread she is receiving now is only a small part of what they owe her.

> Chunni Begum quickly extended her *katora*. 'What? So little milk you've put in the tea and you didn't butter the roti either, you wretch. And so much water you draw too. Now remember to be careful, do you hear?' (p. 128)

These are Mastur's special female characters, impoverished, suffering hardship, and yet filled with unusual strength and courage, revealing, despite their sad lot, an indomitable verve for living.

Much more than any of her contemporaries, Mastur has also chosen to delve into the sexual and emotional frustrations of young women, women whose lives are unfulfilled because they are poor, because they have no obvious talents that make them marketable in a society where women are indeed marketable, because they are economically dependent first on fathers and then on husbands. In 'Trust' we meet Razia who seeks only true love and is in agony when her first husband turns away from her at the instigation of his overprotective mother and sisters—an old and familiar story. 'Not to know love is no crime,' she anguishes, 'but to give love and then snatch it away is the worst of all crimes.' In Safdar, a man who occasionally sees her moping in her doorway and begins to show concern, Razia finds renewed hope. She falls in love with him and marvels at the depth of her emotion. 'What a strange and fulsome love it was. Even an ocean is incapable of braving the force of a lover's adoration.'

Betrayal follows Razia like an ominous shadow. When the truth being concealed so cleverly by Safdar becomes apparent, she is shattered. Again she feels 'darkness ... at the base of her vision.' What has Razia done to deserve this? Nothing, Mastur suggests, but then again Safdar, although a loving husband and a caring, affectionate father to Razia's child from her first marriage, is also neither set on a pedestal by Mastur nor is he painted as a blackguard. It is obvious that Mastur doesn't wish to place the blame on men; rather she berates the society's mores, the class divisions, the lack of education among both men and women, the unfortunate circumstances that allow one woman to have an attentive, loving husband and another to have a husband who beats her regularly after getting drunk and will not allow her to leave the house while he is out. As Razia joins the ranks of those who are living a loveless life, she clasps the most abused one among them and says, '*Arri* sister, why are you still angry with me? Let's be friends now, our quarrel is over at last.'

A slightly different kind of betrayal undermines the young protagonist's struggle to find love and respectability in 'Harvest.'

One of the most haunting stories in the collection, it revolves around Kaneez's unremitting search for a husband, and consequently love, a home, and respectability—all the things her society deems it necessary for a woman to have to justify her existence. Her approach is unconventional; she doesn't mind marrying men who only want her for short periods of time so that she is 'wife' for a while and is then 'let go.' Of course the choice is not hers, she takes what she can get and this is all that she can get. She is an orphan, she is poor, her mother is old and frail, and there is no source of income for the two women. The story is complex, and, weaving through layers of meaning, brings Kaneez to the door of Din Muhammad who needs a woman to take care of his ailing wife Sakina. Another marriage for Kaneez, a six-month contract this time. 'She's an orphan, she'll have enough to eat for six months,' Din Muhammad assures Kaneez's mother, a poor widow who cannot give her daughter the means to find 'honour' but is reluctant to say yes to the match and pile more dishonour on herself and her 'family's name.' But Kaneez is adamant, and not because she doesn't sympathize with her mother's feelings; she is more realistic about her situation and her mother's. 'If *Abba* were alive, you too would be married with honour, but now that you have no honour who will marry you?' Kaneez tells herself, and then consoles herself by conceding that 'at least a few days will be spent living honourably.'

Her wedding, this time, is a cheerless, sparse event. She remembers the time when her father was alive and how he had put up a swing for her on which she 'used to swing for hours with her friends, talking of weddings.' None of the usual celebrations for her. Her heart is crushed.

> *Arri* Kaneej, you were fated to suffer bad luck. All the girls went to set up their houses, there were such celebrations at their weddings, the bridegrooms came with flowered diadems on their heads. And you, you're making your own *ladoos*, and who will play the drum? (p. 89)

But, she is not ready to give up just yet. In her desire to receive love and attention from Din Muhammad, who seems completely engrossed in his wife and is heartbroken over her illness, Kaneez flirts with him and uses every artifice she can draw on to make herself indispensable to him, his wife, and their two children. She is confident that Sakina, who is very sick, will die.

> '*Arri*, how beautiful she is, but she has no life left in her, all skin and bones she is, she's nearly done for I think, how many days will the poor woman live?' (p. 94)

Tenacious and never ones to give up easily, women like Kaneez inhabit spaces where all women have gone, at one time or another. If not physically, certainly emotionally and psychologically. In exploring the lives of these characters, Mastur enters a realm which very few writers, male or female have dared to. She picks at the sexual turmoil that festers in a society where women's sexuality is a taboo subject, certainly in literature. In 'Springtime of Life' she puts the reader into the young female narrator, Bittan's head. The story begins on the crest of her emotions.

> The whirling smoke from the smouldering, soggy kindling was moving toward the small skylight in the kitchen and she was sitting on a stool nearby, trying to blow life into the flames with hot hurried breath. Finally, youth's simmering breath succeeded in fanning the flames. (p. 129)

Bittan is like Kaneez in many ways. She too wants to be married. But her reasons extend beyond the desire for home and respectability. Bittan is a woman who feels her sexuality, who senses its needs, who wishes for sexual fulfilment. Unable to seek satisfaction on her own, she must wait until her family weds her. In the meantime, her emotions are raging, her mind and her body are experiencing changes that leave her restless and irritable. The family, however, seems oblivious of her needs, although her mother can detect that something is amiss.

But now it was as if her life had changed. Even the tiniest bit of work irritated her; if her mother complained she would start muttering as well. She had begun to hate *Amma*, her brother, *Bhabi*, and the baby. She stayed awake until two or three in the morning, tossing and turning in bed. Her body was racked with aches and pains and her heart beat violently. She wondered what was wrong with her. Her mother knew, but feigned ignorance. (pp. 130-31)

The story reaches a climax, when, unable to hold back her anger at the indifferent and unsympathetic treatment meted out to her by her parents, her brother, and her sister-in-law, Bittan blurts out, 'Why have you kept me at home like this? Why don't you marry me off then, who's stopping you?' thus cutting up 'lips which had been sewed together with modesty all this time.' The mother and the sister-in-law respond as if they have both been struck by lightening.

'*Hai!*' *Amma* beat her chest.
'The day of judgement is at hand. An unmarried girl asks for a husband with her own mouth.' *Bhabi* placed a finger on her nose in amazement and then she led her chest-beating mother-in-law out of there. (p. 134)

But Bittan is finally calm. 'She saw them all and felt satisfied, as if a large stone had been lifted from her chest.'

The protagonist in 'The Heart's Thirst' faces a similar dilemma. Shut up in her house, this young woman, also living like Kaneez with a widowed mother, is troubled by isolation, poverty, and loneliness. She cannot work because the mother fears her daughter will lose her honour if she leaves the house alone and so this young woman is doomed, like Tennyson's Lady of Shallot, to observe the world from afar; she peers at it through a chink in the tattered sackcloth curtain on the front door and that too only after the mother has left for work. As she gazes longingly at the beautiful clothes women strolling past her door are wearing, her heart constricts with envy.

It soon becomes apparent that the clothes are not the only things that catch her eye. The *paanwallah's* lewd glances from across the street throw her into a tizzy. At first she is horrified and beset with dreadful feelings of guilt and keeps the door shut for three days. Her worst moments occur when she is faced with her mother's desire to preserve her daughter's honour. However, all efforts by the mother to find a suitable match for her daughter have failed and it becomes obvious that like Kaneez and Bittan this young woman may also have to take matters into her own hand. Her interest in the *paanwallah* stems from the knowledge that she may be doomed to a life of spinsterhood for ever, although she does not admit it openly. So, despite her guilt 'her heart smouldered' and finally on the third day, after her mother has left for work, she opens the door and 'sadly, while observing the excitement of the world, stuck her whole head out carelessly.' The *paanwallah* approaches her with an offer of a suit of 'the heart's thirst' and proclaims his love for her. She rebuffs him angrily and shuts the door in his face, but his words agitate her and she 'felt as if a thousand furnaces had started heating up her body.' Her passion for the suit, which will be the first silken thing next to her body ever, motivates her to accept the *paanwallah's* offer, but he wants more and even though she is desperate to have the suit, she is reluctant to give herself to this man until he marries her.

> 'Put it on, my dearest, so I can see how you look.' He moved closer. 'I'll be your slave for life.'
> 'Talk to *Amma* then.'
> 'I will, but don't torment me now.' He wanted payment on the spot. She tried to extricate herself from his grasp.
> 'You don't love me, here, give me the suit and I'll leave.' She clasped the clothes to her breast.
> The *paanwallah* smiled triumphantly. 'All that will come later.' He lunged toward her. (pp. 146-7)

The exhange proves humiliating, but only for a moment. Soon she wipes her tears and looks at the suit, which was 'soft like a baby's cheek and shimmered like the rays of the moon,' and in the days that follow the 'suit was like her heartbeat.' But reality finally sets in, the *paanwallah* boasts his conquest in public and the young woman must make a serious choice. And she does. After all, she is a Mastur woman and will not accept defeat easily.

The last three stories in this collection, namely, 'In Stealth', 'Bhooray', and 'Lost and Found' have all been crafted in a male voice and are told from a man's point of view. The first two are part of the group of stories which scrutinize women's lives, while the third is from her work on subjects related directly to class inequality. In 'In Stealth', Babuji, a man who 'must have been fourteen when he began a life of debauchery,' decides to mend his ways when he is thirty and, although vehemently opposed to marriage earlier, does get married, even falls in love with his wife. And thus begins a tale of ironic twists. The wife does not return his affections, she is cold and distant, and never has a smile on her face. The more he courts her the more she is repulsed. Her behaviour leads some of the neighbours to suspect that she has a secret lover, while others attribute her unhappiness to the fact that she doesn't have children. Bewildered by her actions and egged on by the neighbours, Babuji begins to treat himself with mail-order drugs and syrups so that he could produce offspring, but five years pass and there is still no sign of offspring. Once again, Mastur's ability to examine sexual themes with great probity becomes evident in this narrative. Babuji's wife, disgruntled with his fawning and unappreciative of his gifts, turns to the young manservant who had been hired to take care of household chores when she became too ill to do the work herself. She recovers rapidly, but, for some unknown reason, Babuji does not seem to be happy.

> But, no one knows why, the more she recovered and the greater her happiness, the more Babuji was overcome by despondency. He should have been happy that the wife, whose face always wore a sullen expression, was now budding with joy. There was a spring in her step, her eyes shone, and instead of griping about housework, she was now always seen giving Rahim a helping hand. So what was the cause of his despondency. (p. 156)

The cause is obvious. Mastur takes a very bold step here to do what she does next. As to be expected, the critics did not receive this story favourably. How can a woman behave in the way she does, how can Mastur portray such behaviour in a woman? For Babuji to be a debaucher since the age of fourteen is all right; not only, sadly, are men seen to be born to such behaviour, but also conversely, women are regarded as creatures who must always keep their expressions of sexual desire under lock and key. No one refers to Babuji as a whore, but his wife will obtain that title easily.

In 'Bhooray', a tragic and moving story of love and betrayal, we see a man who, true to the standards of his society, cannot accept a woman who has tarnished her womanhood by sleeping with other men, albeit to keep herself alive. Bhooray once loved Zahooran, a girl he was betrothed to and left behind in his village at the time of Partition. Many years later he stumbles across her in the women's hospital where he works as an orderly. One afternoon he discovers a pregnant Zahooran sleeping in the veranda not far from where he sits answering the phone. He had forgotten her. At the beginning of the story we find him happy with the life he has chalked out for himself after a long struggle, a life made doubly satisfying because 'he could freely flirt with the young *ayahs* and daughters of old *ayahs*,' something 'he was now adept at'. When he sees Zahooran again, he is stunned to find her in this condition. Strangely unselfconscious about her pregnancy, she professes love for him, a love she tells him she has nurtured all these years of separation. Bhooray is annoyed by her talk.

'Don't talk like that now, you belong to someone else.' Bhooray felt irritated. *What wiles women have,* he thought, *what airs she's putting on.*
'You're saying this?' Zahooran shut her eyes in bliss. 'I'm yours Bhooray, body and soul.' She was trembling. ...
Then he examined her closely. *What's the use of taking body and soul,* he thought. *What's the use of remembering the past?* 'Why are you in the hospital?' he suddenly asked. ...

'Why do you hide the truth? Why don't you just admit that when I couldn't be found your father gave you in marriage to someone else. Don't give me this *filmi* drama.' Bhooray spoke angrily.

'What do you mean?' She arched her neck arrogantly. 'Zahooran is not the sort of woman who would marry a second time. I've been married to you. It was for you that I left my village and lost my parents ... She started weeping. 'This has been forced upon me ... I had to work in the bungalows to keep myself alive, but these city *babu sahibs* are very bad. ... I come here to this hospital and have abortions. Each time I die to live again ... She spoke between sobs. 'Now I've found you Bhooray, I won't go anywhere. Look how raw my hands are from scrubbing pots and pans.' (p. 170)

Bhooray's heart does not melt. He thinks Zahooran is tainted goods now and no longer fit for him. Later, Bhooray regrets his decision to turn Zahooran away, but his regret comes too late. For him, for her.

'Lost and Found' is a moving narrative about a man Rafique, who, no longer young and energetic, is desperate to find some means of providing for his wife and two children. He toils endlessly at the vegetable market, but his aching knees torment him and slow him down. During this time he becomes embroiled in debt to Molla, the shopkeeper, whom he had viewed as his good friend until one day he discovers that Molla was 'not in the least bit perturbed about the sum that was owed him. When he [Molla] was in trouble, Rafique would simply hand him his cottage.' Rafique is devastated; he 'felt as if his own clothes were about to be reduced to tatters, he imagined his wife sitting on the roadside, leered at by onlookers, and he saw his children, frightened by the barking of dogs, seeking refuge in their mother's lap.' In his desperation Rafique plans a scheme to get rich quickly. He will pick up a child from the roadside and then wait until a reward is offered for the missing child, at which point he will take the child to its parents and, proclaiming he had just found it on the road, he will claim his reward. The 'Lost and Found' section of the newspapers has been Rafique's inspiration and the large amounts offered in some instances convince him that if the child he brings home is from a well-to-do family, he will definitely come out ahead in this game. Of course the scheme backfires. Like many of Mastur's stories, the narrative operates on many levels. The story, told effectively and with compassion, is about a poor man's hopes and love, about parental devotion, about friendship, loyalty, and treachery, and about the inequitable class system that breeds the kind of despair that would motivate an essentially good man to stoop really low. It is about survival.

Mastur's stories inform, agitate, provoke, and move. Whether it is her stubborn, tenacious-minded women the reader is faced with, or the warped ideology of a struggling national identity, or narratives about social inequality and injustice, there is very little in Mastur's work that fails to leave a mark on the reader's consciousness. In exploring these subjects, Mastur neither preaches nor moralizes, nor does she offer ready-made solutions. She merely embroiders a tapestry. Ultimately, it is the reader's responsibility to examine her narrative patterns and grapple with answers and resolutions.

## IV

Khadija Mastur wrote five collections of short stories which are: *Chand Roz Aur* (A Few More Days), *Bochaar*, *Khel* (Play), *Thanda Meetha Pani* and *Thake Haare* (Tired and Defeated). Her two novels are *Aangan* and *Zamin*.

The publication details of the stories and excerpts from the author's novels included in the present selection are as follows: 'Cool, Sweet Water' ('Thanda Meetha Pani'), 'Suriya' ('Suriya'), 'Harvest' ('Khirman'), 'Trust' ('Bharosa'), and 'Bhooray' ('Bhoore') from the collection *Thanda Meetha Pani* (Lahore: Nuqoosh Press, 1983), pp. 131–8, 69–77, 9–36, 139–67, and 52–67, respectively; 'The Miscreant' ('Das Nambari'), 'The Hand Pump' ('Hend Pump'), 'The Heart's Thirst' ('Dil Ki Piyas'), and 'Lost and Found' ('Talash-e Gumshuda') from the collection *Thake Haare* (Lahore: Sang-e-Meel Publications, 1995), pp. 244–60, 53–70, 146–61, and 86–99, respectively; and 'Springtime of Life' ('Javaani') and 'In Stealth' ('Chupke

Chupke') from the collection *Bochaar* (Lahore: Sang-e-Meel Publications, 1995), pp. 85–91, and 39–46, respectively. The story, 'They are Taking Me Away Father, They are Taking Me Away' ('Mainu Le Challe Babla, Le Challe Ve') is taken from *Funoon* 20 (Jan–Feb 1984), pp. 209–12. The excerpt from *Aangan* appears on pp. 304-10, and the two excerpts from *Zamin*, on pp. 67–75 and 154–59, respectively.

Tahira Naqvi
New York, December 1998

## NOTES

1. I.A. Rahman, 'A Fighter Presses On,' The Herald (Karachi), Aug 1982, pp. 30–1.
2. Funoon 20 (Jan.–Feb. 1984), p. 43. Hereafter all citations to this work appear in the text.
3. Reproduced as 'Chand Roz Aur Ka Dibacha' in ibid., p. 97.
4. In his 'Khadija Ki Shakhsiyat Aur Fan Ke Rishte' (Interconnections between Khadija's Personality and Art), ibid., p. 63.
5. M. Sadiq, *A History of Urdu Literature,* Oxford University Press, Oxford 1964, p. 591.
6. As quoted in Rahman, op. cit., p. 37.
7. Ibid., p. 31.
8. As quoted in Azhar Qadir, 'Khadija Mastur: Ek Mutali'a' (Khadija Mastur: A Study), Funoon 20 (Jan–Feb 1984), p. 127.
9. See his article 'Khadija Mastur: Ek Mutali'a' (Khadija Mastur: A Study), in ibid., p. 122.
10. Qasmi, op. cit., p. 63.
11. 'Khadija Ke Khutut Jo Nadim Ko Pahli Nazarbandi Ke Dauran Bheje Ga'e, Ma'i 1951–Novembar 1951' (Khadija's Letters to Nadim during his First Incarceration, May-November 1951), in ibid., p. 276.
12. In ibid., p. 58.

# Glossary

*abba:* father; something like 'Dad.'
*amma:* mother; something like 'Mom.'
*ammi:* same as 'amma.'
*anna:* a coin; one-sixteenth of a rupee in value.
*aqiqah:* a Muslim cermony of shaving the head of a newborn on the sixth day after birth, followed, ususally, by animal sacrifice.
*arre:* O!, Hey!; an informal manner of addressing a man.
*arri:* O!, Hey!; an informal manner of addressing a woman.
*ayah:* a nursemaid.
*azan:* the Muslim call to prayer proclaimed from the minaret of a mosque five times a day just before the commencement of the ritual prayer, salat, namaz.
*babu:* a title of respect; a clerk.
*badshaho:* 'Your Highness!'
*bahan:* sister
*bahu:* a daughter-in-law, son's wife.
*baji:* elder sister.
*bare chacha:* elder paternal uncle.
*bari chachi:* wife of the above; senior aunt.
*bare sarkar:* great lord or master; used by a servant or a socially inferior person when addressing or referring to the senior master of a household.
*begum:* lady; wife.
*bethak:* a room for receiving visitors; sitting or living room.
*ahagwan:* Hindu term for god.
*bhayya/bhaiya:* elder brother; reflects endearment and respect.

| | |
|---|---|
| *bhangra:* | a wild, carefree folk dance. |
| *bibiji:* | addressing an elderly lady or the mistress of a house. |
| *bindi:* | an ornament worn on the forehead. |
| *bua:* | sister; paternal aunt. |
| *burqa:* | veil, a kind of mantle covering the whole body from head to toe. |
| *chacha:* | paternal uncle. |
| *chachi:* | wife of paternal uncle. |
| *chalia:* | crushed betel nut. |
| *chana:* | chick-pea, gram |
| *chaprasi:* | peon; messenger. |
| *chaupal:* | something like a community center in a village; public meetings may be held here. |
| *chawanni:* | a four-anna coin; one-fourth of a rupee in value. |
| *chilam:* | earthen bowl of a hookah containing tobacco and live coals. |
| *chota:* | small. |
| *chowki:* | a small stool. |
| *chowkidar:* | watchman. |
| *churan:* | a digestive mixture of powdered herbs. |
| *daal:* | any of the several varieties of lentils. |
| *dada:* | paternal grandfather. |
| *devali (Dewali):* | Hindu festival of lights at which tiny oil lamps are lighted to honour Lakhshmi, the goodess of wealth. |
| *devi:* | a goddess. |
| *dhamma dhum:* | a continuous thud; loud noise or report as of a drum; stamping and thumping of foot. |
| *dhoti:* | a garment for the lower-half of the body; usually a cloth worn round the waist, passing between the legs and fastened behind. |
| *dilli:* | local name for Delhi. |
| *dulhan:* | bride. |
| *doli (Dholi):* | palanquin. |

## GLOSSARY

*dupatta:* a length of cloth thrown loosely over the head and shoulders by women.
*eid:* the Muslim festival which comes at the end of Ramazan, the month of fasting.
*filmi:* pertaining to the cinema or movie films.
*ghee:* clarified butter; a staple cooking medium in Indian and Pakistani dishes.
*gulee-danda:* the game of tip-cat.
*hai:* ah!; a sigh; moan.
*hakim:* a South Asian practioner of traditional herbal medicine.
*haveli:* a large and spacious building; a mansion.
*holi:* a Hindu festival in spring, at which people sprinkle red or yellow powder at one another.
*Hindustani:* someone belonging to the Urdu-speaking class.
*janaza:* funeral bier.
*jharu:* a straw broom.
*ji:* an honorific suffix attached to names or titles.
*kafir:* an unbeliever; infidel.
*kameez:* a tunic-like shirt.
*kheer:* a dessert made of rice and milk.
*khichri:* a rice-and-lentil dish.
*laddu:* a kind of sweet.
*lahol:* part of an Arbic formula repeated by Muslims to ward off evil.
*lassi:* a yogurt drink.
*lota katora:* small, round metal pot for general use.
*mah'ia:* a romantic folk tune.
*manno-salwa:* manna, the word implies food of extraordinary richness.
*masi:* an aunt.
*mohajir:* one who migrates.
*muezzin:* announcer of the hour of prayer.
*nim:* a tree with small, bitter, berry-like fruit; its twigs are used as tooth-brush and leaves, in place of moth-balls to store woollen clothes.

## GLOSSARY

*paan:* betel leaf chewed frequently in India and Pakistan.
*paisa:* a penny.
*pullao-zarda:* rice cooked with special spices and saffron.
*pallu:* one end of a dupatta or sari.
*paani:* water.
*para:* a section of a book; mostly applied to the Qur'an.
*qila:* castle; fort.
*raat ki raani:* a very fragrant flower.
*rehal:* a stand to support the Qur'an or any other book.
*roti:* a type of thin, round baked bread.
*sahib bahadur:* honorific title for a man.
*sa'in:* a mendicant.
*seer/pao:* seer is a weight roughly equal to two pounds; pao is one-fourth of a seer.
*shehnai:* a clarion.
*surmadani:* a container for powder used to adorn eyes.
*thanedar:* a police inspector.
*tongawallah:* the driver of a light, two-wheeled carriage (tonga) pulled by a horse.
*zamindar:* landlord.

# They are Taking Me Away, Father, They are Taking Me Away!

A thin stream of water trickled down the drain, the fluffy soap suds encasing the water like a sheath. After a bath in the poorly-lit bathroom, he had walked across the courtyard while drying his hair with a towel, and pulling a chair into a sunny spot he had sat down in it to warm his freezing body. As he rubbed his hair with the towel, his eyes fell on the drain. The water was flowing in the filthy drain clogged with scum. Suddenly, he remembered the incident that had affected his overly-sensitive mind with such force. For several days afterwards he had not been able to think of anything else. Then, gradually, everything had faded from his memory. But today, the sight of the thin trickle of water accompanied by soap suds brought back the memory of that incident with a jolt. He felt as if a thousand sighs were smothered in his chest and he was engulfed by the same emotions that had overwhelmed him when he was confronted with that incident, and this despite the fact that he had known horrors the mere sight of which would melt even a stone. Nothing had ever touched him the way this incident did.

The city's hustle and bustle had been swallowed by death. Huddled in corners, its face hidden, life sobbed. Desolation proclaimed that the city could never flourish again. Death avowed that no one could escape from its clutches. But members of the Aid Committee declared that life was not so cheap that they should let people be caught in the web of death like insects. Wherever they could go they went; they searched out anguished, helpless lives and brought them to the refugee camp. That day he had combed the isolated nooks and crannies of the city for those affected by the riots and had succeeded in bringing fifty people to the refugee camp. It was the end of the day. After parking the truck at the police station, he began walking in the direction of his house. Exhausted, he walked fast so he could get home quickly and rest. Suddenly he came to a standstill. Twelve or thirteen men stood at the edge of a street drain, peering into it. He came up to them. There was a lock on the front door of the building outside which they were standing. The men were planning to force the lock.

'Three days ago we finished off every child and adult in this house, so how did this one escape?' The man with the grisly face and bloodshot eyes waved his dagger in the air.

'Break the lock then,' the other man said, freeing his foot from his waist-string which trailed to the edge of his *shalwar*. 'But just think, who could be inside when there's a lock on the door?' He tried to make a rational appeal.

'If there's no one inside then is this a magic show being conducted here?' The third man glared with his reddened eyes and pointed to the drain. A stream of water mixed with soap suds slowly trickled in the scum-ridden drain before them.

'It seems as if someone has just taken a bath,' the fourth man said, wiping his dagger with his shirt front.

What should he do, he wondered. The police station was quite far from here and not a single policeman was in sight for miles.

'Break the lock!' Several voices droned in unison.

'But listen to me, this is not humane...' He was trying to shower drops of humanity on emotions that were aflame with the fire of vengeance. But he was cut off before he could complete his sentence.

'When our sisters, mothers and brothers were being bathed in blood, where was humanity then, and where were you?' Several of the men spoke at the same time.

'He must be in bed with his humanity,' the man with the grisly face and bloodshot eyes said with a loud, vicious laugh.

'But look...' his hands rose and fell.

'The lock will be forced open, why are you stopping us?' They looked at him as if they suspected he was not one of them.

'I'm not stopping you, of course you can break the lock,' he mumbled helplessly. He knew no one was going to listen to him and if he resisted further they would rip him into pieces and throw his body aside. In a short while the latch was freed from the lock. They all went in. He followed them. His spirit fluttered and shrieked. He began thinking hurriedly of a way to help the person in hiding and all at once he thought of a plan that might prove effective.

'Look, don't go in there like this, the man may have a gun. I have a rifle, I'll go in the front first and all of you can fall in behind me.' He spoke in a whisper.

The men did as he asked and let him go ahead. He climbed the stairs slowly. One, two, three…the stairs were like an unending chain. Although he had been exhausted mentally and physically from working hard all day, he did not feel the least bit tired at this moment. He wondered how anyone could have survived the bloody attack of three days ago. The moment he saw him this person he would signal him to quickly hide somewhere. He would let him know that death was leaping toward him. Surely there must be a place in this house where he could hide as he had done before.

First floor…second floor…third floor…every floor was vacant. He was the first to enter every room. Everywhere he was welcomed by silence and desolation. It seemed as if owls had taken up residence here. He had seen such pictures created by men that he did not have the energy to seek a new picture within himself. His pace quickened. He left those who were following him cautiously several yards behind. And when he arrived at the top of the stairs on the fourth floor and entered the room facing the stairs, he staggered in shock. A beautiful slender girl sat on the floor before him. Her nose was red, her eyelids were swollen, her eyes were filled with weariness and her body looked frail. Her long hair hung loose, and holding a comb in her hand she gazed with half-shut eyes at a mirror in front of her. A soap-dish, a towel, hair clips and a couple of hairpins lay next to her on the floor. He wasn't sure if sitting before him was a real, flesh-and-blood person, or an enchanting spirit, a fairy. When the girl lifted her heavy-lidded eyes and looked at him and the comb fell from her hand, he became aware of her as a real person and his soul fluttered once again to rescue her. He signalled her to hide and whispered that there were people coming to get her. But the girl seemed rooted to the ground. She made no attempt to move. All she did was to look at him with an expression of helplessness on her face and then she dropped her gaze. The men stormed into the room. The daggers they had been brandishing were lowered. All of them burst into diabolic laughter.

'We dug a mountain and found a rat.' The man with the bloodshot eyes moved toward the girl and he felt as if the earth beneath his feet was shaking. The girl's face turned white.

'Have pity, don't touch her!' Coming between the girl and the man with the bloodshot eyes, he screamed like a madman.

'Why? Will her body be soiled? We do all the work and he reaps the benefit. I say, go your way now.' One of the other men spoke derisively.

'No...no!' He tried once again to put himself between the men and the girl, but the man with the bloodshot eyes placed his dagger on his chest. Then he lifted the girl and threw her over his shoulders as if she were a lamb. The girl did not make a sound, she did not resist, but when the men turned to leave she stretched out her limp arms toward him. He wished that the dagger had pierced his chest at that very moment. Agitated, he leapt toward her again, but was thrust back and the man with the bloodshot eyes wrapped the girl's arms around his neck. As if in extreme pain, the girl shut her eyes.

Within seconds the room was empty. More desolate and more empty than before. They were gone. He was sitting on the floor where moments ago she had been combing her hair. He had failed to reach out and hold her outstretched arms. He burst into tears like a child. There was some stubborn emotion in his heart that made him sob hysterically. He had seen women being abducted, he had heard the cries and laments of so many women, and no one had ever touched his heart. But this girl, with her outstretched arms, had left such a mark—it was as if she had pinched and twisted the soft flesh of his heart.

When he could cry no more he collected the hairpins and clips which had been trampled on and placed them in a corner. Sometimes he stared at them, occasionally picking them up and feeling them with his fingers, and sometimes he caressed the damp towel. Then his gaze wandered to the bed on which the wrinkled sheet told of someone who had lain on it for days, tossing about restlessly, in agitation. This strange and beautiful girl had spent three turbulent days and nights on this bed, he thought. Rising to his feet, he went to the bed and slowly began straightening out the wrinkles in the sheet. The pillow was smudged with tear stains. She had been crying for three days and finally, exhausted, she had washed her face so she could regain enough strength to start crying again. Then she sat down to comb her hair. But why was she combing her hair? Why did she wash her face with soap? If she was tired she could have just splashed water on her face, but she had actually washed her face with soap and water. And she was engrossed in adorning herself. The city was plunged in silence. There was silence in her building. Death had swallowed every one. A frightening desolation pervaded the entire building. Not only were there no signs of life nearby, there were no signs of life for miles. After three days in this quiet, forsaken room, she was now adorning herself. Exhausted and spent. Who was she doing it for? Why? What emotion motivated her? What a strange girl, how beautiful—and when they carried her off she offered no resistance, made no noise. And once again those outstretched arms gripped his heart and his mind. If only he could have that beautiful, tired girl rest her head in his lap, if only he could stroke her swollen eyelids, and do everything that she wanted him to do. The feeling of helplessness overwhelmed him again, tormenting him. He picked up the pillow from the bed and placed it in his lap. Under the pillow was a folded piece of paper, wrinkled and soiled. He picked it up and, unfolding it, began reading. 'My beloved—' He read on quickly, but when he got to the part which said, 'I'll be coming to you soon. I'm yearning to see you, my longing is so great that if even a terrible storm stands in my way it will not be able to prevent me from reaching you—I will come straight to your room, where, adorned and beautiful, you will be waiting for me and—' his hands shook and the letter fell to the floor.

All at once he heard a noise downstairs. There were sounds of *dhamma-dhum*! Perhaps a house nearby was being looted. Picking up the hairpins and the clips, he slipped them into his coat pocket and with faltering steps he climbed down the stairs and silently walked off toward his house.

While still deep in thought, he glanced at the drain again. The water had trickled out and the soap suds, now doused, were no more.

# The Miscreant

By the time news arrives in the small villages and the countryside, it has already lost its appeal. This is not to say that newspapers don't happen to show up in such places, it is just that only the landlords and their educated sons have access to them. And what need do they have to pass the information in the newspapers to the small-time farmers, shopkeepers, and other uneducated folk? These uneducated folk, who have their own confined world in which stories of oxen, ploughs, and personal friendships and animosities abound, they know nothing of what is going on in the rest of the world. Sometimes one of them travelled to the city and returned with all kinds of strange news which was then proudly broadcast to the villagers. But it was curious that the news about the demand for Pakistan immediately spread in all the villages. And how could such news be concealed from this village? What had happened in actuality was that these educated landlords and their grandsons had repented their sins and had not only begun reading the newspapers to the uneducated folk, they had also started making speeches.

In the evening everyone gathered at the village meeting place, the *chaupal;* the *hookahs* began gurgling, the men partook of opium, and the landlord's sons read aloud at the top of their voices from the newspaper for hours and explained matters in detail. Along with this, every now and then a person wearing an air of authority started making rounds of the village. At the landlord's orders, garlands made from wild flowers were draped around the 'leader's neck and thus decked, the leader addressed the villagers in a loud, bellowing voice. The five or six hundred inhabitants of the village scrambled to hear his speech. Among those listening were Hindus as well as Sikhs. The Hindus and Sikhs appeared somewhat troubled, but the faces of the Muslims glowed, as if a red paste had been rubbed on them. Whenever people raised a cry during the speech, the birds pecking at seeds in the fields started, the animals ran this way and that, and the earthen pots of the women drawing water at the well knocked against each other.

The older men and the elders would begin to gather at the *chaupal* as usual. But they had hardly settled down when the young men of the village arrived on the scene, adjusting their turbans as they came. Usually the older inhabitants of the village complained that the young men never showed up at these meetings; nothing could persuade them to come and listen to anything, regardless of whether it was good or bad. They preferred to spend their evenings playing the flute and singing songs of love. But now, the demand for Pakistan had wiped out the grievances of the older inhabitants. Often what happened now was that the young men arrived before the older men did and started talking heatedly amongst themselves. Not about the voluptuous bodies of women and sweethearts, but about Pakistan, and that too as if Pakistan had already been created. Hindu and Sikh men were also part of these conversations.

'And then our government will not require that we pay levies?' A young man would ask.

'Of course not. Because it will be our government.' Fazlu, who was a well-built, six-foot tall young man and who, because of his courage and extreme good character, was regarded as the leader of the young men, would speak forcefully. His manner could lead one to think that he had become the king of Pakistan.

'And brother, you won't take levies from us either?' One of Fazlu's Sikh friends would ask meekly.

'Of course not, my friend. It already makes me sad to see the terrible plight you're in.' Fazlu would lovingly pat his hand.

'When Pakistan is created, don't start thinking ill of us Fazlu *Bhayya*.' A strange kind of fear would flutter in Fazlu's Hindu friend's eyes.

'Come my friend, what are you saying? We grew up together, teased girls together—have you forgotten I was the one who was responsible for the meeting between you and your sweetheart? And now you're talking like this? I'll think of you as one who is the very best.' Fazlu would place his arm around his neck.

'I don't know why I'm scared.' Fazlu's Hindu friend would gaze into Fazlu's eyes as if he were about to leap into them.

'You were always such a coward.' Fazlu would slap his friend's bald head in mock anger and everyone would break into loud laughter. They all talked like this until the older people showed up. Upon the arrival of the older men a very serious discussion about Pakistan's development would ensue and before long the number of oxen would increase, new ploughs would be purchased, suddenly the village would have water pumps, the primary school would reach the middle-school level, and canals would be dug which would inundate the fields in a matter of minutes. And then, late into the night, as if indeed these canals were real, all the men jumped into them and swam home.

With the elections in the assembly, the hustle and bustle at the *chaupal* increased threefold. Fazlu would rope in all his friends and take them to the *chaupal*. If his Hindu and Sikh friends showed the slightest bit of reluctance to come along he would show his displeasure. Who could go against Fazlu's wishes? They would immediately cajole him into spitting out his anger. All of the traditional values of brotherly love were imbued in Fazlu's character; how could he ever imagine that any Hindu or Sikh in his village would oppose the creation of Pakistan? Whenever a calamity occurred, he rushed to provide assistance without giving any thought to religion. He regarded *Bhagvan* and God as the same. And Pakistan was one of God's greatest blessings—how could any man refuse it?

There was news of the impending arrival of a unionist leader. Fazlu didn't pay much attention to the news when he heard it.

But then the chief landlord in the village sent for Fazlu, lovingly offered him a chair in the presence of other landlords from the village and explained why the unionist leader was coming. To bring down the walls of Pakistan, to cut into their votes and inform the British rulers that it was the Muslims themselves who didn't want Pakistan. The man should not be allowed to enter the village, he explained further to Fazlu, because if he did enter he would immediately join forces with the moneylenders and entrap the peasants who were already deep in debt, and then their votes would be automatically diminished. Anxious to show his importance, Fazlu assured the landlord that the leader would not be allowed to set foot in the village.

The unionist leader was indeed not allowed to set foot in the village because on the day of his arrival Fazlu stationed himself along with seventy other men at the spot where he was expected to come from, thus blocking his entry. The leader was flabbergasted. Among the men standing in his way, the Hindus and Sikhs were in greater numbers than the Muslims. The landlord summoned Fazlu and commended him highly.

The elections went very well.

At the *chaupal,* schemes for Pakistan's development continued to be entertained without fail. Thousands of schemes were in the making when suddenly news of Hindu-Muslim riots in Bihar, Nawakhali and Calcutta began pouring in. So many hundred Muslims have been martyred by the Hindus and so many hundred Hindus have been killed by the Muslims. The riots became a topic for discussion at the *chaupal.* Everyone condemned the riots, but Fazlu was the one who couldn't control his agitation. When he tried to imagine that people were destroying links forged over so many years by waving knives, he felt as if his brain was going to explode. These days he was overly solicitous when it came to the Hindus and Sikhs in his village. He could see that, surrounded by hundreds of Muslims, the small number of Sikh and Hindus appeared somewhat subdued and apprehensive.

'Dada, what is happening is really very bad,' he would burst out whenever he ran into an elderly Hindu villager. 'Their brains are addled. Are Allah and *Bhagwan* different that brother is killing brother? If I could help it *Dada*, I would cut the hands of those who are doing the killing, I would throw them before dogs and spit on their faces.' Here a heavy invective would struggle to escape from Fazlu's lips, but he would hold it back. *Dada* would look at Fazlu with affection and then sigh deeply as if thousands of years of tradition were slowly perishing.

'Come now, let's not talk about riots. What does it all have to do with us? Are we having riots in our village?' When Fazlu heard talk of riots from his Hindu friend he got really irritated.

'But what if we did?' his friend would ask in a low voice.

'Then...then Fazlu is still alive.' He would stick out his broad chest and twirl the ends of his small moustache. 'Let's see who can touch anyone in this village. But how can something like this happen, how can something like this happen in our village?' Fazlu would draw a long sigh of satisfaction.

News about the riots took on an increasingly disturbing aspect. The riots were spreading from city to city and Fazlu was losing his peace of mind. Tidings about Pakistan's creation were gaining strength, but Fazlu was not happy at all. He was tormented when he saw how distressed the elderly Hindu villagers and his friends were. For no reason at all he began to think that his friends had distanced themselves from him. These things crept into his mind in strange ways. For example, he made plans to go hunting but his friends couldn't get together on time and he got extremely agitated. This sort of thing used to happen all the time in the past and he never gave it any thought. But now when he got upset his friends would try to make him shake off his anger and he wouldn't relent. He didn't reveal his thoughts to them, but when he was alone he blasted the riots with as many foul curses as there were at his disposal.

Also, for some time now he had begun to hate the newspapers and the landlord's son. There was a time when the sight of a newspaper excited him and the knowledge exhibited by the landlord's son filled him with pride, making him feel as if the young man were his own son. When the landlord's son read the newspaper, Fazlu watched him from a distance with great interest; he felt as though there were blossoms dropping from the boy's mouth. But now the news of the riots had convinced him that both newspapers and education were terrible things. Would there be news of such horrible events if it hadn't been for the newspapers? News which separated friend from friend? And if it hadn't been for education, would the landlord's son have been able to convey these news to the villagers? Now when the landlord's son read from the newspaper, Fazlu felt as if there were embers pouring from his mouth instead of blossoms.

One day when the landlord's son was returning from the *chaupal* after having read the newspaper, Fazlu, who had been standing silently in an isolated part of the street, waylaid him.

'*Malik ji*,' he cleared his throat and began. 'Please don't read the newspaper.' Fazlu's voice was burdened with the weight of entreaty.

'Why?'

'The news that we get is really bad. We are more in number than the Sikhs and the Hindus. Who knows what goes on in their minds when they hear the news. Our love could become tainted, *Malik ji*.'

'Come now, that's not true at all.' The landlord's son laughed loudly. 'It's not just Hindus who are being killed, Muslims are also being martyred. Why should love be tainted? The newspaper is very important, Fazlu, after all how will we know what's happening in the rest of the world, and how will we find out when Pakistan was created? You shouldn't think such useless thoughts. We know that you have a strong bond with your Hindu and Sikh friends, but you shouldn't be so worried.' He laughed, patted Fazlu's back, went on his way.

Fazlu felt like running after *Malik ji* so he could stop him and say, 'You are an animal, you wretch!'

When news about riots took on a gruesome face, Fazlu stopped going to the *chaupal* altogether. But how could he escape the news, because even the children knew what was happening.

'Fazlu *Bhayya*, *Malik ji* has told us that four hundred people have been killed. They throw people into wells, village after village has been destroyed.'

'Were Hindus killed or Muslims?' Fazlu would ask in a muffled tone.

'*Malik ji* said that wherever there are fewer Hindus there the Muslims are taking revenge and where the Muslims are fewer in number there the Hindus are taking revenge...'

Fazlu would silently head on home. These days he did not leave his house very often because wherever he went he felt the fear reflected in the eyes of Hindus and Sikhs pursuing him. The Hindus and Sikhs now seemed so apprehensive that Fazlu's whole being protested. He thought, the world can do what it wants, but why should my village be destroyed? Why should those who had walked shoulder to shoulder with each other now walk about with downcast eyes? He didn't know what to do, how to rid everyone of this fear. Shutting himself up in his house, that is what he pondered all day.

Fazlu heard that tragedy had visited *Chachi's* family; her brother had been killed in Calcutta. He dropped the food he was eating and ran to *Chachi's* house, but no one there was weeping. *Chacha*, *Chachi*, and their daughter whom he called sister, were all silent and apprehensive, as if afraid that if they wept all hell would break loose, that if they made the slightest noise their throats would also be slit. Several of the village elders were also present and everyone stood with heads hung low. For a few minutes Fazlu remained silent. *Chachi* looked at him as though she were saying, 'Fazlu, look, your brothers have snatched my brother, the same brother who brought you a turban from Calcutta and who went hunting with you, the same brother whom you liked very much and about whom you often enquired.' Suddenly Fazlu clasped *Chachi* to him and broke down. It was as if *Chachi* and *Chacha* were waiting for a Muslim to weep with them so that they could give vent to their grief. They wept so much that even the elders could not hold back their tears.

Fazlu was not the same after this incident. He began spending all his time in the company of Hindus and Sikhs. He made every effort to please them and to keep them happy, he ran errands for them and swore at both Hindu and Muslim rioters. He wanted to dispel the clouds of fear that hung over their hearts so that once again the village would resound with the old hustle and bustle. He wished that *Chacha* Baldev would scold him again as he did when he found him out late at night, that *Dada* Sardar Singh would slap him lovingly for not wearing his turban the right way, that *Chachi* would chide him for no reason at all, and the girl he called sister would request that he bring *bindis* for her from the city, that his friends would go hunting with him, plan wrestling bouts with him, and then, pinning him down, laugh merrily. But the locusts of discord were attacking cities and villages, humanity was dead. And in places where there were no actual riots, rioting took root in the minds of people. Desolation sprang up even where nothing had been destroyed. Hunting, wrestling matches and the requests for *bindis* were being slowly swallowed by dread and Fazlu's heart had become as melancholy as a sputtering candle on a grave.

Independence was finally declared on August 15. Independence Day festivities were in progress. Today Fazlu forgot all his woes. Today he could not even see the fear in his friends' eyes. He gathered all his friends in a frenzied manner and got them to make red and yellow streamers. With his own hands he strung up streamers at *Chacha* Baldev and Sardar Singh's house and also distributed streamers to all other Hindu and Sikh households in the village. The *chaupal* was decorated like a bride, the policemen received assistance in decorating the police station and in this connection Fazlu also tolerated a little remonstrance from the *thanedar*. The landlord had special sweets made to celebrate Pakistan and Fazlu, along with his companions, was in the forefront, distributing these sweets. That night decorative oil lamps were lit in every house. A singing and dancing programme had been arranged at the homes of the landlord and the *thanedar*. Ignoring his advanced years, Fazlu also forcibly dragged *Dada* Sardar Singh to the entertainment. Fazlu didn't want a wall of formality to remain standing. He was constantly congratulating the Hindus and the Sikhs, making them aware again and again that Pakistan was theirs too—the dancing and singing continued all night; Fazlu didn't sleep nor did he let any of the others shut their eyes for even a moment.

Suddenly Fazlu's happiness was snuffed out. The trouble in Lahore escalated into dangerous rioting which soon spread all over Pakistan. The Muslims were clearing Pakistan of Hindus and the Hindus were purifying Hindustan. *Malik ji* now said that the Muslims were avenging the deaths of their martyrs. The trains arriving from Pakistan contained not living passengers, but corpses. And then Malik *ji* said that if the people in a village hide the Hindus, people from another village come out to attack them. When the elders heard about this speech they were stunned into silence.

'But *Malik ji,* if anyone dares attack our village I'll smash his teeth!' Fazlu exclaimed passionately. And *Malik ji* merely smiled.

All these horrifying news cast a pall over the entire village. Wherever one went there would be talk of destruction and ruin, people would walk about sighing, their heads hung low. It was as if someone had drained all the blood from the faces of the Hindus; their eyes were dark with misgiving, their faces bore expressions of entreaty—they were begging for their lives. And going from house to house, Fazlu was offering each one a promise of safety.

'*Chacha,* don't be afraid, Fazlu is still alive—*Dada*, Fazlu isn't dead yet—Brother, trust Fazlu.'

One day Fazlu heard that his village was about to be attacked by people from another village. They weren't going to allow a handful of Hindus and Sikhs to remain in a Muslim country, they won't allow them to remain in a country where they were born and where they grew up, where they sang the *mah'ia* at night, sighed longingly for their sweethearts, and where, when they saw the full-grown wheat swaying in the breeze, they kissed the wheat stalks in joy. They can't remain in this place any more. But Fazlu insisted that they remain. He couldn't see his village destroyed.

Fazlu gathered all his friends and devised a plan to protect the village. Everyone had to swear on the honour of their mothers and sisters that they would not make a retreat, even if their own lives were at stake.

Fazlu and his companions spent seven sleepless nights guarding the village. The attack didn't take place, but the good thing to come out of all this was that Hindus and Sikhs began to feel less apprehensive. The expressions on their faces seemed to indicate that they were beginning to trust the Muslims, that although their lives were in danger, there was someone who would protect them from that danger.

Calm prevailed for a while until suddenly there was another uproar one day. Two of the moneylenders had been knifed to death. Their bodies were discovered in the woods on the outskirts of the village in the early hours of the morning. Next to their bodies lay their overturned, shiny brass bowls. Their clothes had caught on the brambles in the nearby bushes and blood had dried around them. The moment the people who had discovered the bodies brought the news to the village, the entire village spilled out to the site of the murders. The Muslim elders stood with their heads bowed low in grief and anger and the young men screamed furiously.

'By God, if we knew who has done this we will blacken his face and put him on a donkey!'

'I will kill them!' Fazlu clenched his fists. All his hard work had been in vain. The Hindus shut their doors in fear. One could hear the women inside crying. No Hindu could be seen standing around the corpses. Fazlu didn't know what to do. The elders decided that everyone would get together at the *chaupal* that night and solicit oaths to see who had done this.

With great difficulty Fazlu and his companions forced the Hindus to open their doors. He assured them that tonight the truth would become known. The murderers would be meted out such punishment as would make the entire village tremble. Afterward the bodies were removed and readied for cremation. The Hindus came out timidly to carry the corpses to the funeral pyre.

That night when the oaths were administered the truth was revealed. Two very poor farmers confessed that this was their doing. The landlord had told them that if they killed the moneylenders they would be released from all their debts and the interest that kept multiplying. Because their families were starving, they were taken in by the devil's advice. After they had made their confession, the farmers placed their turbans at the feet of the elders. They wept in shame, but they were also afraid the landlord might find out they had confessed. Everyone was fuming with anger because no one had the courage to fight such a powerful landlord. The police station belonged to the landlord, and the *thanedar* was the landlord's personal friend.

All this was concealed from the Hindus. Fazlu and his friends were instructed to tell the Hindus that the murder had been committed by people in the nearby village. They came at night and hid in the woods and killed two of their men. But they shouldn't worry. The village will be watched day and night.

They were given thousands of assurances, but the Hindus no longer felt safe. Several families packed their luggage. They were going to leave the village. After Fazlu got tired of telling them they were in no danger, he would make arrangements to get them out safely through the Muslim areas. He and his companions would travel with them all the way, and when the tiny family disappeared from view he would feel as if his own mother were taking her last breath right before his eyes. He would start sobbing like a child.

Some of the families were so apprehensive and fearful that they quietly departed in the middle of the night. In the morning when Fazlu discovered they had gone he would become agitated. Who knows what they will go through—they should have trusted Fazlu at least. That day Fazlu would become so depressed he wouldn't eat anything. All day long he would go from one house to the next in an attempt to prevent others from sneaking away like this. Perhaps it was because of him that fifteen or twenty families were still undecided about leaving.

One day the *thanedar* called in Fazlu and some of his companions. He was throwing a party to celebrate the creation of Pakistan and had invited a few select guests. He entrusted all the preparations to Fazlu, a task Fazlu took on happily.

When everybody had eaten and left, Fazlu and his friends cleaned up and put everything away. They finished around two. On his way home with his friends, he passed by the landlord's house and saw him pacing outside his house. There were several other men with him. Fazlu wondered why all of them were strolling about at such a late hour. It had been a long time since they had eaten and gone home. 'Maybe the landlord has eaten too much of the *thanedar's* food,' Fazlu's friend joked, stifling a laugh.

'You fool, you plough the fields of the landlord to fill your stomach—if he hears you you will starve.' Fazlu too was trying to restrain his amusement.

Just as they moved a few steps further the landlord's sharp voice dropped chains on their feet.

'Come here Fazlu.'

Fazlu quickly went up to the landlord. For a few seconds the landlord was silent. He was looking at Fazlu with a sympathetic expression on his face.

'What did you want, *Zamindar ji*?' Fazlu bowed his head. He couldn't understand why the landlord was looking at him in this manner.

'I was waiting for you. Fazlu, the news is very bad. When I returned I found out that *Devi* Deval's family slipped away at midnight, and the terrible tragedy is that they abducted your sister and took her with them.'

'*Zamindar ji*...' Fazlu stared at him like a madman. 'This is a lie, they cannot take my sister, no one can take my sister.' The six-foot tall Fazlu crumpled to his feet. His only sister, his treasure. She was four when their parents died and Fazlu was the one who raised her. He had suffered a great deal of hardship for her sake, stumbled so many times. That was the sister who had been snatched from him. And snatched by the people for whom he had given up his sleeping and waking hours, for whom he had put his own safety aside.

'If you don't believe me, go and see for yourself, your sister is not at home.' *Zamindar ji* raised his voice passionately. 'Those bastards have abducted the innocent child, the unfortunate girl—now when naked women are paraded, the bastards will push your sister into the crowd as well—that's why they have taken her, so they can humiliate her. How sad that the villains have slit the neck of the very person who had protected them.' The landlord placed a hand on Fazlu's back.

'This is life, master,' bowing his head, the servant standing nearby whispered.

'They took my sister! They cannot do such a thing, *Zamindar ji*...for their sake I have...' Fazlu was speaking as if in extreme pain. He held his head between his hands. With great difficulty his friends lifted him up, and then who knows where he suddenly found the strength, but like someone driven by insanity he sprinted toward his house. The door was shut. He pushed it open and leaped in. The flame in the lamp on the ledge burnt low and his sister's bed, the sheets dishevelled, had been tossed upside down.

Turning up the flame in the lamp, he cried, 'Begma!' When he didn't get a reply he ran frantically from one corner of the house to the other. She was not in the house.

'Begma, my sister!' he screamed again with ferocity and then he pulled at his hair. In the dimmed light he could clearly see his sister walking in the midst of a crowd of naked women, drops of blood dripping from her face and her body.

'I will not spare even one of them, I'll kill them all!' Swiftly he opened a trunk of clothes and pulled out a long, shiny dagger from under the clothes. As he ran his finger along the blade of the dagger a few drops of blood fell to the floor and were absorbed into the mud. He kissed the dagger and ran. His enraged friends followed him.

Fazlu was hurrying through the streets as if he were in a daze. The wolves howled in the woods nearby, the dogs barked, but Fazlu could hear nothing, could see nothing.

First he entered *Chachi's* house. *Chachi* and the girl Fazlu called his sister were asleep. *Chacha*, however, was awake and sat on his bed as though guarding them.

'Fazlu, my son, you could have done this by yourself, why have you bothered the others.'

For a moment Fazlu's raised hand halted in mid-air, but in the very next instant his lamenting sister appeared before his eyes. She was naked. There was blood dripping from her lips. After he had finished with *Chacha*, Fazlu turned toward the girl he called his sister. He ripped off her clothes. He chewed her lips with his teeth. He trampled her body mercilessly and then he hacked her body into pieces and hurled the pieces into the street.

Afterward the sounds of screams could be heard all night and when the rooster crowed in the morning Fazlu had finished taking his revenge. His eyes were red like raw meat, his hair was dishevelled, his mind was completely numb. He was standing motionless on the street leading to the mosque as if he had no home, no place to go to. Tears flowed unchecked from his eyes.

When the elders of the village left their homes to go to the mosque for prayers, their heads were lowered, their faces bore expressions of intense pain. When they approached Fazlu they stopped.

'Go home, son.' They patted him on the head. Fazlu could not comprehend what they were saying. All he could see was the crowd of naked women with his sister in the front.

With great difficulty Fazlu's friends took him home and made him lie down. They sprinkled cold water on his face. The elders of the village stopped by to see him on their way back from prayers.

'Such a nice boy, so decent. What if he loses his mind? If that wretched Diyalu hadn't taken his sister with him none of this would have happened. Would he have seen the murder of so many good friends?' They murmured quietly amongst themselves and left.

Fazlu remained in that state for several hours. The tears didn't stop flowing nor did he speak. All he did was stare fixedly at the ceiling.

'Begma *behan*!' A friend of Fazlu's who was sitting near him screamed loudly and then, picking up his turban, ran outside.

Fazlu could not believe his eyes. But his widowed aunt, *Masi* was with her too. He jumped up and clasped his sister in his arms. Then he began touching her as if to make sure she wasn't a clay image. But the clay image was talking.

'*Bhayya*, I was awake all night, there were such sounds of screaming, it was terrifying. No one knows what happened. None of the women came to *Masi's* house this morning—I'm glad I didn't stay here alone—you were working, I would have died if I had been here by myself. *Masi* came last night, she was so worried and she said, 'Come with me, there's going to be trouble in the village and there's a Hindu family right next door—who knows when Fazlu will return.' I was just worried about you *Bhayya*, I thought, God forbid...' She began kissing his arm wildly.

'Yes Fazlu, I had just finished eating and was about to go to bed when the *zamindar's* man came and he said there's trouble in the village, Fazlu will be working all night, and you go and get his sister, the Hindus are right next door, who knows what can happen, I'm only concerned with your well-being, and she's our sister too, isn't she. And so I go up right away. How right he was. Begma would have been terrified, she was crying all night.' The old woman was out of breath because of the long distance she had walked. 'May God forgive us, what kind of screams were these Fazlu, how did all this happen?' The old woman sat down on the bed.

'*Masi*...' Fazlu could not utter a single word. Pushing Begma aside, he fell on the bed with a thud and began sobbing uncontrollably like a child. 'Killed everyone...killed everyone...O *Zamindar ji*...the girl I called sister...' Fazlu bit down on his lips.

The old woman was looking at him in surprise while Begma, clinging to her brother's arm, wept.

That night at the *chaupal* the elders whispered amongst themselves and tried to pacify the weeping, wailing Fazlu. They knew everything now. They also knew where the wealth of the moneylenders had gone, who had swallowed the goods belonging to someone else.

Fazlu could not get even with the landlord because he made his living by working in his fields. He wanted to marry off his sister, it was the landlord's land that was helping him prepare his sister's dowry, it was this land that had enabled him to take care of his sister after their parents death; how could he get even with the *zamindar*? How could he abandon his sister, the sister for whom he had spilled the blood of his loved ones and taken on in return a lifetime of pain and agony for himself?

The next day Fazlu roamed about the village like someone who was lost. He could not find peace, there was a strange wild look on his face. The empty houses of *Chacha* Baldev, *Dada* Sardar Singh, and their companions seemed to cut right through his heart. Distraught and anguished, he returned home and tried to calm himself by engaging in idle chatter with Begma.

In the afternoon, just when Begma was giving him some *lassi*, there was a loud knock on the door. When Fazlu opened the door he saw a policeman standing there. This was a man he knew well.

'Fazlu *bhayya*, the *thanedar* wants to see you. It's something important.'

'All right,' Fazlu mumbled helplessly. He didn't want to work today. He felt as if he had no energy left. 'You go ahead and I'll be along shortly.' Fazlu wanted a little time. But the policeman didn't budge from his place and so he was forced to accompany him.

'Well Fazlu, how are you sir?' the *thanedar* broke into a loud guffaw the moment he saw Fazlu.

'By your grace, I am well.' Fazlu lowered his head and clasped his hands together.

'Yes, Fazlu *sahib*, I heard that you wiped them all out in the middle of the night. We were asleep, we didn't even know what happened.' The *thanedar* laughed raucously again. '*Zamindar ji* has informed us that you are responsible for all this unrest.' Suddenly the *thanedar's* manner changed. He thundered. 'Look, you bastard, you've had some practice now so you had better be careful, otherwise, if I so wish, you can rot in jail for the rest of your life. It's just that your earlier good behaviour comes in the way. Now remember, you are not to go near *Zamindar ji's* house. I'll pull out your tongue if I hear you have even passed by his house and *Munshi ji*...' He turned to his clerk, 'Put this worthless bastard's name down on the list of miscreants.' The *thanedar* burst into another laugh and gave the bewildered, wide-eyed Fazlu a smack on the head.

# Excerpt from *Aangan*

Pakistan had been founded. Leaders of the Muslim League had left for the capital, Karachi. A bloodbath was being played out in the Punjab. *Bare Chacha,* shocked into despair, sat in the *bethak* like a sick person and kept asking over and over again, 'What is happening? How did Muslims and Hindus suddenly become each other's sworn enemies? Who taught them this? Who took away love from their hearts?'

When he asked Aliya all this, she patted his head and said, '*Bare Chacha,* rest, you're tired.' And *Bare Chacha* shut his eyes as if the river of blood was flowing right before his eyes.

Kariman *Bua* sighed when she heard reports of violence. 'How everything has changed. There was a time when the Hindus would give their lives if the Muslims in their village were threatened and the Muslims would sacrifice all to save the honour of the Hindus. Such was the spirit of brotherhood that it seemed the two had been born from the same mother. But nothing remains now. They both have daggers in their hands now.' There hadn't been any riots in their town, but everyone was terrified. Who knew what might happen and when.

'Where is my Shakeel?' *Bari Chachi* began wailing when she heard that riots had broken out in Bombay. 'Your Pakistan has been created Jamil, your father's country is also free, but who will bring home my Shakeel?'

'Everything will be all right *Amma,* he will be fine. These riots aren't going to last more than three or four days.' Jamil tried to placate his mother, but his own face remained ashen.

In the evening, while everyone was having tea, *Mamun's* letter arrived. He had written to *Amma*, telling her he had dedicated his services to Pakistan and was leaving soon. 'If you are coming with me let me know right away and be ready.'

'Jamil, send him a telegram immediately. It won't take us any time at all to get ready, we're ready now. He's my own brother, how can he go without me?' *Amma's* face was flushed with joy.

Jamil looked at everyone apprehensively, as if the rioters had arrived at their very door. 'But why would you want to leave, *Choti Chachi*? You're safe here. I'll give my life to protect you.' He turned to look at Aliya, something he hadn't done in a very long time. What a pleading look that was. But Aliya lowered her eyes.

'So I shouldn't leave, and live instead in the land of the Hindus? At least it will be our own people governing in Pakistan. And what's more important, I can't live without my brother for an instant. Ah!' *Amma* was beside herself with excitement.

'Aliya will not leave, *Choti Chachi,* she won't go, she can't leave.' Jamil spoke as if in a state of delirium.

'Who are you to flaunt your rights?' *Amma* became enraged. 'Who are you to stop her?'

Jamil lowered his head. 'Yes, yes, you must leave *Choti Chachi.*' Aliya felt she could not go. Centuries would pass and still she would not be able to move from this spot.

'I'll send a telegram right away that everyone is ready.' Jamil got up and left.

Aliya felt like screaming that she was not leaving, that she couldn't leave, that no one could force her to leave. Her throat was lined with thorns, she couldn't utter a single word. She looked around her and then lowered her gaze. But why should she stay? Who should she stay for? she thought and calmly began cutting *chalia. Aliya Begum, if you stayed behind you would be stuck in mire for the rest of your life.*

'Kariman *Bua*, if everyone has had tea, will you . . .' Asrar *Mian* called from the *bethak* and Kariman *Bua* started yelling like a witch. 'I say, will someone send this Asrar *Mian* to

Pakistan as well. Everyone's gone, everyone will go, but he won't go anywhere.'

The sound of Asrar *Mian*'s coughing became audible for a moment and then there was silence.

'Will you really go, *Choti Dulhan*?' *Bari Chachi*, who had said nothing all this time, asked.

'Of course I'll go,' *Amma* replied curtly.

'This is your house too *Choti Dulhan*, don't leave me alone here.' Tears gathered in her eyes. She looked away. Perhaps she was afraid of the loneliness that was to come.

As if in search of a haven, Aliya ran upstairs. The sunlight, now a yellowed hue, had crept up on the high wall of the house across from theirs. The birds seeking shelter in the compound of the high school were making a din.

Once in the fresh, open air, she sighed in satisfaction and began pacing back and forth like a passenger on a platform, thinking about what to do next. Perhaps this was for the best; she would find happiness if she left.

When she came down she found everyone lost in their own thoughts. Only Kariman *Bua* was still muttering as she speedily cooked *roti* after *roti*.

*Where is Jamil? Why isn't he back yet?* Aliya looked at the empty chair. She wondered if this strange man would remember her or forget her.

The wick in the lantern was worn and there were twin flames rolling from it. The glass chimney was blackened on one side. In the dim light the faces of *Amma*, *Bari Chachi* and *Kariman Bua* appeared distorted.

Jamil returned and went to sit in his chair. 'I've sent the telegram *Choti Chachi*,' he said slowly.

'You shouldn't stay out so late,' *Bari Chachi* said, 'you should come home by evening. Who knows when the trouble might start here.'

'One has to stay out late. The Muslims are scared. They have to be told that they should remain resolute and maintain a calm atmosphere. One can't do all this by staying at home.'

'How dreadful,' *Amma* said. 'Now that the country is free all this has started. Well, it doesn't concern me. You did put the correct address on the telegram, didn't you?'

'You shouldn't worry, the address is correct.'

'By God's grace, we are leaving for Pakistan, but you should worry about your family, Jamil. No one is well, and just look at your mother.' *Amma* looked sympathetically at *Bari Chachi*.

'Who is going to Pakistan?' *Bare Chacha* asked in a bewildered tone the moment he set foot inside the house. He had heard what *Amma* was saying.

'Aliya and I will go, who else?' *Amma* replied sharply.

'No one can go, no one can leave this house without my permission. Why will you go to Pakistan? This is our country, we have sacrificed so much for it and now we should leave it and go? At last we have the opportunity to live a life of comfort.' *Bare Chacha* spoke passionately.

'My, my! Since when have you become the protector of our rights? What have you done for us? We have suffered every conceivable sorrow here, you snatched my husband from me, you killed him, you orphaned my daughter, and now you flaunt your rights?' *Amma*'s voice quaked with anger.

*Bare Chacha* lowered his head. '*Kariman Bua*, have my food brought to the *bethak*,' he said, and walked away from there.

'Is this how you want to repay *Bare Chacha* before you leave? He has not ruined anyone. He didn't invite anyone to join him. You listen very carefully to what I am saying today— I love *Bare Chacha* as much as I loved *Abba*.' Aliya pushed away her food and after washing her hands, came to the *bethak*. She paid no heed to *Amma*'s muttering.

'Are you really going, my child?'

'Yes *Bare Chacha*, *Amma* is all set to go, what can I do?' she replied helplessly.

'The Englishman has played a clever hand even as he was leaving. He has uprooted families from their homes. Still, my dear, don't go, explain to your mother, the time has finally come for you to be blessed with good fortune.'

'*Bare Chacha,* I'm *Amma*'s only support, how can I abandon her? She will go no matter what. You don't know how unhappy I am at the thought of leaving this house and how I will suffer. You, you...' She hid her face in her hands and broke into sobs.

'I know that *Choti Dulhan* hates me. I know I didn't do anything for all of you, but the time has come to make amends, to bring the good old days back. I'm being offered a very good job, in addition there is a chance I will get ten or fifteen thousand rupees to invest in the shops. I will wipe out all of *Choti Dulhan's* grievances.' He patted Aliya lovingly. 'Is there no oil in the house? The light from the lantern is getting dimmer. God willing, I'll arrange for power to be reconnected soon. And you should get admission in a master's programme, I think I will definitely help you get admission next year.'

Aliya's heart was breaking. She wiped her tears and sat mutely. A turmoil raged inside her, but she couldn't utter a single word. May God bless you with peace, *Bare Chacha,* she prayed silently, may all your dreams be fulfilled. How could she tell *Bare Chacha* that in reality she too wanted to run away from here.

Asrar *Mian* was at the door of the *bethak.* Aliya walked out of there to the veranda.

Who knows what *Amma* and *Bari Chachi* were saying to each other. Jamil was still sitting in his chair, twisting his fingers. For a few moments she stood in the courtyard and then she went upstairs.

The dew-soaked night was bright with the light of the moon. The moon seemed to be shining in the middle of the sky and as was customary every day, someone was playing a record on one of the rooftops nearby.

'There's a thief after your purse, traveller, beware.'

She began strolling slowly. She felt so strange. As if someone had snatched her powers of reasoning. 'Is this me?' she asked herself and was surprised at her own voice. What madness—who was this she was questioning?

At one point, as she was walking back and forth, she turned and suddenly found herself face to face with Jamil. He was standing still, like a statue. She hastened her step. *What is he here for, has he forgotten his promise?*

'Have you really decided to go?' he asked in a quiet voice.

'Yes,' she replied without pausing.

'You will be making a grave mistake. Don't you remember you said once that memories become very painful when one is far away. I don't think you will be happy there.'

'I will be happy wherever I am. But you promised me that you will not say anything to me.'

'What am I saying?'

'Nothing.'

'You are in my debt, remember that you will have to pay me back.' He turned to go. 'You will be happy there, won't you?' he asked, stopping for a moment.

She remained silent. Jamil continued standing near her for a few minutes longer and then he left. She felt as if she had lost everything.

After she had been strolling a long time she got tired and, coming downstairs, she started writing a letter to Chammi. She had to inform her of their departure from here.

# Excerpt from *Zamin*—I

Her decision to remain in this house was not a recent one. The day she made that decision she did not leave her room all day and all night she cried until she finally fell into the deep abyss of helplessness. This was the night when she realized that a woman's lot is loss, suffering and helplessness. But the thought made her angry. Finally, with great determination, she avowed that just as one erases misspelled words, she would wipe out these notorious labels that are attached to women. After that day she resumed living in that house as if it were her right to do so. Everyone, except for Kazim and Salima's mother, *Khalabi*, had accepted her by now.

Kazim teased her. 'Do you think you're Napoleon? It would be something if you vanquished me and *Khalabi*. They're stupid, those who think you are one of them and who agree with everything you say.'

'Vanquish you? You're nobody. As for *Khalabi*, I am not interested in her at all.' Sajida responded very calmly to Kazim's sarcasm and busied herself in some task or the other, ignoring Kazim as he were just a clump of clay.

'I,' he said, swelling up his chest arrogantly, 'I am very important Sajida *Begum*! You'll soon find out how important.'

He used a threatening tone and for just a moment Sajida found herself turning weak with fear, but she immediately pulled herself together and felt strong again.

When dinner ended amidst a chorus of political discourse, she went with *Ammabi* to her room. She felt as much affection for *Ammabi* as she felt hate for Kazim. For some reason she saw *Ammabi* as a restless, thirsty dove in search of water. In any case she was compelled to spend most of her time in *Ammabi*'s room these days because Salima was studying for her M.A. exams and needed privacy.

'Do you really love me Sajida?' *Ammabi* asked one day, surprising Sajida with the suddenness of her question.

'Love?' She collected herself. 'You can call it what you wish *Ammabi*. I feel peace when I'm close to you and I get a whiff of that same fragrance of love from you that I felt on *Abba's* person.' Feeling helpless, she lowered her head.

A peaceful expression appeared momentarily on *Ammabi's* face and was gone in the next instant.

'You know that my own children don't love me,' she said sadly, a vacant look floating in her eyes.

'How is that possible, *Ammabi*?'

'Everything is possible. Kazim is his father's son, and Nazim, well he has distanced himself from me because I don't know how to fight for my rights. That silly boy doesn't know that one can achieve a great deal by fighting, but one cannot receive love in that way.'

Sajida suddenly remembered something Taji had said. 'Salima's mother is like my mother, *Baji*.'

'Who snatched your love from you, *Ammabi*?' Sajida gently took *Ammabi*'s hand in hers. It was cold as ice.

'There was no question of anyone snatching it. We were children when we were engaged and when I was older I began to love my fiance just as every young girl does. But he was in love with my cousin, Amina. Do you know Amina?'

'No.'

'Salima's mother, your *Khalabi*. But no one knows this. We were married, Nazim was born, and then when I was pregnant with Kazim, Amina was widowed. Malik brought Amina and Salima to our house. I was happy, and the world also applauded his action.' She became lost in thought.

'What happened then *Ammabi*?'

'What do you think? I discovered the truth. After Amina's arrival he started drinking heavily. I cut myself off from him. I hated Kazim because Amina was raising him and also because he resembled his father. *Uff!*' She began rubbing her face with her hands. 'The hell we create with hate is worse than the real hell. Am I wrong?'

'No.'

'And Nazim wanted me to escape from this hell. As soon as he was old enough, he began urging me to leave his father, get a divorce, remarry and—' She broke into tears. But a minute later she dried her tears and sat with her head lowered as if tormented by a sense of guilt. Why was she was telling Sajida all this, who was she to her?

'*Ammabi*, I'm like your own daughter, don't you trust me at all?' Sajida asked gently, but she was immediately beset with feelings of remorse. It's the same tongue that utters the name of God and the same tongue that also delivers curses. *Ammabi* sat silently with her head still bowed. God knows what she was thinking. Sajida didn't know what to say. Malik didn't even have the moral courage, she thought, to admit his love before he was married. He abandoned two lives at the gates of hell and drowned himself in a sea of alcohol. What an easy way to avoid facing reality. What a crass way in which to celebrate love. She wondered if he still thought about all this. For the first time Sajida felt sorry for *Khalabi*. Who thought about her, who was there who saw her as a prison cell in which her emotions, her thoughts, her tears, her longings, were all serving a sentence as punishment for the crime of love?

'Now that you're here my loneliness has been diminished somewhat. I've been alone for twenty years. Salima is a very nice girl and she has tried her best to get close to me. But for some reason I haven't been able to make her mine, even though I know she doesn't like her mother.'

Sajida gave no reply. Salima's face, with its embarrassed look, floated before her eyes.

Sajida got up to leave when Nazim slowly walked into the room.

'Please stay Sajida *bi*, I'll go.' He cast a penetrating look at Sajida.

Sajida left without a word and returned to her room. Moonlight from the window played on her bed. She lay down without turning on the light. Perhaps love has been the cause for the most oppression in the world, she thought. How much tragedy, loss, and contention had resulted from the actions of those who professed love, how much had been plundered in the name of love, and still people didn't stop loving. Moved by her own stubborn feelings, Sajida broke into tears and after she had wept a long time, her heart told her, 'You will never be able to forget Salahuddin, Sajida, your waiting will never end.'

She got up and walked to the window. The trees and plants were all shadows in the moonlight, but under the large *peepal* tree she saw two bundles. What was that? Perhaps someone was sitting there, but who? she wondered curiously.

After a short while the bundles moved, stood up and walked past her window. She was rooted to the ground.

Taji walked away in the direction of the garage and Kazim came to the veranda. A little later she heard the door of the gallery open and shut.

Sajida fell on her bed. Taji's mother had pushed her toward the caravan and had said that she should clasp the hands of a good man in her country. She kept thinking of this. How could she explain to Taji that the hands that were giving her support were not to be trusted.

Early in the morning when she returned to her room with her bedding, she became aware of a great stillness around her. Last night when she had taken her bedding to the lawn to sleep there, the fragrance of *raat ki rani* had filled her with nostalgia about her own home and, feeling distracted, she had muttered vague replies to Salima's queries. In one year she had trained herself to find release from the pain of remembrance. Because inactivity treats memory like a rival, she tried to keep herself busy all the time.

She came to the gallery quickly where *Khalabi* was dusting the vases. She followed her to Kazim's room.

'Look how untidy these three keep their room,' *Khalabi* said. 'They're grown up but still they have no sense of neatness. And

Kazim,' she said, smiling lovingly, 'he's like a two-year old. I get all tired and sweaty from cleaning his room. Nazim is the only one who maintains some tidiness around him.' *Khalabi* cleaned Kazim's room with loving care while Sajida watched her from afar. 'Your Kazim is not a baby, he's the oldest,' Sajida said sarcastically, but the sarcasm was lost on *Khalabi*.

'Yes, although he thinks he's a philosopher. And he's so good at his studies, and so naughty he won't let anyone be quiet for long. He's not serious like Nazim. I've raised Kazim, you know, I took him when he was born, when Salima was two. *Baji* didn't take Kazim in her lap even for a minute. When I weaned Samina I thought I wouldn't have any more milk, but by God's grace, rivers of milk began to flow.'

'I know everything,' Sajida said dryly.

'What do you know?' *Khalabi* asked in astonishment.

'How you've raised Kazim. I think if you weren't around, this house would have gone to rack and ruin, and as for Kazim, he probably wouldn't have survived.' Sajida maintained a normal tone.

'May God bless him with my life as well. You're right. If it hadn't been for me this house wouldn't be what it is today. *Baji*, the poor thing, has always been frail and weak, and she has always remained aloof. Anyway, what need does she have to work when I'm here to take care of things.' *Khalabi* spoke cheerfully.

'Have you listened to the news today?' Nazim's words, spoken dejectedly, broke in on them.

They were both taken aback to find him in Kazim's room at this time of day.

'The *Quaid-i-Azam* has passed away,' Nazim informed them in a melancholy tone and quickly left the room.

Sajida felt that *Quaid-i-Azam*'s body was lying right next to her heart and she couldn't even cry.

'Oh my God, what will happen now!' *Khalabi* dashed out of the room. Sajida followed her. '*Arre*, we didn't even have a chance to settle down—did you hear, *Quaid-i-Azam* is dead, Malik. Where are you?' She screamed and started crying.

*Khalabi's* scream unnerved everyone. *Ammabi* appeared on the threshold of her door for a moment and disappeared. Taji was standing next to Kazim, her hands covered with dough. Sajida couldn't remember when he came or from where.

'Kazim *Mian*, what will happen now? I won't go back to my mother.' Taji broke into sobs.

'You silly girl, you won't go anywhere!' Nazim looked at her angrily and then shut his eyes. He was reclining silently in an armchair in the veranda.

'Well, there goes this bungalow, make preparations to move into the quarter, that horrible man won't allow us to live here any longer.' Recently Malik had started drinking in the morning as well; he teetered on his feet.

'What horrible man?'

'That man—your father—whose bungalow we're living in,' Malik yelled. Nazim turned away his face.

'You come to your room, Malik.' Salima appeared just as *Khalabi* was taking him back to his room. Her eyes had reddened.

Schools, colleges and offices were all closed.

'Salima, you're crying too, I see,' Nazim said. 'People on the streets are banging their heads against walls and sobbing hysterically.'

Salima said nothing.

'What will happen now, *Bhai Mian*?' Kazim asked. This was the first time Sajida had seen him look fearful. For a moment she felt great satisfaction.

'Yes, what will happen now?' Nazim looked disdainfully at Kazim. 'How strange that with *Quaid-i-Azam*'s passing, many of the people see the death and destruction of this country. Why don't people realize that this country owes its existence to the struggles of a great many people. They've lost their sense of selfhood at the passing of just one leader. True, we need to mourn, but isn't this attitude our country's misfortune also?' Nazim swiftly rose to his feet and, giving the front door a push, he left the house.

When Sajida made her way to her room she saw that Taji, leaning against the door, was still weeping. Sajida placed her hand lovingly on her shoulder. 'Don't cry Taji, nothing will happen, nothing at all. You'll continue to live here, in Pakistan. You'll never go back to your mother.'

Taji didn't say anything. Keeping her head bowed, she walked away slowly and Sajida came to her room and sat down on her bed. Today, for the first time, Nazim's comments had made her feel good. She felt at peace. Suddenly she remembered what Gamu used to say. 'Drink hot tea, eat soft *roti*.' How can anyone dare to threaten a country which is inhabited by such people?

# Excerpt from *Zamin*—II

Nazim and Sajida's arrival made *Zamindar Sahib* and Lalli very happy. In the evening Nazim argued with *Zamindar Sahib* for hours in his lawn. *Zamindar Sahib* was adamant that big and small, rich and poor, everyone had been created by God, and Nazim tried to explain that God had created only human beings and the division of big and small was one that human beings had brought about themselves. 'The one who plunders is rich while the one who is plundered is poor. How hard your tenant farmers work on your lands to provide you with a luxurious lifestyle, but look at their own condition; they hunger for life's most basic comforts.'

One day the argument took a rather nasty turn. *Zamindar Sahib* was saying in a loud voice, 'You're talking about the rights of the poor? When they are clubbed, their rights will be finished, they will cease to exist.'

'And *Zamindar Sahib*, what if the club makes a turnaround?' Nazim replied angrily, adding, 'But blinding riches prevent one from thinking about the future.'

*Zamindar Sahib* retorted, 'If you continue to harbour these opinions in Pakistan you'll be spending the rest of your life in jail.'

After this unpleasant exchange Nazim didn't meet *Zamindar Sahib* nor did Lalli come to visit. Nazim was still so weak that he spent the major part of his day in bed. His liver and his intestines had both been damaged while he was in jail. He read most of the time and played with Asad sometimes. Sajida had managed to get work as a teacher in a nearby school and somehow they all managed to make do on her meagre salary. Sajida felt that Nazim was getting worse, but she didn't say anything to him; she didn't want him to be burdened physically or emotionally. It broke her heart to see him drag his leg when he walked.

Housework, taking care of the children, teaching, watching over Nazim—she didn't have the time to entertain any forgotten memories. When the movement against the Qadianis picked up and schools and colleges were closed, she got a chance to spend more time at home. She didn't mention anything to Nazim, but she was always fearful. One day while she was heating the food she heard a knock on the door. Her heart beat violently. They hadn't come again for Nazim, had they? Every time there was knocking on the door her heart beat uncontrollably.

She opened the door. It was *Zamindar Sahib*. He patted her head lovingly. 'You may be angry with us, but when we call someone sister we stand by our commitment. Is Nazim *Sahib* in?'

'Come in *Zamindar Sahib*,' she said cheerfully and brought him in to Nazim who was reading the newspaper with a look of extreme distress mapped on his face.

'There are terrible clashes with the Qadianis,' *Zamindar Sahib* said, 'you've seen the news, haven't you? A lot of people have died. There's been looting, and look at the police, they're shooting at their own people. I say, let the looters do what they want, the Qadianis aren't Muslims—our government has gone too far, it has arrested such prominent religious scholars all because of these people who are fated to go to hell.' *Zamindar Sahib* delivered his speech in one breath.

'I agree that these religious scholars should finish off all the *kafirs* in the world, but *Zamindar Sahib*, tell me something — how spacious will that hell be where all these people are headed? Heaven is only for people like you, isn't it?'

'Look here Nazim *Sahib*, this is no time for humour.'

Suddenly they heard the sounds of uncontrolled weeping coming from the direction of the compound. Bewildered, Sajida dashed to the door. A bloody corpse had been brought into the compound. Women standing around the rope cot were beating their chests and wailing. As they pounded their chests they challenged the young men. 'Go, go and kill ten to avenge the death of one and become martyrs.'

Sajida felt her head swimming. Blood, riots, the streets of Delhi, the refugee camps—everything spun around before her eyes. Somehow she steadied herself and returned to the room.

'What's happened?' Nazim supported her as he helped her into a chair.

'A corpse has arrived, soaked in blood.' She leaned against the back of the chair and shut her eyes.

Nazim immediately turned on the radio. 'Martial law has been declared in Lahore.' Martial law regulations were being announced on the radio.

'The most frightening achievement of inept leaders,' Nazim said, shutting his eyes in pain.

'I'll be leaving now to check things at home,' *Zamindar Sahib* said, 'the servants had gone out to see the excitement firsthand, I hope the fools won't be killed for nothing.' He got ready to leave.

'Don't worry, bullets recognize also the servants of landowners.'

*Zamindar Sahib* left without responding to Nazim's remark.

The sounds of weeping were heart-rending. With what difficulty the children of the poor are raised, Sajida thought, and how easily they're pushed forward to take the bullets, and those who push them don't receive a single scratch. The noise of weeping continued through the night. She had given Nazim a sleeping pill, but she herself tossed about restlessly all night. All kinds of thoughts were in pursuit of her sleep like ghosts. She also wondered what the Deputy Commissioner was doing. How happy he must be with this *holi* that was being played with blood!

Because of the martial law, at the funeral the next morning only nine or ten men were present to carry the *janaza*. The screams of the women had now turned to sobbing. Nazim kept saying over and over again, 'I hope this martial law doesn't prove to be the black cloud of the future.'

Sajida listened quietly to everything he said. For a whole year he had been pacing about restlessly in a two-room house.

'Why don't you rest for a while.' Sajida lost her temper. 'If you can't do anything then what's the use...'

And, his spirits dampened, Nazim went and lay down on his bed in silence.

No sooner had the terror that goes with martial law been diluted somewhat than another bit of bad news was broadcast. Daultana *Sahib* had resigned from his position as Prime Minister.

'How many governments have been dismissed since Pakistan came into existence, and which government is offering its resignation now?' Nazim asked absently.

'I don't remember,' Sajida replied apathetically and continued helping her son Asad with his clothes.

In the evening Nazim's friends arrived. The silence in the room was suddenly broken. A heated discussion about martial law and Daultana's resignation ensued. Sajida rushed to make tea so she could sit down with them and hear their point of view. Everyone was saying something or the other; it was as if they had all been given the opportunity to speak after days of silence. But Nazim said nothing.

'Are you still terrified of martial law?' a friend asked.

'I'm not terrified of anything,' Nazim replied in a placid tone. 'I was just listening to what you all were saying. Now let me tell you that Daultana hasn't resigned. As if on a special mission on behalf of someone in Karachi, the Defence Secretary, Iskander Mirza, made him write the resignation letter. The letter was waved from the balcony of the Government House. Also, poor Khawaja Nazimuddin found out about martial law after the fact. Now he's only Prime Minister in name.'

There was silence in the room for a few moments. Everyone was thinking that now the bureaucratic government would rule without any constraints. Suddenly someone knocked on the door, startling them all.

Nazim addressed his friends. 'You should stop visiting me for a while. I'm lying here helpless like a defeated pawn. You'll get into trouble for nothing. One can feel satisfaction only if one suffers after having accomplished something.'

'I'll see who it is,' Sajida said, rising to her feet. Going to the door she asked, 'Who is it?'

'Lalli.'

Sajida quickly opened the door. Lalli came in and leant against the door. 'Your brother says that the CID is still after Nazim *Sahib*, he shouldn't have so many people gathered here at one time and they shouldn't be talking so loudly because in the quiet of the evening the voices travel far. And here, keep these sweets. Nazim *Sahib* can't move about too much, you can serve these to your guests with tea.' She handed the box of sweets to Sajida and left.

'Who was it?' Nazim asked.

'Lalli had come with sweets for our guests and she was saying we shouldn't talk so loudly, the voices travel far in the quiet of the evening.'

'Your *Zamindar Sahib* isn't spying on us, is he?' Nazim asked in a worried tone.

'No, he doesn't do things like that, but if I oppose him then he could become my enemy, although I don't know what he could gain by being hostile to someone ordinary like myself.'

Perhaps everyone was finding the sweets too bitter to swallow. One by one all of Nazim's friends left.

Sajida shut the door and came to lie beside Asad. Nazim was in deep thought.

'Can I ask you something?' Sajida said softly.

'Yes.'

'What did they want you to tell them when you were jailed in the fort?'

'All that they already knew.'

'What?'

'That I'm on the side of democracy, justice and equality, that I oppose all restrictions on the written word and I'm for freedom of expression, that I criticize the government.'

'So what was so special about that?'

'They couldn't understand that if I didn't become a member of the assembly and was not able to obtain an acre of land through agricultural reforms, why and for whom did I support democracy and equality and interfere in the affairs of the government.' Nazim spoke as if to himself. 'They were upset that I dream of seeing Pakistan as an exemplary nation and that I wish for its existence and its progress. They suspected a conspiracy in all of this, and they wanted to discover what that conspiracy was.'

'And?'

'And nothing. When I finally convinced them that like them I too would devour Pakistan as if it were *mann-o-salwa*, all of the other tortures that I was to be submitted to were forgotten and I was free!'

'Nazim, is it possible for your hunger to become so intense?'

'No, but I did not have the strength to suffer more torment. How long can a man lie on a slab of ice, and—' He paused momentarily. 'And it's better to tell a lie and be free than exist in jail. Is there anything else you want to know?'

'No.'

They were both silent for a long time afterward.

For half a mile from their house there was no habitation. One could clearly hear the planets at night. The barking of the dogs and the sound of the planets startled Asad from sleep. Sajida clasped him to her breast. Nazim was observing her with a dazed look and she could see the pain and torment he had suffered in the past stirring in his eyes. Sajida felt ashamed for having questioned him. She shut her eyes, pretending to be asleep. Nazim tossed and turned in his bed well into the night.

# Cool, Sweet Water

The war is over. The trenches that had been dug everywhere have been filled up. The houses that had been reduced to rubble by the bombs are now being rebuilt. When the war started it was autumn, then came winter and now it is spring. People appear as busy and happy as they did before the war. Businesses that had slowed down are doing well once again. Who knows if people still remember the agonies of war now that six or seven months have passed? The hustle and bustle of life makes you forget everything easily. But what can I say about the others? As far as I'm concerned, even now when I see moonlight caressing the earth it seems that it has lost its shimmer; I feel as if the moon is still complaining about our neighbouring country. If someone proclaims that the moon says nothing and hears nothing and all this is just nonsense attributed to poets and writers, then that's all right; these are matters that are related to the imagination. I am a writer, the emotions that I experience in relation to the moon are unusual. When I heard that the Russian spaceship Luna 9 had landed on the moon, my respect for the reach of man's intelligence increased, but a sigh also arose from a corner of my heart. I looked again and again at the moon and, believe me, my frail eyesight managed to catch sight of the Russian flag on the moon's surface. I was also able to see the corpse of the old woman with the spinning-wheel; her spinning-wheel had been smashed by Luna.

Who knows what will happen after man's conquest of the moon. What will the gains be, what the losses. But all I feel at the moment is that the people who inhabit the earth have lost everything. Any attempt to associate the moon with images of beauty bewilders me; in my imagination no lover appears weeping in remembrance of the beloved in the light of this shimmering ball of love and passion. When I compel myself to imagine this scene, I begin to ponder about the kinds of metal available on the moon and I wonder what chapters regarding man's preservation and destruction will be written with the aid of those metals. Who knows when the surface of the moon will become a battlefield.

I was still drifting in the darkness hovering over the image of the moon when the Russian flag was also planted on Venus, the star that is the first to appear on the sky in the evening. How can I now look at someone's shining eyes and proclaim that they are filled with stars? How will I say, 'You people, when you are tired of enduring the hardships of this world, you will have no beautiful vision left, you will talk of the metals found on the moon instead of sitting in the moonlight and conversing about the beloved, and when you are tormented by thoughts of the beloved at night, instead of counting the stars you will think of building a bungalow on Venus?'

Oh yes, where did I begin and where have I rambled to. I was saying that to this day I see the moon as a doubter. Even now when I hear the firecrackers go off in the neighbourhood at a wedding I am reminded of the boom of guns and the explosions of bombs. I go into the kitchen and see the lantern hanging by a nail on the wall and I still remember the seventeen days of darkness. We made each other out in the light of this lantern, bumped into furniture as we walked around, and so many times suffered bruised knees, cuts on fingers. No one has wiped clean the glass chimney of this lantern. I don't want it to be cleaned ever so that I can remember that the nights of war are pitch dark.

I love peace, I hate war. But I love that war as much as I love peace which is fought for freedom, for honour, for the survival of one's country.

Oh yes, so I was saying that the war is now over, but as long as I live my memories will live with me. Now how can I forget the eight-year-old boy who was flying a kite on the roof of the house next door. There were so many planes flying that day that one couldn't hear a thing. Even though I knew these were our own planes my heart trembled with fear and foreboding. I screamed to the boy, 'Come down from the roof!' He said, 'When the enemy's planes appear I'll bring them down with my kite, I'm not afraid like you.'

For a moment my trembling and pounding heart was stilled, but in the very next instant when another plane flew overhead and the frightening sound of the siren echoed, I screamed fearfully, calling out for my son Parvaiz who was nowhere to be seen. I couldn't leave the house because I was afraid my daughter Kiran might get scared. Thank God Parvaiz was in the other room, studying. Leaving his books in the other room, he came to be with me. I don't know what was wrong with me in those days. I kept a constant watch over the children. I wanted to cleave my chest and hide them in there, I wanted to protect them from the shadow of war. Again and again I remembered a scene from a film in which there were corpses littered everywhere after a bombardment and walking among them a child, crying for who knows whom. For some reason when I had Parvaiz and Kiran by my side, I was besieged by an overwhelming desire to protect them. I kept thinking of the young boy who had been flying a kite on the roof. Was he still flying the kite? O God, what is this strange passion for freedom which has never been vanquished by anyone, and does it also blend into the souls of tiny beings? I don't know if rulers of powerful nations also think like this or not. They probably think that big fish can swallow little fish. They probably see very little difference between people and fish, although Vietnam proved to the whole world that this adage which has come out of ponds and seas is of no account.

A few days after the war started, Zaheer decided to take the children away from Lahore so that they would not be frightened by the thundering booms that continued day and night. I resisted strongly because I didn't want to leave my loved ones behind, but the look of terror in the eyes of my dear daughter, my

Kiran, convinced me that it was important to take this little creature away from here. The next day my two children and I started off for Multan by car. Only I know how I clutched Lahore to my breast and bid farewell to it. I became very emotional at that time and began weeping. The journey was very trying; I was sitting in the car exhausted, my face hidden in the *pallu* of my sari. Suddenly the car came to a halt with a jolt and when it didn't start again for a while I raised my head to look out of the window. A long line of army trucks loaded with soldiers was ahead of us, the trucks passing one at a time because of poor road conditions. I wondered what front they were headed for and how many of them were going to return. I said goodbye to them in my heart and hid my face again, but in the very next instant the sound of clapping drew my attention to them. The soldiers in a truck in the rear were dancing a *bhangra* and as I watched them the soldiers in the other trucks began dancing *bhangra* as well. They were laughing boisterously. Some had cigarettes between their lips. There was such fervour in their clapping—oh God! I was watching them and I couldn't believe my eyes. Oh God! Are they really going to fight cannons and bullets? I stared at them in disbelief. In truth, there was no trace of anxiety on their faces. Their faces were illuminated with the bloom of flowers.

Finally the trucks packed with soldiers got on their way, but I kept watching them until they had disappeared on the horizon, kept listening for the sound of their clapping, kept asking myself, *Am I afraid of death?* For the first time the thought of death was like the taste of honey.

How badly one sleeps during war. It was our second night in Multan. Our hosts and all the children were asleep. I had been awakened by the rumble of planes. I got up and looked out the window and in the distance saw red lights in the sky. I thought I should wake up the hosts and ask them what this was when suddenly there was the sound of a tremendous explosion. The window panes rattled and the walls shook as if they were about to fall on our heads. There was no reason to make inquiries any more. Everyone was awake and walking about. My children were calling for me. I quickly advised everyone to huddle together under the tables in the gallery.

Then there was another explosion, which was severer than the first one. The children under the tables knocked into each other. I put my arms around Kiran and held her close and whispered in Parvaiz's ear, 'Don't be afraid of death. You remember those dancing soldiers, don't you?' He laughed and sat up straight. But I felt he was trembling. A few minutes later there were more explosions, but they weren't very strong, the sound now coming as if from afar. Then, suddenly, we heard a plane fly over the roof. I remembered all my relatives who were not with me. I experienced a deep sense of disappointment. How sad to die far away from home, in a strange place. I saw everyone's face in my imagination, but the faces disappeared in the twinkling of an eye. Soon there were two planes flying over the house. I thought of God, I prayed for this moment of danger to pass, and I felt great peace.

Gradually the roar of the airplanes became less distinct and then disappeared altogether. For a while after that there was neither an explosion nor did we hear another plane flying over the house. Complete silence prevailed, disturbed only by the occasional barking of a dog and the sound of weeping coming from the house next-door.

Moments later the all-clear siren went off and we got up. My hostess, who had been bending over her three-year-old child during all this, spoke for the first time. '*Apa ji,* how dear our children are to us. If the roof had fallen in the explosion it would have come down on me, but Munna, snug under me, would have been completely safe, wouldn't he?' She left the room without waiting for my reply.

The children went back to sleep in no time, but I remained awake all night. I kept wondering about the place where the bombs had actually fallen. How had the innocent women and children fared there? Troubled by this thought, I hugged my sleeping children and held them close. In the dark I thought I could see the bodies of dead children, I could see wounded children thrashing about in pain.

The night passed in torment. Early in the morning I got ready and left with my hosts to see the places where the bombs had fallen.

Two or three miles outside of Multan we came across a crowd of people. A great many mud homes and thatched dwellings had been razed to the ground. The women were retrieving things that were buried in the rubble. There were pots and pans scattered everywhere.

The children looked bewildered. Many of the them had bandages around their heads and on their feet. Some women squatted with their hands folded, watching the demolished dwellings as if they had lost everything, as if these were not just ordinary dwellings but palaces. The men were informing the visitors that there had been no loss of life.

I stood there quietly, anxiously observing what was going on around me. Despite the large crowd, I felt as though I was isolated. But I was relieved to hear there had been no loss of life. About seventy yards from where I was standing, a group of people had gathered and all of them seemed to be looking down at something. On questioning the steward I found out that this was one of the spots where a bomb had landed.

Later, when the crowd had thinned, I too approached. A small crater had formed where the bomb had fallen, and sitting next to the crater was an old man with a sheet spread out beside him. Strewn about on the sheet were innumerable coins. As soon as he spotted me, the old man cried, 'A donation *Begum Sahib*, a well will be dug on this spot, and out of it will come cool, sweet water.'

I placed whatever I had in my purse on the sheet and the old man, as if moved to sudden liveliness, started calling out loudly:

'Cool, sweet water, *sa'in*, cool, sweet water!'

# Suriya

I don't know why my old sweeperess left and how the new sweeperess arrived to take her place. I wondered how she could have left when I had never scolded her for not doing the work properly. Later I discovered that she had had a fight with the cook and he had told her to leave. Because I have never tried to question the cook's rights in this house, I kept my annoyance to myself and, albeit reluctantly, ignored the whole matter. The first sweeperess had been cleaning in our house for over four years and she handled the work well and with much care. The new sweeperess was a pretty young girl of about eleven or twelve. The first day she came with her mother. One couldn't tell by looking at the mother that she had been born to this profession; a strange kind of dignity was reflected on her face.

They began working with great diligence, but it angered me to discover that they didn't know how to clean the floor properly or how to brush the rug.

When they requested permission to leave, I called them in and asked somewhat angrily, 'Since when have you been working? Is this any way to clean?'

The mother remained silent, her lips pressed together tightly. But the girl's tongue was loosened immediately. '*Ammi* doesn't know how to do anything. She only takes care of the work at home. *Daḍi* and I tackle the cleaning at the bungalows. Today *Ammi* was with me and that's why nothing was done right, but from tomorrow you'll see the kind of work I do. Everyone says, "Suriya, you're very clever." I'll make you happy, you'll see.' Her round cheeks glowed as she spoke. The mother did not protest her daughter's remarks and, seemingly accepting of her inadequacy, she remained silent. This young girl's grown-up chatter made me laugh.

The next day Suriya cleaned the house so well that everything shone. I wondered with surprise how she had become so competent in one day. I became convinced that the day before she had not done her job well only due to laziness. Well, it was fortunate that she had come to her senses after just one round of rebuke.

Once she had completed her chores Suriya looked at me proudly and said, 'Everything is all right, isn't it *Bibiji*?'

'Well-done,' I said, in an attempt to encourage her. 'You've done a very good job of cleaning today.'

'Everyone says, "Suriya, you're very clever." Even my grandmother can't do the work so nicely. In the beginning when she went to the bungalows she would be turned out after two days.' Hearing her work praised, she spoke with greater pride.

'What did your grandmother do before?' I asked.

'Nothing, she mostly did the housework. There's a lot of work in the house.' For some reason her face fell.

'So now there's no more housework?'

'No *Bibiji*.' She was quiet for a few seconds. A thoughtful expression floated over her face. 'You see, the people in our family, they complained that we were just sitting around like princesses at home, doing nothing, and they said other things too. That's why my grandmother and I started working. My grandmother gets thirty rupees, I'll get twenty rupees. I'm right *Bibiji*, aren't I? We'll get something by working, we'll not lose anything, will we?'

'Of course, you're right. It's good to work.' Prompted by this display of wisdom, I promptly agreed with her.

So many sweeperesses had come and gone. They each had some strange habit or the other. Not a day would go by that one of them would not ask for something. *Dupatta, shalwar,* a few annas, a little *ghee,* a little flour, and if they didn't get anything else then there was always a request for food. If they got something they would feel elated and if they were refused, they left shamelessly, without any signs of remorse or embarrassment. Ever since she had come Suriya had never asked for anything. Once or twice when the cook offered her some food, she refused, saying, 'I had a lot to eat at home before I came.'

After every ten or fifteen days, Suriya's mother or grandmother would come just to ask if Suriya was doing the work properly and if I had any complaints at all. They would leave happily after I had reassured them that her work was satisfactory.

Suriya had been working for several months now. I became so fond of her that whenever I had some time I would engage her in conversation. Her mature ideas and serious ways sometimes made me feel as if she wasn't a young girl of eleven or twelve but someone at least fifty years old. Her good manners surprised me. It seemed as if she had seen life closely and that she was experienced in the ways of the world. But when I showed amusement at the seriousness of her tone, she would stare at me foolishly, and at that time, because she couldn't understand the reason for my amusement, I would see her as only a very young and naïve girl.

One day, happy with her work and gratified by her conversation, I gave her a rupee as a reward, but she put the rupee on the table as if it were something vile. 'I have enough in my house, *Bibiji*, I'll take only my salary, nothing else.'

I insisted, but she wouldn't even look at the rupee. I felt insulted by her action. Who does she think she is, I thought angrily. I wanted to slap the miserable creature. 'What do you have in your house, then?' I asked, curbing my anger.

'There's a lot in my house, *Bibiji*. There's a cow, and she delivers at least seven *seers* of milk every morning and seven in the evening. *Ammi* sells the milk we get in the morning and what she gets in the evening she churns to make *ghee* and *lassi*. And *Ammi* has a trunk as big as your storage room where she stores six new cotton quilts, six bed-pads, and ten quilts. When other family members have a lot of guests, they borrow bedding from us. And we have many pots and pans and dishes, with floral designs, which *Ammi* has set out on the upper shelves.

The mirror is this big.' She extended her arms to indicate the width of the mirror. 'And my *Ammi* has five beautiful suits from her dowry, with gold edging and...'

'And your *Ammi* will give you those suits for your dowry,' I teased and she lowered her head shyly. The truth was that all my anger had evaporated and I was envious of Suriya's household. We hadn't had unadulterated milk for years, were tired of consuming Dalda all this time and couldn't even remember the fragrance of pure *ghee,* and had never entertained the idea of keeping a cow in the house because of the fear that after we had had the luxury of unadulterated milk and pure *ghee* for six or seven months, the cow would become pregnant and then we would have to go back to milk from the market and Dalda *ghee*.

'And *Bibiji*, there's a huge earthen bin in our house which is always full of grain, and at Christmas last year *Ammi* had a beautiful embroidered suit made for me which I will wear again this Christmas. You know what Christmas is? You know it's like *Eid*?'

'Yes, you silly girl, of course I know what it is.' I couldn't help laughing, but for some reason her face assumed a melancholy expression at the mention of Christmas, her eyes clouded and she fell into deep thought.

'What's the matter Suriya, why do you look so sad?' I asked lovingly.

'It's nothing. Just that it's still a long way off to our *Eid*.'

'Is that all?' I broke into a laugh, thinking at the same time that despite her overly mature demeanour, she was a child after all.

I became very busy. There's always a great many chores to attend to, but this time we had so many guests that I had very little time to myself. Suriya would come, finish her work quietly, and leave. She would never talk to you unless she was spoken to first. During this time her grandmother came once, but when she saw all the guests she left without asking about Suriya's progress.

Today I finally had some time to breathe and just as Suriya was getting ready to leave, I called her to come and sit with me for a while. I didn't feel like talking, but I could hear the clap of thunder and I was afraid the poor girl would be soaked to the skin if it started raining. When I observed her closely I realized that she looked frail and sickly. Her cheeks had lost the freshness of childhood and her eyes were ringed with dark circles.

'Suriya, what's the matter with you, why are you looking so thin and weak?' I was worried about her.

'No *Bibiji*, nothing is the matter,' she said. She lowered her gaze to her hands and rubbed one hand with the other.

'You've got a cow in your house, don't you have any milk to drink?'

'*Ammi* is always pestering me to drink milk, but milk makes me sick.'

Now I was convinced that Suriya was really sick. It would be advisable to get her treatment because people like her only become conscious of illness when they're about to depart from this world. I was feeling very sorry for this sweet little girl. 'Come on, I'll take you to the doctor, we'll take your mother along as well.'

'Oh my God! Why should I go to the doctor? I'm scared of the very word doctor—he gives injections, he gave my youngest sister an injection and she died three days later. My mother still cries when she remembers.' She sighed deeply as if she were a wise old woman.

'Then you rest at home for a while,' I suggested. 'I'll make other arrangements for a few days.'

Suriya's face suddenly turned pale. For a few moments she stared wildly at me and then broke into sobs.

'You're getting rid of me *Bibiji*,' she said, sobbing, 'I love you *Bibiji*, I won't let anyone else do the work in the house.' Having said her piece she covered her face in her *dupatta* and sat down as if she was very tired.

'Oh, you silly girl. Who's getting rid of you?' I pulled her toward me and patted her head. 'How can I let my Suriya go?'

She wiped her tears and began smiling. This was the first time she had been so close to me. A strong odour emanating from her clothes sickened me. I had never imagined that her clothes would be so filthy and hadn't even noticed until now that she always wore the same clothes when she came to work.

'All right, don't cry now and sit down.'

When she sat down I advised her that she should bathe every morning and change her clothes after every two or three days. One can get sick also from staying dirty, I told her.

'I have a lot of clothes at home *Bibiji*. When I go home I take these clothes off and put on something else. I put on these clothes when I have to clean.'

'Well, that is all right then.'

She stayed for a while longer and then left. After she had gone I kept berating myself for saying I would let her go. How much better if I had hadn't said that. Suriya's tears tormented me all day. Anyway, I consoled myself by saying that when she came tomorrow I would treat her with a lot of affection.

The next day when Suriya was about to leave after finishing her chores, I told her to come and sit near me. But I hadn't started talking to her as yet when her grandmother arrived and seated herself down on the floor next to Suriya.

'Is she doing the work properly, *Bibiji*?' she asked.

'Yes, she's doing very well. I don't think anyone else can do the work as well as she does.' My gaze travelled to Suriya's face after I had finished praising her and I saw that she was smiling smugly.

'You go home now,' Suriya nudged her grandmother with her elbow. 'There's so much work at home, and you're just sitting here, doing nothing.'

Suriya's grandmother did not move. She was staring at me. There was something in her eyes today that I couldn't comprehend.

'*Bibiji*,' the grandmother said in a subdued voice.

'What is the matter?'

'*Bibiji*, could you give me an advance of five rupees from Suriya's salary? We haven't cooked food in the house since yesterday, and it's not possible to do any work now on an empty stomach and Suriya's mother is also...' There was more she wanted to say. There was such pleading in her voice. But suddenly Suriya got to her feet in anger and before I could say anything, she lunged at her grandmother. She was pummelling her grandmother with all her force, she was scratching her face and screaming. 'How shameless you are! You've already started begging. You couldn't wait, did anyone from your family ever beg? May you die of hunger, may you die and may you...'

I tried to get Suriya away from her grandmother, but she wouldn't stop. She scratched her grandmother's face until it was bleeding. Her grandmother submitted silently to the beating. She didn't lift a hand to resist. But all the while tears flowed from her dimmed eyes.

When I finally pulled Suriya away, she hid her face and ran out weeping. I was stupefied. I had no idea what was going on.

'What is all this?' I asked Suriya's grandmother.

'It's nothing really *Bibiji*, 'she said between sobs, 'ever since we have fallen onto hard times and have had to occasionally go hungry, Suriya has stubbornly refused to get help from any one. She says it's better to die than to ask for help.' She began wiping the blood from her face with her dupatta. '*Bibiji*, we had never done this kind of demeaning work before. We had everything in our village. Our own cow, our own house, a little land in which Suriya's father planted garlic, onions, and vegetables. He sold these in the market, there was no dearth of money. He also worked as a tenant farmer. We would get grain for a whole year. Our trunks were full of quilts and sheets. Suriya's father treated his daughter like a princess. And then *Bibiji*, one night we discovered that war had broken out. The Indian army came into our village. We fled from there with only the clothes on our backs. And now we've been here a long time, living in a hovel. When the other women saw that we didn't even have enough to eat they, got us to take up this line of work. But even now Suriya thinks she is the old Suriya of the village. She'll be starving for four days, but she won't ask for help, but me *Bibiji*, I'm an old woman...' She started crying again.

I was stunned into silence. I could neither speak nor weep. Waves of pain rose in my heart. How I longed to clasp Suriya to my breast.

With great difficulty I got up and brought Suriya's grandmother a month's advance and gave her an extra ten rupees. 'Buy some flour with this.'

She showered blessings on me and, wiping the blood from her face, left.

Suriya never again came to my house. I waited many days for her. I even saw her in my dreams.

The armies went back. Those who had left their homes were told to return. Several sweeperesses came to my house and went, but even now when one of them asks for something, Suriya's voice echoes in my ears.

'I have enough in my house, *Bibiji*.'

# Trust

All of June had gone by without a drop of rain. But this morning there was a heavy dust storm followed by so much rain that the city was deluged. The children in the neighbourhood took off their clothes and frolicked in the downpour, the grime on their skin becoming congealed as they rolled their sun-scorched bodies playfully in the cool, wet mud.

As soon as it stopped raining, the women picked up their buckets and hastened toward the hand pump. Work had been at a standstill since morning, all of them were in a hurry, and each one wanted to be the first to fill her bucket. Numerous water-pots and buckets collided simultaneously with the spout of the hand pump. But, despite the commotion, the women continued to chatter about leaking roofs, drenched household items, and goats bleating in panic. They were also cursing the landlady who demanded rent on time, but who had neglected to have the roofs repaired. Every once in a while the children hurled sludge at the women, who paused in their conversation long enough to respond with a barrage of coarse profanity. And just as all of them were busy gossiping and filling their buckets, Razia arrived with her luggage piled on a cart. When the cart's wheels came to a standstill in the open courtyard after spraying mud in all directions, Razia, who was soaked from head to foot, got off and first helped her daughter down. Then she squeezed her *dupatta* dry and, draping it hastily on her shoulders, she came forward to give the driver of the cart a hand when he began unloading her things. The women at the water pump abandoned their buckets and water-pots and gathered to scrutinize the new tenant. At this moment they seemed to be in no hurry whatsoever.

'I say sister,' Razia began eagerly. 'Safdar came last night to inspect the quarter. He said, "It's a nice place, you'll be happy there." ' He's at work right now. He said "I'll come at night and transport all the luggage myself, don't try and do it yourself, you'll get tired." It started raining when I was on my way here, now if I get sick he'll be angry.' A warm smile spread on Razia's face. 'So what if he's angry, he's tired too from working all day.' Razia's glance appeared to be seeking approval for her comments. Then she started embracing her neighbours as though she had known them for a long time and continued chattering, 'I say sister, what have you done to this child? Do you know, you should give the baby a little butter every morning. Safdar used to do that with Safia. That's why my Safia was so chubby, so heavy that we made bets when we picked her up, we just couldn't stand straight when we carried her.'

'Really?' Shaadan Pathani exclaimed as she extricated herself from Razia's embrace. She looked with amazement at the thin, skinny Safia who was sitting crosslegged on the ground, scooping out wet mud and rolling it into thin strands between her palms. With a sigh of relief Shaadan clasped her son to her breast, swore at Razia in Pashto and broke into a laugh. The poor woman had been living in Lahore for fifteen years and none of the women had learned her language. But she had picked up some broken Urdu and Punjabi. She spoke in Pashto only when she wanted to give vent to pent-up feelings.

'But *Masi*, your back is still straight,' Peelu said with a chuckle, and everyone started laughing. Rarely did anyone bother with poor Peelu, so she laughed and joked and forced herself on the group. Because she was a Christian, all the other women regarded her as inferior, and the fact that her father was employed as a road-sweeper only made matters worse.

'I say, your back doesn't remain bent forever,' Razia said irately and proceeded to unlock her door. Pulling out the *jharu* from her luggage she said, 'I have to prepare Safdar's supper, sister, I'd better clean and cook now or else when he comes he won't let me work, he'll say "You must be exhausted from bringing in all the luggage by yourself."

Perhaps no one heard what she was saying. The women were too busy examining her luggage from a distance. A misshapen bed with oversized legs, a brand new shining transistor radio, two trunks, a bedroll secured with twine, a sack filled with pots and pans, a table, a chair, and two bamboo cots with worn string ends dangling loosely here and there.

The women were agog at the sight of such magnificent household objects. They had nothing more than rope cots, simple bedding and a few utensils in their quarters.

'Play the radio, *Masi*,' Peelu requested with the eagerness of a child.

'I say, what do I know about this radio—when Safdar comes he'll turn it on himself. I begged him not to buy it, but he bought it anyway. He said, "You'll listen to songs and you won't feel so lonely." Razia chuckled haughtily. 'Now listen sisters, I better get to work, my daughter must be hungry, and I have to arrange the furniture, sweep the floor, and put everything away.' Razia took the *jharu* in her hand and disappeared into the darkness of her lodgings. Within minutes clouds of dust filled the room.

The women returned to the hand pump. It was nearly eleven, but the cloudy weather seemed to have slowed the passage of time. The women were now filling their buckets and water-pots with great alacrity, returning to their quarters in haste. Except Peelu, who, forgetting everything else, continued talking about the transistor. How strange, she thought, that now she would be able to hear songs in her courtyard. Normally she'd have to make rounds at this bungalow and that, and be forced to run innumerable errands for the upperclass ladies without asking for wages just so she could satisfy her craving for music.

After Razia had meticulously arranged the furniture, she washed her hands and face. Then she unwrapped the *rotis* from the yellow flowered bread cloth and sat down with Safia to eat.

'Eat properly, don't drop crumbs or else people will say you're the child of a sweeper.' She scolded Safia for no reason, upsetting the poor child who started sobbing. Clasping her to her breast, Razia tried to pacify her, which was not easy. Finally the girl was quietened. Razia began cursing silently. 'O *Amma*, may Allah make your offspring also pine and want for love. My loss isn't so great, but you deprived this child of her father.'

Because she was tired she went to bed after supper with Safia at her side. Once more she hugged the child, but Safia, irked by her affection, appeared restless. She wanted to go outside and play with the other children.

'All right then, go and play if you don't want to sleep,' Razia said lovingly. Her heart still ached from the harsh words she had used with her daughter. She began thinking of the old days. If it weren't for Safia she would never care to remember those days. What more did she want now that she had Safdar? And he loves Safia as if she were his own daughter, Razia thought, trying to comfort herself. She turned on her side and made an effort to sleep. But today her rebuke had brought back memories of Safia's father and her own mother. Her past rankled in her eyes like sand, robbing her of sleep.

Since she was the sixth daughter and the tenth child of her parents, everyone cursed her when she was born. Everyone prayed for her death, but she stubbornly continued to live. She never ate her fill at her parents' home, no one ever spoke to her with affection. When *Amma* sent off five daughters to new homes, each with a dowry consisting of a water pitcher, a brass bowl, and one suit of clothing, Razia wept without restraint. Her heart ached; at ten she was consumed with the desire to be sent off first. When her older sisters returned to visit, they whispered amongst themselves of their husbands' love. They talked of things that dumbfounded her, and when they said that their husbands had meat cooked once a week specially for them, Razia screamed. The taste of meat and the odour of love made her curse her sisters. 'Liars! Bitches!' She had never received a single morsel of meat, nor any love to sustain her. Her brothers yanked her plait and pummelled her, and her mother constantly scolded her, wishing upon her the death of a cat or a dog. She ran from her house to take refuge at the neighbour's. But who was there in the neighbourhood who had the time or the desire to comfort her, to hold her? The women in the neighbourhood spoke affectionately with her only when they needed to have their children's diapers washed. If she refused, they too drove her out, saying, 'Get out, go and sit in your mother's lap.'

When Razia was fourteen, *Amma* arranged for a pitcher and a brass bowl for her and, cursing and wailing, pushed her out into another's house. Razia felt as if she had discovered heaven. Her husband told her that her face was like the moon, he said he was her slave, and he avowed that if he was ever unfaithful, may God punish him. Razia was delirious with amazement. She couldn't comprehend how her face, which she always thought was like that of a witch, was now like the moon, and that she who had been trampled under foot by everybody could now have a man telling her he was a slave at her feet. And when she was convinced all this was indeed true, she felt a pride and joy that made her feel as if she were flying on clouds. In the morning she told her sisters-in-law how much their brother loved her. Then, without waiting to be sent for, she dashed off to her mother's house and recounted to everyone the story of her husband's intense love for her. Her sisters, who had come to attend her wedding and who, after years of married life were now like left-over lentils, secretly cursed her, but Razia's brother's wife couldn't conceal her jealousy and made a grab for Razia's tinsel-sprinkled hair. Sobbing, crying, and cursing everyone, Razia returned to her house. At night she told her husband what had happened. He was so furious he immediately went to his in-laws' house, stood outside their front door, and swore and railed at Razia's family without giving them any opportunity to respond. Then he came back and told Razia she was never to set foot in that house again.

All day long Razia sang her husband's praises. The slave sitting at her feet was oblivious to the world. And her sisters-in-law and her mother-in-law were prostrate with grief. The mother, intent on snatching her son, and the sisters, anxious to have their brother back, became alert. Their tongues grew long and sharp. But when Razia's husband saw tears in Razia's eyes, he rebuked his mother and sisters harshly, and at that moment Razia wished her mother-in-law's and her sisters-in-law's tongues would become longer and sharper still. Razia felt heavy with the weight of her pride.

A year passed happily. But how long could this last? Finally the prayers of the mother and the sisters were heard. The husband grew weary of the ever-recurring tussles. How long could he ignore the mother who had raised him? After all, this too was a sin. One day when Razia complained to him about her mother-in-law, he beat her. At first Razia couldn't believe what had happened, but when he started beating her every day, Razia's eyes were opened. Her pride lost its wings, suddenly she crashed to the ground with a boom. She sobbed and wailed and pleaded, but who was going to hold her now? This was when Razia was pregnant with Safia. Her husband began staying out at night. When they observed her helplessness, her mother-in-law and her sisters-in-law approached her lovingly and comforted her. Razia saw that their grief at her situation prevented them from doing any housework. Overwhelmed by this show of affection, Razia faithfully and wearily completed all the household chores. When her husband came home she hid in corners and cried. Not to know love is no crime, but to give love and then snatch it away is the worst of all crimes. Every fibre of her being screamed, 'O cruel one, turn around and look at me.'

And when Safia was born, Razia felt she was completely ruined. She might have been able to retrieve her husband's love if she had given birth to a boy. She lost all interest in the house. Once she was back on her feet, she spent most of her time sitting on the threshold of the front door. That was when Safdar started walking past her on some pretext or another, and before long he was wiping her tears. Despite attempts to hold herself back, Razia fell in love with Safdar. What a strange and fulsome love it was. Even an ocean is incapable of braving the force of a lover's adoration. She found new wings. Once again, she looked at everybody around her, but she didn't say anything. She was frustrated that she couldn't tell anyone about Safdar. Then one day when her mother-in-law cursed her, she threatened her by saying she would have Safdar beat her.

This brought on an attack in which everyone participated and finally her husband divorced her and threw her out of the house. And Safdar's open doors welcomed her in.

Once the waiting period was over, Safdar married Razia with great pomp and ceremony, thus proving all those wrong who had suggested that he would abandon her after the waiting period. When they heard news of the wedding, Razia's ex mother-in-law and sisters-in-law tossed over live coals, and for some reason her ex-husband repeatedly picked quarrels with them and didn't go out all day.

The memories made her feel restless and troubled. Razia let out a sigh. Then she got up from the bed and went out to look for Safia. She found her engrossed in making a tiny dwelling with the moist mud.

The earth still exuded a fragrant aroma and patches of thick, dark clouds still swirled about in the sky. Women had climbed on the roofs of their houses and were throwing down cowdung cakes and firewood that had become soaked from the rain. The children below picked everything up and took it inside. Old women sat on rope cots under the thick-leafed trees, gurgling their *hookahs*. Beyond the roofs of the quarters you could see clearly the tops of magnificent bungalows, their red, green and brown walls streaked with rain.

For a while Razia quietly watched the scene before her. Then she put a lock on her door and walked into the quarter next-door. At first she couldn't see anything because it was so dark. Then, as her eyes became accustomed to the darkness, she was able to make out the form of a thin, lean woman sitting on a *chawki,* eating.

'I didn't see you when I came,' Razia said in an easygoing manner and sat down beside her.

'I observe *purdah,*' the woman said, swallowing the morsel in her mouth.

'What? you have spinach! I say sister, until I eat spinach I can't rest.' Razia quickly broke off a piece from the *roti* in the woman's plate and began eating.

The woman gave her a disapproving look, then continued eating. All she had were these two *rotis,* and here was this woman, wanting a share for herself. She seems to be a Punjabi, the woman thought. These people have no manners. For one thing, they use their hands instead of their tongues to talk and then, to make matters worse, they call her a Hindustani. If she could help it she'd snatch the piece of bread from Razia's hand. She really could not stand Punjabis. She had given up everything to come here and be a Pakistani, but no one gave her that satisfaction. She remained a Hindustani.

'I say sister, why does this child look so limp?' Razia asked, wringing her hands to shake off the crumbs from her palms.

'He has fever.'

'Oh my, oh my, give him some quinine. My Safdar starts giving me and Safia quinine as soon as the hot season begins. This is from mosquito bites.' She got up and touched the boy's forehead.

'Who's going to bring us quinine? The boy's father leaves for work early in the morning, and I can't go out.'

'Safdar doesn't insist that I observe *purdah*. I could get quinine for you myself, but I don't know where the shops are. In a day or two I'll know where everything is.'

'Here, have some more *roti*.' The woman was deeply affected by Razia's loving manner.

'No sister, I can't eat any more. Look how hot the child is. If I knew my way around, I'd have got the medicine for him right away. But when Safdar comes home in the evening I'll ask him to get it.'

'He'll get it?' the Hindustani woman asked incredulously.

'Why sister, if I tell Safdar to stand on one leg all night, he'll do it.' Razia started laughing. 'Getting quinine is nothing.'

She rose to leave. 'I should go and see what Safia is doing. Safdar is very fond of her. When he comes home, he'll say, "Why did you leave her alone?"' She dashed out of the quarter without turning to see how the Hindustani woman's face had darkened. The woman was wiping her eyes. Her husband had never spoken to her affectionately, and had such a suspicious nature that he did not allow her to leave the house in his absence.

The clouds were still rolling in the sky. On the road next to the bungalows, cars zoomed by with a show of grandeur. Old women, sensing the silence of the afternoon and the cool breeze, had stretched out on their rope cots and were beginning to doze. Shaadan Pathani's goat, tethered outside, bleated shrilly as if terrified of the darkness of the overcast sky. With an occasional peek into people's quarters along the way and exchanging conversation with whomever she encountered, Razia finally made her way back.

Exhausted from playing, Safia was now leaning against the closed door of their quarter, fast asleep. Razia brought her in, put her to bed and lay down next to her. There was a loud clap of thunder and then it began to rain. The children's voices gained momentum. After a while she fell asleep and when she awoke she found Safdar sitting on a chair, dozing.

'Why didn't you wake me up, Safdar?'

'You were sleeping after a long, tiring day,' Safdar said, taking out three rupees from his shirt pocket and handing them to her.

Quickly Razia lit a fire in the brick stove and made tea for Safdar. Then, pouring the tea in the saucer, she held the saucer to his lips so he could sip the tea. At this moment she looked so radiant one would think someone had made her drink a whole bottle of wine.

'Get me two annas worth of quinine,' she said, putting the cup and saucer down.

'Why?' Safdar asked anxiously, and taking her wrist he felt for her pulse.

'Stop now, there's nothing wrong with me. It's that poor Hindustani woman, her son has fever and I promised her I'd get the medicine for her.'

'Let her be, why worry about her,' Safdar said lazily, and clasping Safia to his breast, he lay down. Safia was still sound asleep.

'*Hunh!*' Razia whined. 'Don't get it then, she'll say I was a liar, she'll say, "Safdar doesn't listen to her, what she said was just an empty boast."'

'Whoever calls you a liar will have to answer to me.' Safdar pinched Razia's cheek lightly and jumped up from the bed. 'I'll get it right away.' He left the room.

It had got dark earlier than usual because of the clouds. Razia lighted the lantern and placed it on a niche in the wall and began preparations for the evening meal. Safdar had brought home meat as he did every day. Today the smell of meat made Razia sick. There hadn't been a day since their marriage that Safdar had made Razia miss meat. He knew how much she liked meat.

As she took off the wrapping from the meat, Razia remembered that when she had told Safia's father that meat was cooked once a day in her sisters' households, it wasn't long before he too provided her with an abundance of meat. As the long beef fibres got stuck between her mother-in-law's teeth, she cursed and swore, and Razia felt secretly elated. But then a day came when Razia crushed mint on the grindstone every day to eat with *roti,* weeping as she ate.

While she was washing the meat, Razia shuddered and looked around her fearfully. Then she let out a long sigh and told herself that what had happened was now in the past and not all men are the same.

After throwing out the dirty water, she shook Safia's shoulder. 'Look, your father is home. Get up now, wash your face and hands and come and sit by the stove.' Razia didn't want to remember anything now.

Razia was browning the meat when Safdar returned with the quinine. She took a small chunk of meat from the pot and put it in his mouth. 'Taste it, see how delicious it is,' she said coquettishly. She pulled out the firewood from the stove and went to the Hindustani woman's quarter. 'Here sister, give him half a pill each time, the fever should wear down by tomorrow morning. Your husband isn't home yet?'

'No, it's still early, he'll roam about on his way home. Sit, will you.'

'I can't, Safdar is home...do you think he's going to be content without me?' Razia winked with a laugh, checked the child's fever and left.

* * *

In four or five days Razia collected a great deal of information about the compound where she lived. The compound was the property of a benevolent woman who had set up these quarters constructed of unbaked bricks for the poor. The rent was only fifteen rupees a month. Any damage and wear and tear were the tenant's responsibility. All night long people stayed awake to plaster the roofs, a punishment meted out to those who wished to enjoy the cool breezes of the monsoons by using their roofs for sleeping outdoors.

On hearing all this talk about leaking roofs Razia immediately filled a few baskets with soil and stored them under her bed. Who knows when the roof might start leaking.

Every month the landlady, accompanied by two of her servants, came to inspect the compound. Before she left she collected the rent and issued further orders for more repairs. Razia was anxious to see her. She had heard Peelu say that the *begum* was pretty just like her.

In the morning, after Safdar ate his breakfast, kissed Razia, and went off to work, Razia experienced a wave of restlessness. These days, the minute Safdar left, she would go to the Hindustani woman's quarter. She had been married for two and a half years, but she still couldn't tolerate being in the house without Safdar.

The Hindustani woman had told her many secret stories about the people living in the compound. For example, who was having an affair with whom, whose husband had mistresses on the side, and which men beat their wives. And in telling this, the Hindustani woman carefully concealed the story of her own beating by her husband. After sharing all these secrets with

Razia, she extracted a promise from her that she would never breathe a word of any of this to another soul. She regarded Razia as her sister, which was why she had told her everything, she said.

Razia believed all the stories she was told. She had put her trust in the Hindustani woman's devotion the very first day she met her. For hours Razia talked to her about Safdar and the Hindustani woman listened cheerfully, heaping blessings upon her. No one knows what's in the heart. You keep your eyes on what is visible. Razia did not have the slightest inkling that the Hindustani woman hated her. This was the devotion that had begun with quinine pills. There was much bitterness attached to it, much helplessness. If she didn't need Razia to do things for her, like a witch she would have scratched Razia's face, she would have slashed her tongue and thrown it before vultures. Despite being married all these years, she had never heard a single word of love from her husband's mouth.

Some more time passed and soon Safdar and Razia's love became a joke among the inhabitants in the compound. She was overjoyed when the women teased her and she responded coquettishly, 'All right, I love him, so what?' The unmarried girls didn't leave her alone either. '*Masi*, your Safdar hasn't come yet?'

She had been happy since her arrival in the compound. The neighbourhood where Safdar had got her a quarter before was a dismal place. All around them were bungalows, busy *begums*, and overworked servants. Razia tried everything, but no one would sit down for two minutes to talk to her. No one wanted to hear that Safdar adored Razia and that she was the most fortunate woman in the world. She thought that these *begums* were very strange, she felt sorry for them, the poor, starved, spent creatures. Safdar had told her a great deal about them; she knew that here wives were not loved.

On summer nights when Safdar's spotless, white bedding was laid out on the cot outside his quarter in the courtyard, he lay down and immediately turned on the transistor and in no time all the fun-loving men and women from the compound gathered around his cot. Razia lovingly invited the women to sit on her cot and the men found a place to sit with Safdar. Songs continued to pour from the radio while men talked about politics, offering opinions on the forthcoming presidential elections, rising prices and finally all conversation ended at the question of having enough to eat. 'What do we care who comes and who goes? The government that lowers the price of grain is the best government,' Safdar would say wearily and turn his attention to the songs on the radio. But Shaadan's husband persisted. 'No, grain can be more expensive, but we won't accept a woman's rule. This is our disgrace. God created woman to be lower than us.' No one gave the Pathan a reply. The Listener's Choice programme on the radio could not be ignored.

Sometimes Shaadan's husband brought home some of his Pathan friends from his woodstall and all of them sang songs in their native Pashto late into the night. Shaadan ran from one person in the compound to the other, inviting them to come and listen to the songs, offering them cups of black tea. Razia never participated in this get-together. She would say to the Hindustani woman, 'Why should I go, sister? Don't I have a radio in my house? Their singing gives me a headache.' The Hindustani woman agreed with her to her face, but how could she tell her the truth, how could she tell her that she loved those songs, that she longed to be a part of anything that went on outside her quarter.

But ever since Razia's transistor radio had made the people in the compound swarm around her, Shaadan too, moved by jealousy, organized a singing programme at least once a month. After having listened to Razia's incessant boasting she was now determined to show everybody that her husband was no less affectionate. While talking to the women about her own husband she made fun of Razia. 'She may be getting the shoe from him every day but will she tell?' These days Shaadan was so careful that when her husband beat her and swore at her she bolted the door from the inside so that no one outside her quarter could hear anything. Like a mound of raw cotton that is being thrashed, she quietly submitted to a pounding from her husband and didn't utter a word of protest.

* * *

Today when Razia went to the Hindustani woman's quarter she told her that Shaadan had been there and she was making fun of Razia, insinuating that she may be beaten every day by her husband but the beating wasn't going to make her stop boasting about her husband's love for her.

Razia became incensed when she heard such a serious accusation. 'That misbegotten wretch! She's saying that because she's probably getting a beating herself every day. My Safdar hasn't even touched me with a stick made of flowers. I'll go right now and have it out with her.'

'I say, no one has heard of her being beaten since you came, but before that she used to be thrashed to no end. That mark on her forehead, that's from a beating. She was in bandages for eight to ten days.'

'I'll teach the misbegotten creature a lesson she won't forget easily,' Razia said, suddenly rising to her feet.

'For God's sake, don't mention my name, Razia. I've told you all this out of love for you. I was extremely distressed when I heard things said against you.' She grasped Razia's hand and forced her to sit down again. 'Sister, you should exhibit fortitude. No one knows how long I have had to hold myself back. Everyone makes fun of my *purdah,* all the women mock my accent. Why are people here like this?'

'Sister, things like this don't happen in Quetta,' Razia said proudly although she didn't know where Quetta was. At the time of Partition she was very young and no one in her house mentioned the subject either. Everyone was concerned with putting food in their stomachs; who had the time to grumble about territorial divisions?

After a few moments of quiet Razia got up again. 'Let me at least ask her, sister. You can cut my tongue out if I mention your name.'

'*Arri*, how many people will you ask? All the women are envious of you in their hearts. So what if they don't say anything out loud, and ...' the Hindustani woman didn't continue because Razia left without waiting for her to finish.

It was afternoon. The women lay on the rope cots under shady trees, fanning themselves lazily as they dozed. The children were wrestling near the hand pump and splashing about water collected in small bowls and ladles.

'Where are you going *Masi*?' Peelu asked her. She was sitting next to her mother, crocheting.

Razia did not give her a reply. She was trembling with rage. She stopped only when she had reached Shaadan's quarter. There was a lock on her door and the goat tethered to a peg outside was chewing cud with its eyes shut. 'Where is she, her husband's darling? Just look at that face of hers! She's developed a very long tongue!' Razia was screaming loudly.

'What's the matter?' the old, widowed seamstress asked, startled out of her drowsiness.

'Just tell me *Masi*, where is that princess?'

'She's over there on the other side, near the big tree,' Peelu answered instead in a merry tone. She got up and began walking alongside Razia. The other women also hurriedly scrambled to their feet.

'Now, tell me sister, what have I done to wrong you that you should speak such nonsense against me? Inside your quarter your husband thrashes you with a shoe every day. My Safdar hasn't even raised his little finger to hurt me.'

Shaadan Pathani was dozing with her baby clasped to her breast. Taken aback by this sudden onslaught, she came out of her snooze in a fluster, picked up the *dupatta* from the side of her pillow and immediately covered her head with it. Her face was beet-red.

'First tell me who says I said that.'

'It doesn't matter who said it. Tell me, you spoilt darling, when did you see me getting a beating?'

'Well, if you don't tell, then I will. Why, is your husband descended from the heavens that he doesn't beat you? You lie.'

'You're the one who is lying, you are the one who gets a thrashing.' Razia swung from the Pathani's hair.

At first the women tried to separate them, but when they refused to listen, the women withdrew to one side and calmly watched the spectacle.

In the beginning the two women exhibited equal strength, but the Pathani was after all a Pathani. She punched and clobbered Razia until Razia's beautiful face was swollen and blood flowed from her mouth. This was when Razia freed herself from the Pathani's grasp and started howling and screaming loudly.

'Ahh, you see sisters, she's made my face swell, all of you are witnesses, there's blood flowing from my mouth. Just wait until Safdar comes home in the evening, I'll have him give her a beating she'll never forget. *Arri*, he does what I tell him to, and here this misbegotten creature says he beats me!'

'You must be misbegotten, woman, your mother too!' Shaadan replied breathlessly and lunged toward her. But Peelu restrained her forcefully and compelled her to sit down on the rope cot. Then she dragged Razia to her quarter.

Now it was Shaadan's turn to start sobbing violently and all the women gathered around to calm her. But she would not quiet down. Perhaps she was thinking that once again tonight she would have to bolt her door from the inside and submit to a beating. Her husband punished her whenever she fought with someone. In this place people were always ready to get their heads bashed at the slightest provocation and run to the police station. Only once, driven by a desire to show off, the Pathan fomented a fight and his entire savings were wiped out in trips to the police station. To this day he was not able to compensate for that loss.

Razia returned to her quarter and fell on her bed in a fit of weeping. Safia saw her mother's condition and quickly ran out. Seating herself next to her on the bed, Peelu tried to soothe Razia. She didn't want to leave; she was anxious to see what Safdar would do when he found out what had happened.

'*Masi*, should I clean the lantern?' Peelu asked. 'It's getting dark.'

'Yes,' Razia said between sobs. 'I'm not going to do anything until Safdar gets home.' Her soul ached for Safdar. Only he could rid her of this pain. It was Safdar who had lifted her out of the hell of hatred and placed her under the cool shade of love.

Peelu cleaned the lantern, lighted it and hung it from the nail on the wall. 'Now stop *Masi*, don't cry any more,' she said, rubbing Razia's back. But Razia's sobs grew in intensity with each passing moment.

Around five o'clock Safdar came home. He lowered his eyes when he saw Peelu and placed the grocery bag on the table. He was about to sit down when he heard the sound of Razia's sobbing; he became agitated.

'What happened *arri*?' He nearly screamed and gathered Razia in his arms. 'Come, say something.'

Peelu got up and walking over to the door, sat down on the threshold.

'That Shaadan beat me up.' Razia turned her swollen face toward Safdar. 'She said you don't love me, she said you give me a beating with a shoe every day. She was tainting your name, and when I asked her for an explanation this is what she did to me.'

'Who does she think she is!' Safdar rose to his feet and puffed out his chest.

'Everyone is jealous of your love, everyone...' Razia cried in an agonizing tone.

'I'll chop off the hands of those who hit you.' He rushed toward the door and despite Razia's efforts to hold him back he was gone.

Razia glanced at the surprised Peelu and wiped her tears. 'You see? Didn't I tell you that if Safdar knew there's no telling what he might do?' Leaving the door of her quarter unlocked, Razia ran after Safdar.

'I'm not afraid to die, I'll swing by the hangman's rope, but I won't rest until I've cut off the hands that beat my wife!' Safdar paused before Shaadan's quarter and roared. Beating his chest with both hands he invited Shaadan and her husband to a fight. All the men and women in the compound gathered around him.

'You stop your woman, your woman came to fight, I too am not afraid to die!' Shaadan's husband, the Pathan, screamed.

'All right, come on then, let's decide this once and for all.' Safdar pulled up his *shalwar* and tucked it in swiftly and lunged at the Pathan's throat.

The Pathan's threat had gone unheeded. He looked at everyone in distress.

'Now look brother, these women fight all the time, but you and I are of the same faith, why should we fight. I'll punish my wife. If I fight and there's bloodshed, that will make us sinners in the eyes of God, and the world will also say that a brother took his brother's life.' The Pathan removed Safdar's hand gently from his throat.

'All right Safdar, let him be, he's calling you his brother. But you, tell your wife she shouldn't say stupid things, all right?' Razia's heart melted.

Safdar lowered his head and walked back to his quarter.

'You see *Masi*, I was telling the truth when I said that Safdar loves me so much. Who knows what he would have done just now.' Razia addressed the seamstress and then she looked around at everyone as if saying, 'There now, burn with envy.' She strutted off toward her quarter.

At the very moment when Safdar was applying the turmeric paste that he had prepared to Razia's face, the Pathan was beating Shaadan with such force that despite her efforts she could not hold back her screams. And the women standing outside her door quaked, their hearts aflutter.

This was when, clasping her younger sister to her breast, Peelu mimicked the loving manner with which Safdar had gathered Razia in his arms. Such a shameless man!

All the women in the compound sympathized with Shaadan. They hated Razia's very countenance, their hearts were bursting with hostility toward her.

The swelling on Razia's face went down the next day and forgetting everything, she roamed about in her usual cheerful manner. '*Arri*, sister, all night Safdar was awake, staring at my face,' she told everyone, but no one seemed to care, although nearly all of them secretly wished that their faces could also be swollen like Razia's. But Safdar was not afraid to lose his life for her, so who was going to incur her displeasure? But when she wasn't there, they made fun of her, swore at her, and assured Shaadan that Razia isn't a real woman, she's a whore. A real woman is one who is a man's slave and who receives a beating at his hands. Hearing all this talk made Shaadan feel better; she agreed with them excitedly. 'God created woman to be smaller than man.' Since the day of their fight, Shaadan had turned away from Razia for ever, it seemed. If Razia happened to pass by, she hid her face behind the flap of her *dupatta*.

In the meantime Peelu continued to spy on Razia under cover of friendship. No sooner did Safdar come home than she began to make trips to Razia's quarter.

'*Bhai* Safdar, put on the radio so we can hear songs.' She would hear a few songs and then run out of there to enact for the women Razia's loving manner toward her husband, giving details of the way she walked in Safdar's presence, her sweet talk.

Now when Safdar played the radio at night and Razia invited the women to come and listen to the songs, no one came. Making up some excuse or the other, the women stayed away. Razia took great pleasure in their envy. The men did come, however, and, sitting next to Safdar on his cot, they listened to the music and talked.

The only friend Razia had left was the Hindustani woman. The minute she saw Razia she dropped whatever she was doing and sat down to chat with her. Now Razia bought inexpensive oil, combs for cleaning out lice and hair pins for her with her own money. And when the Hindustani woman tried to pay her for all these things, Razia would put her arms around her. '*Arri*, Safdar says to me "Everything is yours, if you want you can squander it with both hands," so if it's all mine it's yours too, isn't it?'

\* \* \*

The rainy season was over and it was already quite cold. The days had shortened to such an extent that birds now began the noisy return to their nests around four o'clock. Lamps were lighted in the quarters and the compound became vacant early in the evening. The prevailing quiet was broken every now and then by the squeaking sound of the hand pump and then silence reigned again. When the sun advanced in the morning the men left for work. The women came out to sit in the sunny compound and when their bodies had soaked up enough warmth they became busy with housework. Razia too came out in search of sunshine after Safdar had left for work and, sitting in the company of the other women, she took out tangy orange wedges she had hidden under her shawl and sucked on them.

'It's the fourth month,' she would say with a meaningful laugh, 'and my mouth tastes bland if I don't have anything tangy to eat. That's why Safdar brings me so many of these sour, tangy oranges.' And then she would forcibly hand each woman an orange wedge.

'*Masi*, every day you give us an account of what Safdar brings and then you give us an orange wedge each,' Peelu finally said one day. 'You should give each one of us a whole orange,' she demanded, breaking into a laugh as she winked at the woman sitting next to her.

'I'll do that too, what's so difficult about that? By God, Safdar will surrender all his money for me if he's asked.'

The next day Razia actually satisfied Peelu's request. She didn't rest until she had coaxed all the women into eating a two-paisa orange each.

After Razia had left Shaadan saw all the orange peels strewn about and swore heavily while those who had consumed the oranges justified their actions, saying, 'When someone insists you eat, you have to comply.' Later they joined Shaadan in cursing Razia. Was there anyone among them who had the nerve to give away even two annas for nothing? Mistri's wife Basheeran was divorced by her first husband simply because she quietly slipped two rupees from her husband's pay to help her mother.

Winter's first rainfall came at night, but the clouds were scattered by morning. The cold set everyone's teeth chattering and to top it all a cold wave from Razia's Quetta also arrived. Safdar hadn't left for work as yet because of the chill; by now he had downed several cups of tea.

'Come outside *Masi*, the sun is already high,' said Peelu, coming in just as Safdar was getting ready to leave.

'*Arre*, how can I come just yet? Sit down, I'll go with you in a few minutes.'

'What will happen if you come now? Safdar *Bhai* will lock up and bring you the key.' Peelu spoke mischievously from the doorway.

'You go ahead, I'll be along shortly.' Razia winked at Peelu and laughed.

'It's very chilly in here, why don't you go,' Safdar said lovingly.

'What? Leave you here and go?'

'All right, I'm leaving as well.' He picked up his bag and bumped into Peelu as he tried to get out in haste. Her *dupatta* covering her mouth, Peelu was laughing as she darted from there.

When Razia arrived in the compound to sun herself Peelu had already informed everyone how coquettishly Razia was talking to Safdar this morning, what doting airs they were putting on. Nearly all the women made one nasty remark or another, but Shaadan's eyes filled. Averting her face, she quickly dried her tears on a corner of her *dupatta*. When she saw Razia approach she turned her back to her and began nursing her baby.

'I say sister, I don't feel well at all these days. With Safia I had no problems at all, but this time I don't know what to do. All night Safdar wakes up to check on me. The slightest moan from me and he sits up and starts to press my legs and back and...' Razia was talking while she peeled an orange, but none of the women responded to her words, no one paid any attention, no one had even glanced in her direction. Now, how long could anyone listen to her prattle? The expressions on their faces seemed to be openly saying that the women would like to give vent to their feelings by scratching her face. Razia had caused such a tumult in their loveless lives.

For a long time Razia sat among the women, talked, and then left with a heavy heart. She didn't care about the cold weather and went to visit the Hindustani woman in her quarter. They are jealous of her. Today this thought disturbed her. If this continued she would lose everyone. Who will she talk to then? With whom will she share her stories about Safdar?

The Hindustani woman put away her pots and came to sit beside her.

'It's very cold here sister,' she said.

'What is there to do outside? No one talks to me. Everyone is jealous of me. Why are they jealous, sister?' Razia broke into tears.

'May your enemies cry!' The Hindustani wiped her tears. 'What can they do except be jealous? In their houses they receive a beating every day. Why do you care about them?' The Hindustani woman tried to console her. Then she heaved a long sigh. At this moment she was really feeling sorry for the tearful Razia.

'But sister, I didn't ask them to get beatings. Why am I to blame?'

The Hindustani woman said nothing. Perhaps she couldn't think of anything to say. She too was jealous of Razia, was she not?

'I'll go now sister, there's a lot of work to be done at home.' Because she was feeling unhappy, Razia returned to her own quarter. She lay in bed for a long time. Today the past was assaulting her again.

\* \* \*

The clouds gathered again early in the evening today. The lightning and thunder were frightening. Razia had put in an extra large pile of firewood in the stove which was slowly burning as the night wore on. On the bed next to hers slept Safdar while Safia slept beside her.

When the thunder subsided somewhat Razia too dozed off, but she was restive; she didn't sleep soundly these days because she was full-term and all night her body ached. No matter how much she tried, she couldn't find a comfortable position in which to sleep.

She had been dozing only a little while when she woke up with a start and became anxious when she saw that Safdar was not in his bed. She sat up, but in the very next instant Safdar appeared.

'*Arre*, where did you go off to in this cold?'

'Go back to sleep, do you hear—all night you're keeping watch.' His tone was suddenly brusque. 'I went to pee,' he added gently. He got into bed and pulled his quilt over his face.

For a moment Razia glanced at his face in the dim light of the lantern and then told herself that he was tired from working all day. So what if he raised his voice to her?

The next morning the clouds had scattered. Safdar was calmly drinking tea with Safia. Razia was hovering around him like a moth.

'Safdar, you know, I'm feeling really sick today.'

'Don't do any work, just rest all day.'

'Safdar, you spoke so loudly last night, I got scared and I thought, "Can he really scold me?"'

'I did it for you, I wanted you to sleep comfortably.' Safdar lowered his gaze and started putting his things in his bag.

'I know, I know you could never scold me.' Razia laughed like a little girl.

After Safdar had left she made the beds, put away the dishes, washed the teacups and when she was about to place them on the shelf in the wall her heart missed a beat. The transistor radio was not in its place. The silk cloth that was used to cover it was lying in a corner of the shelf. Razia turned everything upside down in her search for the radio, but it was gone. Razia was troubled by foreboding thoughts. What if the radio had been stolen? Again and again her suspicion turned to Peelu. She was in and out of their quarter all the time. She decided she was not going to question her. When Safdar came home in the evening, he would ask Peelu himself. Who knows, maybe he had taken it for repairs. Recently it had been making a grinding sound.

Locking the door of her quarter, she came out in the sunlit compound.

'I say sister, it's difficult to move around any more. Safdar was scolding me, he said I should rest, but I can't lie in bed all day long.'

No one bothered to reply, but Peelu inched closer to her.

'So why did you get up? Why didn't you stay in bed? I say, you're lonesome without Safdar.' Peelu laughed.

'I don't know what happened to my transistor. Maybe Safdar took it for repairs, he was saying there was something wrong with the sound.'

'Well then, it will be fixed when you get it back.' Peelu began playing a game with small stones. 'Will you play *Masi*?'

'No, I can't bend any more.' Razia gazed at the faces of women who were talking amongst themselves. A few minutes later she returned to her quarter.

The day dragged. She couldn't even do any work today. She told herself that today Safdar would have to cook supper himself.

The minute Safdar walked into the room she got up with a moan. '*Arre*, did you take my transistor to be fixed?'

'Yes, I took it.' Safdar put his bag on the table and sat down in the chair.

'Then why didn't you bring it back? I was going crazy looking for it all day, I thought it had been stolen.'

'I sold it. You're going to need money for the baby, aren't you?'

'Oh, why did you sell it? What about the money I've saved?' She suddenly became sad.

'You'll have the head-shaving ceremony for your son with that money, you'll get a goat for the *aqiqah*, you'll have a party for everyone in the compound. Maybe you can have a band as well.' He began laughing. Razia's cheeks glowed with joy.

'And then everyone will see how well you've celebrated our son's *aqiqah*.'

'Hmm.' He took off his shoes and lay down on his bed.

'This time we'll buy a really big transistor, Safdar.' Razia began making tea for him.

'Yes.'

'Are you sick?'

'I'm just tired,' he said with his eyes closed.

Razia gave him tea and sat beside him. He finished the tea quickly and lay down again. But, holding his hand in hers, Razia continued talking. 'You didn't ask me how I was today. I tell you, I had a rotten day, and when you leave I feel worse. Now you should get a few days' leave, my heart is so restless, and these women don't talk to me either, they're all jealous of your love and...' Razia fell silent. Safdar was fast asleep. She pulled up his quilt and went out to call Safia who was still in the compound playing with other children.

Seeing Safdar sleeping so soundly, Safia decided to do some cooking and when the food was ready she tried to awaken Safdar, but he wouldn't budge. After a few *'hunh, hunhs'* he fell asleep again. Razia was certain now that he was sick. The thought that he was so quiet was driving her out of her mind.

She fed Safia and then went to bed on an empty stomach. She lay awake late into the night and when she finally ambled into sleep she dreamt there were two goats tied to a peg outside her door, and she was sitting on the bed with a baby in her lap who resembled Safdar. Suddenly one of the goats bleated loudly and she woke up.

The open doors of the quarter were banging in the wind and nothing was visible in the darkness outside. Safdar was not on his bed. Razia sat up. 'He's gone out again to relieve himself. What if he catches a chill...why didn't he pee inside, I would have washed it in the morning.' She stared at the darkness beyond the doors.

She sat waiting a long time but there was no sign of him. Finally fear gripped her heart. To go out like this in the middle of the night—what if something should happen? There are all

kinds of dangerous people about at this time of night.
She was about to go out to look for him when he returned. Shutting the door, he went straight to his bed. 'I had a stomach ache, why are you up?' he said softly.
'You didn't even have any supper. You must go to the doctor in the morning. Do you want me to apply heat to your stomach?' She made a move to get out of bed.
'No, no, you're not feeling well. Go to sleep.' He covered his face with the quilt.
How could Razia sleep? She spent the rest of the night sitting up. When Safdar awoke the next morning he seemed to be in very good spirits. He had a hearty breakfast and as he was leaving for work he tweaked Razia's cheek. She felt buoyant when she saw him look so refreshed. 'How out of sorts he was for two days,' she said to herself.

*  *  *

Quickly she finished all her work, locked the door, and joined the women sitting in the sun. She was anxious to tell everyone the big news about the sale of the transistor and the elaborate *haqiqa* celebrations she and Safdar were planning.
'*Arri*, what do you know, that silly man went and sold the transistor. He said "You celebrate your son's *aqiqah* with the money, invite people to a party...the radio isn't important, we'll get another one," and he said, "You can also get a band."' Razia gurgled with laughter and cast a glance at Shaadan, who was sitting with her back to her. No one appeared to be affected by Razia's news.
'Oh *Masi*, he sold it?' Peelu asked wistfully. She seemed to be the only person who was startled by what Razia had said.
'Yes, but so what? We'll get another one, may God prolong Safdar's life.'
'Why *Masi*, we could have had so much fun if you had your radio. Yesterday my father also bought a radio. It's just like the one you had. It works without electricity. We could have played the two together. Well, never mind, now you can listen to my

radio.'

'Come then, show it to me,' Razia said with interest.

Peelu ran to her quarter and soon returned with a transistor. Razia looked at it and became numb with shock. She herself had scratched a mark on a side so that she could always recognize it. So no one could ever steal it.

'Razia, this looks just like your radio,' Basheeran said, peering closely at Razia's face.

Razia sat still with the radio in her lap, her eyes transfixed at some point before her. A darkness grew at the base of her vision, the row of quarters in front of her disappeared, then the tall, overgrown tree slowly drowned in the abyss of darkness. 'Let the *aqiqah* be, Safdar, who's going to bother with goats, the goats are dead, who are we to invite to the party now...' she murmured so quietly under her breath that the women could only see her lips moving.

'When Abba comes home at night then I'll play the radio for you *Masi*.' Peelu snatched the transistor from her lap and, clasping it to her breast, ran with it to her quarter. All the women were looking at Razia with questions in their eyes. The minute Peelu left they all crept closer to her in sympathy, and glancing meaningfully at each other, they sighed deeply.

'I'll say nothing now, Safdar, I don't want your son to lose his father...' Razia's lips were still moving.

'*Hai, hai,* the poor creature, how happily she used to run around all the time,' Allah Rakhi proclaimed. 'I swear I was never jealous of her.'

'Isn't that what I said—is it possible for men to be like this? Ahh, the poor woman.' Basheeran wiped her tears with a corner of her *dupatta*.

'*Arri*, why are you sitting like this? Why don't you say something? Come to your senses.' The seamstress shook Razia's shoulder vigorously. She flinched and stared at everyone as if she did not know them. Allah Rakhi, Basheeran, the seamstress—all the women had tears in their eyes. Razia slowly edged closer to Shaadan Pathani.

'*Arri* sister, why are you still angry with me? Let's be friends now, our quarrel is over at last.'

Razia clung to Shaadan and wept so passionately that Shaadan too broke into sobs.

# Harvest

Sitting in a corner of the room, her head lowered, Kaneez was wiping the tears from her eyes with the edge of her *dupatta*. *Amma*, standing nearby with her hands placed on her hips, was glaring at her. Kaneez lifted her head once, looked helplessly at her mother, and then hid her face between her knees again.

'Think carefully, girl. It's easy to say yes, but when you return after six months people will say you ran away to find a husband, did a terrible thing, and then, what is worse, you left him. *Arri*, why are you bent on making the life of this old woman miserable?'

'I've been in the house for so many days, *Amma*,' Kaneez murmured, 'people are talking even now, and who knows I may not come back.'

'If you don't come back where will you go, girl?' *Amma* scowled angrily at her.

'Give me an answer *Amma*, I'm late already,' Din Muhammad called from the veranda. The September sun fell sharply upon his person. 'She's an orphan, she'll have enough to eat for six months at least.' Din Muhammad's voice rang loudly.

'I'll find some place to go *Amma*, give him an answer first, he's been waiting a long time,' Kaneez spoke restlessly.

'You'll come back after you've dishonoured me, there's no other place you can go, you crazy girl. Why don't you go somewhere from where you won't have to return? You had so many husbands but you couldn't stay put with anyone.'

'Just go and say yes, tell him he can come tomorrow and wed me.' Kaneez stood up in sudden exasperation. Then she sat down again, and pulling up the leg of her *shalwar*, began scratching her ankle.

'You misbegotten creature, you won't listen to any one, will you.' *Amma* left the room swearing and muttering alternately under her breath. 'I accept, Din Mohammad!' she announced in a piercing voice.

Kaneez ran to the door of the room and peeked at Din Muhammad who was rearranging his turban on his head.

'All right *Amma*, I'm leaving now. I'll come back tomorrow, have her ready.' Setting his turban down carefully on his head, Din Muhammad left the house.

Kaneez emerged from the room. The front door was still open. Nonplussed, she looked about her. 'Tomorrow you'll get married for real, Kaneej,' she murmured to herself.

'Grind some sesame seeds to make *ladoos*, when that husband of yours comes tomorrow, what will I give him?' Her mother glowered at her with a bitter expression in her eyes.

'Why are you upset *Amma*?' Kaneez replied tartly and going up to the storage room she began taking out sesame seeds from the bin.

Her mother left the room without another word and Kaneez sat down to grind sesame seeds. *If Abba were alive, you too would be married with honour, now that you have no honour, who will marry you?* Kaneez sighed deeply. *Well, it's all right, at least a few days will be spent living honourably.* Kaneez tried to comfort herself. For some reason, today, after a long time, her thoughts returned to her father again and again and every detail of his death raced before her eyes.

That day when *Abba* returned from work he forgot to bring fodder for the goat. After gulping down a glass of water he left immediately. Her mother tried to stop him, saying, 'Don't go now, it's going to rain, you'll get wet, and it's already dark.' But *Abba* paid no heed and left. Then Kaneez cooked his *rotis* and waited and waited, but there was no sign of him. Night fell and it started raining. It was dark outside and there was heavy thunder and lightning. Her mother ran to the door several times, getting soaked each time. Kaneez kept comforting her. 'He must be sitting under a tree to protect himself from the rain,' she said. More time passed. The rain stopped, but *Abba* didn't leave his place under the tree and that was when she set out with her mother to look for him. She carried an oil lamp under her *dupatta* and, treading carefully in the muddy puddles, she made her way toward the forest. The gusts of wind were at odds with the lamp, but Kaneez didn't let it go out and, her eyes peering at every tree, she continued on her way. Then she saw her father stretched out peacefully under a tree. She called out to him, but he didn't get up. The bundle of fodder lay beside him and drops of water were dripping over his clothes from the branches above. When her mother looked closely at *Abba* in the light of the lamp she saw green-coloured foam on the edges of his lips and on one of his fingers she saw two fresh drops of blood. '*Arri*, he's been bitten by a snake.' *Amma* started crying as if her heart had burst.

Kaneez flung the pestle aside and began removing the seeds from the mortar. *Who knows how much poison there was in him, black like these seeds, you know.* The seeds seemed like writhing black snakes to Kaneez. *Arri, why didn't the snake bite you, what purpose do you have in this world? If Abba had been alive he would have earned money and Amma would have lived honourably. What did you earn girl, you squandered everything, hunger devoured whatever was left.*

And then Kaneez remembered how quickly hunger had made her deceitful. When their goat, its horns braced, returned to the house on the evening following *Abba*'s death, Kaneez ran to her with the pail and after quickly milking her, she drank more than half the milk herself, giving less than half to her mother, and still she tossed and turned all night; tormented by hunger, she couldn't sleep all night and early the next morning she got up and milked the goat and drank the milk again. *Amma*, who had been crying all night, was now asleep. When she got up from her bed around midday she saw the goat's udders hanging like empty bags. Kaneez rubbed the udders for hours and finally managed to squeeze out only a half-quart of milk. *Amma* was beside herself when she saw the small quantity of milk. 'Sell this wretch to a butcher, she's also deserted us.' And Kaneez had said, with great cunning, '*Amma*, maybe she's dry. God willing, we'll get another goat, how many days can we eat if we sell her?'

When the goat returned from the grazing field her udders were heavy and taut. In three or four days *Amma* discovered that the goat wasn't dry and she screamed in anger. 'You misbegotten creature! *Arri,* you're the one who's dry, you couldn't control your appetite for even a few days. Your father never made me work and now you want me to start working to satisfy your hunger and dishonour the dead man, and the family will also say he died without leaving anything for us.'

'What a good life we had indeed!' Kaneez muttered sarcastically. 'Every day it was the same maize bread with a little coriander *chutney*, and on special days maybe a lump or two of raw sugar. Go and nurse your honour. There's no way of keeping our stomachs full without hard work.' Kaneez tried to make her mother see the truth.

Her head hung low, her mother fell into deep thought. 'But I'm suffering from pain in the joints, how can I perform any kind of labour, and if you work what will your father's spirit say?'

'Oh *Amma*, spirits don't come back to say anything. Don't you worry, I'll care for you.' And the very next day Kaneez left the house to look for work.

'May God forgive me,' Kaneez muttered as she scooped the sesame seeds from the mortar and then her thoughts wandered again. *How people tormented me because I was an orphan, they all treated me like I belonged to them but not one of them kept me home. The villains didn't even give me water after they beat me. But you, wretch, you too didn't go and drown yourself in a pool of water. What a strange thing life is, you can't take it with your own hands, girl.* Kaneez sighed and tears rolled down her face and fell into the seeds. *Arre Din Muhammad, you'll eat these ladoos which have Kaneej's tears mixed in them. Swear by my tears you won't abandon me.*

Kaneez hid her face between her knees and sobbed violently, but when *Amma* came in with firewood she wiped her tears and sat down to start a fire as if she had not been crying just moments ago.

It was evening now. She placed a small pan on the stove and began making *ladoos*. Her mother, seated on a rope cot under the *nim* tree, was lost in thought. The lines on her brow had deepened.

'*Amma*, don't be sad, I'll take care of you,' Kaneez said, removing the pan from the stove. 'There's a year's store of grain in the storage room, and it's just you now.'

'You worry about yourself, I'm not important,' *Amma* murmured softly and, picking up the water-pot, she went outside.

After making the *ladoos* Kaneez began pacing up and down in the veranda like a restless passenger at a train station. The moss that had formed on the walls during the rainy season had dried and was crackling, saltpetre oozed through the cracks in the brick walls, and the *nim* tree was bursting with foliage. She remembered that *Abba* used to put in a swing for her on this tree during the monsoons and she used to swing for hours with her friends, talking about weddings and frowning at the mention of mothers-in-law.

Sighing heavily, Kaneez lay down on the rope cot. *Arri Kaneej, you were just fated to suffer bad luck. All the girls went to set up their houses, there were such celebrations at their weddings, the bridegrooms came with flowered diadems on their heads. And you, you're making your own ladoos, and who will play the drum? Amma is hiding herself from everyone so that no one will know you're getting married for six months.* Picking up the *nim* leaves that had fallen over her *dupatta*, she crushed them between her fingers.

Gradually evening fell. *Amma* hadn't returned from outside nor did Kaneez get up from the rope cot. Weeping and wallowing in her own despair seemed to provide an odd comfort. The goat had come in and was soiling the whole veranda with her droppings, but Kaneez didn't feel like getting up to tether her.

As soon as *Amma* entered the house and saw this scene she muttered something under her breath. Mother and daughter spent a restless night. The next morning instead of going to work, she went with *Amma* to the fields. On returning she swept the room and the veranda and put down two rope cots under the *nim* tree. In her own way she was making arrangements for the bridal party, but her gaze was pinned to the front door. *He should be along shortly, but what if he doesn't come?* Kaneez's heart sank with fear. *Arri, no one in this village will marry you even for six months.*

Her mother sat silently at the entrance of the room. Kaneez washed her hands and sat down beside her. 'I'll take care of you, dear *Amma*.'

'Be quiet wretch!' *Amma* said irritably and then, placing her head between her knees, she broke into tears. '*Arri*, if you hadn't been like this today you would have been married honourably to someone in our family, you would have had your own home, your own village. You'll return again in dishonour after six months.' Wiping her tears *Amma* got up and going to the trunk with the red flowers in the storage room she opened it and started rummaging through it.

Steeling herself, Kaneez stood where she was. In the past she had heard not only other people but her own mother too, saying all kinds of things about her and to her, but she had never taken any of it to heart. However, today she felt like screaming that she was not like that, that she had always yearned for a home and for honour.

'Here, your father had this suit made for you. Bathe and put it on. Din Muhammad said nothing would be given or taken, so what suits of clothing are you waiting for?' *Amma* handed her the red flowered suit made of Japanese fabric and, taking out rice and lumps of raw sugar from the bin, she began placing them in a wicker basket.

'*Amma*, don't get all upset, don't be afraid, I won't come back.' Kaneez tucked the clothes under her arm. 'Let them come, then I'll wear these, don't you worry now.' She put the suit on the rope cot on her way to the veranda. She carried the earthen water-pot to the *nim* tree and positioning a rope cot on its side, she sat down to bathe behind it. After she had finished bathing, she straightened the cot and going to the storage room she began drying her hair with a dirty *dupatta*. *Amma* was still seated on the threshold, sighing. Who knows what she was thinking at this time. Perhaps that winter was just around the corner and the pain in her joints would be triggered by the cold, that she would lie on the cot all alone in this house and moan, that there would be no one there to massage her scalp with mustard oil, no one would bring her a glass of water, and if today her Kaneez were married in their family, in their own village, she would send for her during winter. And so her thoughts rambled.

'*Amma*, don't mope like this,' Kaneez said softly, throwing her hair back. Her gaze, pinned to the half-open front door, searched for Din Muhammad.

The sun hadn't climbed high when Din Muhammad appeared along with four men. *Amma* asked them to sit on the cots and stood nearby. 'You must have left early, which was wise. It gets so hot. You didn't have any difficulty along the way, did you?'

'No, we had no difficulty,' Din Muhammad replied in a low tone, 'now you hurry up *Amma*, we'd like to start back before noon, we have three miles to travel.' Then he started talking to his companions.

*Arre, how early you've come, couldn't wait, could you*, Kaneez said to herself. She was going mad with joy. *When the people in the village find out that Kaneej has been married and has left with her husband, how disappointed they will all be.* She hastily changed into the suit with the flowered print, stuck the copper nose ring with the three beads into her nose, and when she looked at her image in the mirror while she was applying red powder that came in a paper packet to her lips, her gaze lowered of its own accord. *Arri Kaneej, how much fun it would have been if the girls had been here at this time playing the drum.*

The witnesses came and stood by the storage room and Kaneez said '*Hunh*' so loudly they all heard her. *Amma* suddenly sat down and then, rising to her feet, she picked up the plate of *ladoos* and left the room.

When *Amma* returned she picked up the rice and lumps of raw sugar from the winnowing basket and tied them in a corner of Kaneez's *dupatta*. 'Get up now, it's time to go.'

Kaneez didn't move for a long time. Her heart ached. What kind of a wedding is this, with no one to give away the bride and then the fear of the six-month arrangement clawed at her heart—she checked the rice in her *dupatta* and got up. '*Amma*, no one should know I've been married for six months.'

'*Arri*, why be scared now, you should have thought of this before. When you come back, won't everyone know?' *Amma*'s voice cracked. 'Come on, it's time to go.'

When *Amma* led Kaneez out by her arm, Din Muhammad and his companions stood up. They said *salaam* to *Amma* and went out quickly. Kaneez embraced *Amma* and followed them.

After walking along a long path for a while, she turned around and saw *Amma* standing in the open doorway, wiping her tears. She had not cried when she said goodbye to *Amma*, but now her eyes filled with tears. Brushing away her tears, she stopped to look at *Amma*. *Amma, I'll take good care of you, don't you worry.* For some reason her steps suddenly became heavy.

Din Muhammad stopped. 'Why are you crying girl, walk fast or it will get too hot.'

*One's man is one's own, girl, he's so mindful already.* Kaneez's pace quickened. When she stopped and turned back at the next path her house and her village were no longer in view.

She was drenched in sweat as she walked. The red powder on her lips was washed out by sweat and the sun scorched her dark complexion until it looked black. The dust from the path covered her *shalwar* all the way to her knees. Still she had no sense of exhaustion; she was going home with *her* man, who inhabited her dreams. Striking the ground with his long wooden stick, the young man with the clipped moustache walked ahead of her, and Kaneez's eyes were fastened on his back. She saw nothing but him. There were ploughs in the fields, herds of sheep went this way and that, and leaning on their wooden sticks, the shepherds observed her with interest.

'Look girl, that's our village there,' Din Muhammad stopped suddenly while walking, and then continued on. Kaneez hastened her step. *Arri, he's comforting me, he knows how tired I am—you know, I'll never be tired walking alongside you,* Kaneez thought passionately.

At the next crossing the four men shook hands with Din Muhammad and went on their way. 'Look, there's our house,' Din Muhammad said, turning to look at her after the men were gone, and then he started walking alongside her. 'Will you manage the house? I have two children and Sakina has been very ill.'

'Don't you worry, I know everything,' Kaneez replied slowly.

'You won't quarrel, will you?'

'I won't embarrass you, don't you worry.' Kaneez said. Her heart sank. The house was not far now, but she was exhausted. She felt she couldn't walk another step. *Arre Din Muhammad, you could have said something nice at this moment, he's only making sure—if I was going to fight why would I have agreed to come? You don't know Kaneej.* Kaneez wiped her tears and glanced at Din Muhammad who had now gone ahead of her. She thought, *I'm ill-fated, can anyone get happiness by fighting for it?*

It was past noontime. They were both entering the village now. The women were drawing water from the well and the village water-mill turned noisily. Din Muhammad stopped in front of a house, then opened the door and went in. Kaneez followed him. Din Muhammad leapt forward and bent over Sakina who was lying on a cot in the veranda.

'How are you feeling?'

Kaneez stood like a stranger in the veranda. Two young children who had been playing with dirt, got up to stare at her with interest and amazement.

'You brought her then?' Sakina made an attempt to raise herself on her elbows but fell back.

'Yes, I've brought her, but don't get up, you will tire yourself.'

Sakina didn't respond. Drawing out a *dupatta* from under her pillow she placed it over her face as if she didn't want to see anything.

'*Arri*, you're the one who said that the home and the kids were being ruined.' Din Muhammad was visibly agitated and again and again he tried to remove the *dupatta* from her face.

'You go and wash, I'm not feeling very well. I'll be all right soon.' Sakina removed the *dupatta* from her face and taking Din Muhammad's hand in hers, she gave him a probing look.

Kaneez was standing in the veranda as if she could hear or see nothing. The crows perched on the wall were making a din and the cow tied to a peg in a corner was mooing loudly for some reason.

'Come in Kaneej, why are you standing there?' Sakina said feebly, and, taking short steps, Kaneez came and sat down by Sakina's bed. The bundle of raw sugar and rice fell into her lap.

'Lift up your veil, girl,' Sakina said with interest, 'Let me also see your face.'

Kaneez stole a glance at Sakina through lowered eyes. *Arri, how beautiful she is, but she has no life left in her, all skin and bones she is, she's nearly done for I think, how many more days will the poor woman live?* Kaneez heaved a sigh of relief.

Sakina's deteriorated physical condition had comforted her greatly, but still, Sakina's beauty rankled in her eyes.

Din Mohammad ate and, wiping his hands with the red towel, he went out. Sakina raised herself on her elbows and said, 'I've been sick for a long time, there hasn't been anyone to take care of the house or the children.'

'*Arri*, don't you worry at all, I'm here now to serve you,' Kaneez said quietly and then got to her feet. 'Tell me all there's to do.' She began unknotting her *dupatta* to take out the raw sugar and rice. She didn't even notice the look of hatred in Sakina's eyes.

Setting the lump of raw sugar along with the rice in a plate, Kaneez patted the children on the head and then sat down with them next to the water pot to wash their faces. 'Raja *babu* will have his face washed, then he'll eat sweets' she recited in an effort to make them submit to the washing.

After drying their faces and hands with her *dupatta*, she took them into the storage room, took out pretty suits from the trunk and changed their clothes. How nice they looked with their faces clean. The older boy's complexion was just like Sakina's while the younger had taken after his father. Kaneez felt a surge of maternal affection for the younger boy. She held him close and began kissing him. *Ah girl, in a few days these unfortunate children will be without a mother, but I won't let them suffer, after all they are my Din Muhammad's children.*

Happy, the children went out and Kaneez turned to survey her house. Three large trunks with heavy padlocks, an expansive bed with heavy copper legs, and at the foot of the bed a new bed-pad and quilt. On a shelf was the Quran resting on a *rehal*, on another shelf a gas lantern and on the third shelf a mirror and a *surmadani*.

Kaneez wanted to open the three trunks and see what they contained. Who knows what they might be filled with. After all, these were all her things. After seeing the dismal condition she was in, Kaneez had become convinced Sakina would leave the house only as a corpse.

Everything was coated with dust. The children had created a mess everywhere. Who knows when the room had been swept last. Kaneez's pity was aroused. *If a woman is sick all the time, this is what will happen. Arri, that's why the poor man had to marry a second time. What comfort can a woman like this give him?* Feeling bashful, Kaneez adjusted the *dupatta* over her head. *Ah, what a house you have got, like a palace, such things there are here that one can not tear one's gaze away from them.*

She came out in the courtyard and saw Sakina who was lost in thought. Sakina turned to look at her with a start. 'Those two bullocks tied to the peg outside under the thatch, are those ours?' Kaneez asked. Forgetting everything else, she had assumed the role of mistress of the house.

'Why girl, why do you ask?' Sakina looked at her with an expression that seemed to say, *What's it to you, they're mine, not yours.* 'Now go and start the supper, it's getting dark and Dinu eats early. Milk the cow as well.' Sakina turned her face away.

*Ah, the poor woman, how sickly she is, with no hope of seeing tomorrow, there's not much life left in her.* Kaneez went to the courtyard and started rinsing out the milk pail. *Arri, this house is mine now and I'll serve you as well.*

Kaneez felt a strange kind of pride while she was milking the cow. *My, what a large animal, looks like an elephant. What's a goat in comparison, gives a mug-full of milk and kicks as well.* She remembered her own goat and the thought of her mother's loneliness began to trouble her. *Who knows how poor Amma is managing, but daughters can't live with their mothers forever.*

It was evening. The crows sitting on the brick wall of the courtyard flew off cawing. From the road outside came the tinkling sound of bells tied around the necks of goats and cows. After rinsing the *daal* quickly she set it on the fire to cook and then left to go to the well with two water-pots. There was very little water left after she had washed the children's hands and faces.

Placing the water-pots on the rim of the well, she stood nearby and waited for her turn. The other women were in a great hurry. '*Arri*, have you come from the other village?' one of the women asked. 'You're Din Muhammad's woman, aren't you?'

'Yes,' Kaneez replied proudly, pulling her *dupatta* down on her face a little.

'He brought her today,' the other woman said, 'there's no trusting this world, he should have waited until Sakina was dead.' With that she set her water-pot on her hip and walked away.

*What is bothering the witch?* Kaneez gave the retreating woman an indignant look and turned to pull the rope.

When Kaneez returned home she saw Din Muhammad was sitting near Sakina with his youngest in his lap. Sakina's face was turned away from him. He kept touching her shoulder to get her attention and was also tugging at her *dupatta*. Kaneez felt as if someone had kindled a fire right next to her heart. She began making *roti* hastily. She was telling herself to be sensible. *Arri, you already knew, so why torment yourself now? You've been brought for six months, you're like a traveller, staying the night and leaving in the early morning.* Kaneez sighed and, patting the two boys, she started feeding them.

After feeding the children she placed a *roti* and a bowl of *daal* on a platter and extended it toward Sakina who was still lying down with her face averted from her. Then she stood up and silently watched Din Muhammad through lowered eyes.

'Get up and eat a little,' Din Muhammad said, helping Sakina into a sitting position. She conceded diffidently and Din Muhammad began making small morsels of food for her which he fed her himself. After every morsel Sakina showed her reluctance to eat any more and Kaneez stood nearby watching them helplessly, wondering what was left in this dried out woman that was making Din Muhammad crazy about her.

'That's enough Dinu, there are knives going through my stomach.' After a few morsels Sakina clutched her stomach in agony. Frightened by her reaction, Din Muhammad quickly made her lie down and ran to get the bottle of *churan* from the shelf for her.

Kaneez picked up the platter of food and walked away to the stove. How her heart ached. *Dinu hasn't eaten anything, that's why he's so weak. She won't eat and won't let him eat either. If it had been me I would have forced myself to eat, even if my stomach were going to burst. How false your love is, Sakina. Who knows how she's weaved her magic, otherwise who would pursue a sick woman like this.*

Kaneez remembered several men whose wives were sick and who no longer bothered with them. One or two of those men had been trailing her as well.

It was late into the night when she finished tidying up and feeding the cow. There were sounds that seemed to be from other planets and far, far away several male voices rose in song to the accompaniment of cymbals. 'Beloved, you are living with my rival, *ho...ho.*'

Kaneez listened intently. *There, they're singing songs in honour of your wedding. What a wedding yours was, no drums and you didn't even sit in a doli, no one even called a bullock-cart for you, and you were married.* Then suddenly she recalled that this was her wedding night, she still had to set up her bed. *Arri, where will you sleep—what will you say to him? Ahh, how sweet it feels.*

'Take Chota to sleep with you, girl. Set up your bed in the courtyard, and be careful he's properly covered, there's a lot of dew at night, Chota shouldn't catch a chill.' Racked with pain, Sakina spoke to her as she lay in bed, tossing her head in Din Muhammad's lap. She was groaning loudly at this time.

Kaneez felt as if a knife had emerged from Sakina's stomach to be plunged into her own heart. For a few moments she stood motionless and in silence. In the still of the night the sound of the turning of the well's pulley could be clearly heard. *Didn't Amma say think well before you do this —what's the use of being unhappy now?* Kaneez asked herself.

She set up her bed in the courtyard, shut the front door and, clasping Chota to her breast, she lay down.

'You won't forget me, will you?' Sakina was whispering softly. Dinu's reply was inaudible. Kaneez glanced at the veranda. They were lying down next to each other, their faces close.

Kaneez heaved a long sigh. *Who knows what date of the lunar cycle it is, maybe the moon will appear late at night, it's still dark now.* Kaneez was consoling herself. *I wonder what the people in my village must be thinking. They must be saying, there, Kaneez is married now. They must be regretting that they didn't come forward with a proposal. They must be remembering. But what good is all that now? I kept saying, take me into your house and no one would agree to do it.*

She lifted her head once again. The two of them were still in the same position. *Maybe they've fallen asleep, the poor man has to sleep, if a man remains awake it's other things he thinks* about. She's weaved some magic to keep him in her power . . . but, how long can she live?'

The exhaustion from the three-mile walk that morning quickly put her to sleep, but she woke up early the next morning. After milking the cow she started a fire and put the milk on it to boil and then immediately sat down to churn the yogurt that had set overnight. In the meantime Din Muhammad returned from his ablutions in the woods. He ate the leftover *roti* from the night before for breakfast and after gulping down a glass of buttermilk, he got ready to leave. 'Take care of Sakina,' he said. Going outside, he untied the two bullocks from under the sloping thatch and quickly drove them out.

Kaneez had watched him expectantly as he ate and also when he was leaving. She longed for him to say something, Sakina was asleep, he could have said something.

After Din Muhammad left, Kaneez gathered the cow dung from where the cow was tethered and, mixing yellow earth with it, she applied the mixture to the floor of the storage room and the veranda before Sakina and the children woke up. Ever since her arrival she had been irked by the patches of flaking earth she saw all over the place.

She felt very peaceful. Pleasant daydreams invaded her thoughts and she began comforting herself: 'It's just a matter of a few more days, girl, in the cold of winter you will be sleeping clasped to Dinu's breast on this bed right here. Sakina isn't going to live long.'

When, after washing her hands, she was hugging the children, Sakina woke up. A look of kindness swam in her eyes for a moment and then disappeared. Groaning, she called Kaneez who ran to her with a glass of warm milk. 'Ah Sakina, how pale you look after a night of pain, here, drink a little milk, it will take away some of the weakness.'

Sakina took two gulps with great difficulty and instantly grabbed her stomach. 'I'm not fated to eat or drink any more,' she said with a groan, 'cook *roti* quickly now, you'll have to go to the fields with food. Take Chota with you, he'll show you the way.' She fell back painfully. How many fears, how much hatred emerged in her eyes, how many inadequacies there were that poisoned her.

Chota's hand clasped in hers, Kaneez was about to leave for the fields with two thick *rotis* soaked in *ghee* and a container full of buttermilk when Sakina began tossing like a snake. 'Return immediately after giving him the food, come back before the sun climbs over the wall there, do you hear,' Sakina said, pointing to the veranda wall. Kaneez turned and saw that the sun was near the wall already.

Kaneez arrived in the fields to find Din Muhammad reclining under a tree. He looked tired and his face was covered with a film of dust. Kaneez sat down beside him and, untying the bread cloth, placed the *rotis* before him. Din Muhammad gave her one look, then lowered his eyes and began eating. 'How is Sakina?' he asked.

'She's all right,' Kaneez replied softly. 'I've travelled such a long distance, why don't you ask me too, *hunh*?' Kaneez sighed deeply.

Din Muhammad didn't say anything and after he had finished eating he wrapped the dishes again in the lunch cloth. 'Do you like my house?' he asked softly as if afraid someone might overhear.

'It's not your house, it's my house Din Muhammad,' Kaneez said with a lift of her head, using a tone of voice that made Din Muhammad lose himself in her eyes for a moment. 'All right then, I'm going now, Sakina said I should return before the sun climbs over the wall.' She rose to her feet.

'You will serve her well, won't you?'' Din Muhammad's face fell on hearing Sakina's name.

'Trust me, will you.' She took the little boy's finger in her hand and started on her way home.

When she got back she found Sakina's gaze pinned to the door. 'Why did you take so long?' Sakina nearly screamed.

'It's a long way Sakina. I left as soon as he had finished eating.'

'What did you talk to him about?' Sakina stared at her.

'*Arri*, what is there for me to say, I'm here only to serve you.' Saying this she picked up the water pot, set it on her hip, and went out to draw water from the well.

On Din Muhammad's return from the fields in the evening, Sakina left her bed in a state of agitation and stared into his eyes as if searching for something. Din Muhammad placed her head on his chest and she continued whispering who knows what to him until in a few moments he was wiping his eyes with a corner of his turban.

*Arre, why should you cry, may your enemies cry instead.* Kaneez looked about her frantically but didn't say anything. The *roti* on the *tawa* was burning. She wanted to wipe off Din Muhammad's tears and wring Sakina's neck in order to snatch away the few days of living that were left to her.

At night Sakina didn't eat anything because of the pain. Din Muhammad did not eat either. Kaneez fed the children and remained hungry herself. Anyway, who was to say to her, *There now, eat something.* Sakina sighed deeply all night long and Din Muhammad would give a start in his sleep every time he heard her sigh.

The next day when Kaneez took food to him he didn't even glance at her; his head lowered like a bullock's, he started eating.

'You're very tired, aren't you, why don't I press your feet when you're done eating,' Kaneez said, edging closer to him. The little boy was playing at some distance in the half-ploughed field.

'Sakina has asked you not to talk to me, so don't, but I'll talk, she hasn't made me swear, has she? Who else will I talk to if not you? Isn't that true?'

Din Muhammad still didn't say anything. Just once he raised his eyes to look at Kaneez and then he called out to his son.

Kaneez moved closer to him. Din Muhammad lifted his son into his lap and kissed him.

'Who are you kissing him for, *hunh*?' Kaneez teased him and then broke into a merry laugh.

Din Muhammad gave her a baffled look. 'Go home now,' he said. Then he put down his son and walked away toward the bullocks.

*Ahh, how much I like you. Why do you run from me? Aren't we married? I've walked miles to be with you* —sitting alone Kaneez was left with her thoughts. Then she gathered the dishes and clasped the little boy's finger. She was overwhelmed by Din Muhammad's decent behaviour. *If it were another man who knows what he would have done to you, but they aren't men are they, they're animals.*

The people in the village were surprised that Kaneez was able to take care of the house and the children and had served Sakina so well—no one ever heard any sounds of quarrelling or bickering. When she went to the well and the women asked her about Sakina's condition, she would describe her ailing condition to them with such despondency that they would be reduced to tears. Sakina's health deteriorated with the onset of the cold weather. Kaneez heaved long sighs of relief, but who knew what was in her heart. Din Muhammad was happy to see that his Sakina was being served well, but when Kaneez took food to him in the fields and tried to talk him into paying her attention, he remained distant.

Once winter came everyone slept inside the same room. At one end of the room was Sakina and Din Muhammad's bed, at the other Kaneez slept on a cot with the little boy. She cooked and served early in the evening and then heated the room by burning cow dung cakes. Afterward she lay in bed and watched from a distance as Din Muhammad bent over a groaning Sakina, massaging her body, pressing her limbs, kissing her, shedding tears at her pain. Kaneez writhed in torment, agonizing. Her husband had been taken from her by a sick woman but she could not utter a word of protest. She was waiting for Sakina's death. Many people had told her that there are certain kinds of magic which lose their potency only when the person who weaves the spell dies.

As soon as it was dark Kaneez finished all her work quickly and, tying up the cow in the courtyard, she would slip into her bed. The moment Din Muhammad came home and sat down next to Sakina, a shot of electricity charged through Kaneez's hands. 'Ah, who knows what those two are doing, what will

Sakina be saying?' Finishing in minutes the work that would ordinarily take hours to do, Kaneez would retire to her cot, but Sakina would start remembering some errand or the other. However, today she didn't say anything and, her head resting on Din Muhammad's shoulder, she stared silently at the oil lamp. Again and again Din Muhammad asked her what she was looking at. Kaneez felt like screaming, 'Those who are dying stare just like this at lamps why are you worried?'

'When the oil is finished the flame is extinguished, the oil in my life is also being depleted.' Finally Sakina spoke up at Din Muhammad's insistence.

'If you talk like this I'll jump into a well. You've forgotten everything, Sakina.' Din Muhammad was getting agitated.

Kaneez was listening with all her might. *What has she forgotten Din Muhammad? What did she say to you, ah, won't you tell me anything? Aren't you my man? Tell me, I'm your woman, Din Muhammad, I have only been dreaming of you.* Kaneez was tossing about restlessly and Sakina continued to stare at the oil lamp.

'Tell me,' Din Muhammad was still urging Sakina to give him an answer.

'Then promise me you'll take me to Agra for treatment next month after you're done with the harvest, promise you'll keep me in the big hospital there. If you want the oil will never be depleted.'

'A lot of money will be needed for treatment in the city, but why didn't you say this earlier. For your sake I'll sell the bullocks, the cows, the plough, I'll pawn every tiny grain of wheat, I'll stay hungry but I'll take you, I promise I will.'

'May your enemies stay hungry!' Kaneez sat up suddenly. 'Who will sell my bullocks and my cow? How will you get all this again, Din Muhammad? The people in the village will make fun of you, and it's the rich people who go to the city for treatment.' She didn't know how she said all this. Her body was being ravaged, how could she see her home being plundered also.

'*Arri*, who are you to speak? Since when is this your home, you misbegotten creature! I've had you brought here just for six months to wait on me.' Sakina screamed like a witch.

'Don't you dare open your mouth again, I'll pull your tongue out!' Din Muhammad roared.

'Why shouldn't I speak? If you sell everything you'll starve and how can I see you starve? She's always putting strange ideas in your head, she's put a spell over you. She'll die, but she'll leave you with nothing.'

'She'll die?' Din Muhammad lunged toward her like a madman and grabbing her plait he started beating her brutally. 'Get out! Get out right now!' he screamed. Just for a moment Kaneez stared at him with her wide-open eyes and then hid her face in both her hands. She made no effort to protect herself from his blows. Awakened from his sleep, the younger boy clung to Kaneez, sobbing violently.

'Stop now Dinu. Why are you making Chota cry, I'm still alive, I won't die simply because she says I will.' Sakina's voice was unnaturally calm.

Din Muhammad let go of Kaneez and, sitting down on his bed, he covered his face with the blanket.

*You cruel one, is that all?* Kaneez looked at Din Muhammad with a wounded look in her eyes and, clasping Chota to her breast, she went back to bed.

The next day when Kaneez took Din Muhammad his lunch he didn't look at her at all. He ate silently with his head flung down and, sitting nearby, Kaneez watched him intently. It was only when he returned the empty plates toward her that their eyes met briefly. His lips twitched and then he quickly turned his back and walked away.

*You, cruel one, if you hit me then you should also clasp me to your breast*, Kaneez said to herself as she wearily walked back to the house. *He's embarrassed, he won't look me in the eye— arre, fool, I'm not a stranger, I'm yours. And it's not your fault, it's Sakina who has cast a spell over you.*

After the beating Din Muhammad couldn't bring himself to talk to Kaneez. She would take his food to him every day and talk endlessly—'Dinu *re*, look how fat the wheat stalks are, Dinu *re*, Chota needs a new set of clothes, Chota looks so much like you, *re*, Dinu *re*, are you angry with me? Don't leave me, look I've made your house shine, Dinu *re*, hold me close at least once—Dinu *re*—'

Who knows if Din Muhammad heard any of this or not. He would hand her back the food containers and walk away into the fields.

By the time the crop was harvested Sakina became extremely weak. Din Muhammad sold the entire crop and the next day he was taking Sakina to the city. He had also arranged for a bullock cart for the ride to the station. Kaneez was happy that Sakina was leaving. She would die in the hospital. Kaneez remembered that several people from her village had been taken to the hospital in Agra. When they left they were in very poor health and they never returned alive from the hospital. Kaneez was sure that Sakina would also not return. And how happy she was at the thought that although he had beaten her, he still didn't sell the bullock or the cow. So what if he had sold the entire crop. She would buy the wheat she needed and she would make money by making *ghee*.

The next day when Sakina was leaving early in the morning, she spoke to Kaneez after what had been a long silence. 'I'm leaving the children in your care Kaneej, don't be mean to them. One can't trust life.' Then she embraced the children and started weeping.

'Kaneej will die but she won't let harm come to them,' Kaneez said, and holding the weeping children close to herself, she went inside.

Din Muhammad helped Sakina into the bullock cart and then came in and looked at Kaneez as if he wanted to say something to her.

'Now don't tell me to take good care of them, they're mine—you go now.'

About eight or ten days passed and there was no sign of Din Muhammad nor was there any word from him. Kaneez waited anxiously. In her dreams she saw Sakina dying, even heard the sound of her last breath, and she sighed with satisfaction, but when she woke up she felt very strange. She felt as if she were going mad. She would feed the children, but often she would forget to eat herself. In the afternoon, moved by a strange feeling, she would absentmindedly wrap food in the bread cloth, fill the container with buttermilk and then immediately untie the knot she had made and start crying. '*Arre* Din Muhammad, you're running after her!' No one knows to whom these entreaties were addressed.

In those days she also thought a lot about her mother. *Who knows how she is, how she spent the winter, who heated pads for her swollen knee. Ah, you should have come and visited me once at least—maybe she was afraid I would go back with her.*

But she would hurriedly put *Amma*'s memory aside. She was afraid of her village now, she didn't know why, but the thought of her village turned into the shadow of a ghoul.

On the tenth day Din Muhammad arrived early in the morning. Kaneez was surprised to see him. He had lost considerable weight. His complexion was so pale it seemed he had been ailing for a long time. The moment he walked in, he clasped the children to him. All Kaneez could do was to stand at a distance and watch them.

'Sakina's condition is very bad, she's had the operation.' Din Muhammad looked at Kaneez. His eyes filled with tears.

Kaneez didn't say anything. She sat down at Din Muhammad's feet and began wiping off the dust from his shoes. *What have you done to yourself, Sakina isn't going to get well now, why are you driving yourself mad?* Kaneez felt a great calm. The news of the operation had convinced her that Sakina would not return.

'Bring me food quickly, I have to go to work.' Din Muhammad pulled away his feet. 'I haven't eaten anything.'

Kaneez hurriedly put *roti*, onions, and a little butter before him and then sat down beside him. Seeing him after so many days made her tongue-tied. She couldn't bring herself to say even a word.

Din Muhammad finished his food quickly and, rising to his feet, he loosened the cow's rope from the peg and began driving the animal out of the door. Kaneez ran and positioned herself before him. 'Where are you going? Even the dust from your feet hasn't come off yet.'

'I've struck a bargain for the cow, I have to sell it, I have to buy a lot of medicines. There's no time to rest.'

'But what will the children do for milk without the cow? The cow is the pride of your home, I won't let you sell it.' Kaneez caught hold of the cow's rope.

For a moment Din Muhammad gazed helplessly at Kaneez and then pushed her away so hard she fell against the wall.

As he was going out the door Din Muhammad turned to look at Kaneez who was still slumped against the wall. 'Don't wait up for me, I'll go to the station directly.'

Kaneez gazed wistfully at Din Muhammad as he walked away with the cow, a cloud of dust rising behind him. When he disappeared from view she braced herself against the door and struggled to her feet as if she had suddenly become an old woman, as if she had lost all her strength. She was mumbling under her breath, 'All right, sell the cow—Kaneej will buy another cow, she won't let the pride of your home be shattered.'

The courtyard looked forlorn without the cow. Kaneez brought in the two bullocks from the shed outside and tethered them to the peg in the courtyard, but still it wasn't the same as it had been when the cow was there.

Din Muhammad had been gone for six days. In all this time Kaneez had applied a clay coating to the floors of the veranda and the courtyard, swept the walls of the house and got rid of cobwebs. Every day she brought in fodder from the fields for the bullocks, and still she didn't tire of work. At night she would be so exhausted she'd have difficulty falling asleep; all her worries jumped on her when sleep evaded her. She missed Din Muhammad and again and again she wondered how he would take Sakina's death. How important it was for her to be with him at a time like this, so she could console him, wipe his tears. How will he deal with everything alone?

When ten days had gone by Kaneez lost interest in work. She roamed around the house in a daze. All day long the children played *gulee-danda* in the street and Kaneez, left alone, was assaulted by fears—what if Sakina's condition improved, she agonized. Din Muhammad didn't come home immediately after the operation—how could Sakina have survived for so many days? Was she made of stone? Will she not die?

Her eyes were pinned to the door, hoping for an answer. If Chota sometimes closed the door accidentally during play, she would run and open it again. 'No, my dearest, don't shut the door, your father is coming.'

On the eleventh day Din Muhammad returned. He looked around as if searching for the children and then he sat down on the cot. Kaneez leapt toward him. 'How is Sakina? What is the matter with you, you're unrecognizable.'

Kaneez was staring at his face for an answer and he was sitting silently on the cot. There were dark circles around his eyes, his cheeks were shrunk, and a black crust had formed on his lips.

'*Arre*, say something, how is Sakina?' Kaneez was getting very agitated.

'She betrayed me, she left me, the cruel one.' Din Muhammad spoke as if in a dream.

'*Hai* poor Sakina!' Kaneez pounded her chest, pulled at her hair, but there wasn't a tear in her eyes. Although she was pounding her chest with a great deal of force, she felt no discomfort.

Still beating her chest, she sat down at Din Muhammad's feet, but Din Muhammad did not weep nor did he console Kaneez. His face was expressionless. Perhaps he had wept too much already, perhaps he had come to terms with his grief.

How elated Kaneez was to see Din Muhammad sitting quietly like this. *Everything is connected to life, who mourns a dead person for more than three or four days, girl, everyone forgets*, Kaneez thought happily, and started to wipe the dust from Din Muhammad's feet with a corner of her *dupatta*. 'Life is not to be trusted, it changes from moment to moment, now don't you grieve,' Kaneez said, trying to console him.

'I suffered so much for Sakina's sake. One night the villagers surrounded me and beat me up, the wounds are still visible.' He rubbed his head with his hand. 'Her cousin begged and begged her to stay with him, but Sakina stayed with me. Her old lover poisoned himself and died and she didn't even go to his funeral. She said "I won't leave your side even for a minute"—O you cruel one, you left me forever, didn't you.' Din Muhammad looked about him foolishly, then lowered his head.

Suddenly he started and said, 'Oh Kaneej, there's something important I forgot.'

This something important was the reason Kaneez had been worshipping Din Muhammad all this time. Her eyes were saying, *Ah, tell me that something important quickly.*

Din Muhammad pulled out a crumpled piece of paper from his pocket and extended it toward Kaneez. 'Your work is finished Kaneej. The six months are over. Here, I've had the paper drawn up, you can leave now.'

'Oh Dinu!' Kaneez could not say anything more. It was as if she had no more to say.

Turning, she sought Chota for a moment with her eyes, then she rose, stuffed the paper under the drawstring of her *shalwar* and said, 'Yes, I'll go now, before it gets dark.'

# The Hand Pump

Night was about to fall. The area around the hand pump was being cemented and only a little more work remained to be done. Their chores forgotten for the moment, all the women from the neighbourhood stood around watching. The youngsters were restive with the desire to touch the handle of the pump, but Chunni Begum stood in their way with her 'No, no!'

'Don't you dare touch it, the cement is still not set properly, it will be ruined, do you hear?'

The youngsters chafed their hands in disappointment.

'You old woman, it's not an arm that it will come off,' the brickmason said, breaking into a loud laugh. 'It's a hand pump, a hand pump.'

'You do your work, I say. Is the platform around the pump still soft or not? Will the masonry not collapse if someone stepped into the masonry?' Chunni Begum convinced the brickmason and the mothers began screaming at their impetuous children. 'You wretches! Keep off for a while. She arranges for water and all you can do is cause problems for her? May you die! I'll break your hands, you wretches!'

Having dealt with the boys, the women started singing Chunni Begum's praises.

'In reality Chunni Begum is an angel.'

'You'll see, when she dies she'll be a martyr,' a woman whispered with deep feeling, her eyes filling with tears.

'This is how people from good families behave. Who in this world spends one's hard-earned money on others?'

The landlord is so stingy, he wouldn't have a hand pump put in for us. We begged and begged, but always his answer was "Why don't you people collect money and have your own pump installed".'

'Do you know...' a woman began but stopped in mid-sentence because the brickmason had risen to his feet, brushing off his shirt front as he stood up.

After Chunni Begum had carefully inspected the brickmason's workmanship from every side, she retrieved money from her waistband and started counting.

'Here's four rupees, count it,' she said, placing the money on his palm with an air of generosity.

'I won't take a paisa less than five rupees.' The brickmason stuffed the money into Chunni Begum's fist.

Money exchanged hands repeatedly and the heckling continued for a long time. The women of the neighbourhood cursed the brickmason on Chunni Begum's behalf.

'All right then, we'll just rip out the hand pump, we don't want even a single *paisa*.' The brickmason finally accepted defeat at the hands of the women and advanced toward the hand pump. He threw the money on the platform with such force that it left a mark on the wet cement.

'You wretch, here, take your rupee!' Flustered, Chunni Begum handed him the last rupee in her pouch, shook the empty pouch out, and twisted it back into her drawstring.

The minute the brickmason left, Chunni Begum plopped herself next to the hand pump and lifted up both her hands toward the sky.

'You have saved Chunni Begum's honour, You have saved her from servitude, may I live only to glorify Your name!"

Chunni Begum lowered her hands and wiped her eyes. At this time the birds were flying in haste toward their dwellings.

'Chunni Begum, God will grant you a place in heaven. How we had to make the rounds at this bungalow or that and be rebuffed by servants and cooks before we could get a drop of water. How our shoulders ached when we had to carry water from such distances.'

The women began once again to praise Chunni Begum, but the encroaching darkness quickly silenced them and they went home to take care of the cooking. The children, on the other hand, continued to loiter in the area of the hand pump.

Chunni Begum picked up a thin stick to frighten the children and, setting up her cot close to the hand pump, she lay down. The children were not afraid of anyone, least of all this flimsy-looking stick, but for some reason they were keeping their hands off this strange contraption. They continued to wrestle playfully with each other not far from the hand pump, Chunni Begum kept shaking her stick at them and only when they were overcome by pangs of hunger did the boys leave.

Chunni Begum stayed awake all night. Happiness and fear had together snatched her sleep. Even if a dog happened to go past her she started and involuntarily raised the stick in her hand; she thought it was one of the mischievous boys. 'Arre, I hope he isn't here to bathe secretly, I hope the good-for-nothing doesn't climb up on the platform and urinate.'

After she had chased the dogs out of the compound she lay down on her cot and patted herself on her back for her cleverness.

'Why, what if the money had been spent on useless things? The arthritis isn't leaving me in peace, in a few more days everyone would have thought that I was handicapped and soon I would have been receiving charity from people. My honour has been saved, no one will call me helpless now.' She gazed proudly at the sky. 'May I live only to glorify Your name Allah—Chunni Begum has always eaten only that which she has earned from her work.'

Chunni Begum had learnt to feed herself with her own earnings since she was ten or eleven. Her widowed mother was the cook in the *haveli* and as soon as she would finish cooking Chunni Begum would scrub and wash the pots and set them aside. Her mother adored her. She would say with pride that if it weren't for Chunni Begum, old age and arthritis would have caused her death from starvation.

Suddenly, while she was toiling tirelessly one day, Chunni Begum was surprised by a new feeling. She came to the realization that the period for indulging in sweet dreams was at hand. Around that time Bitya Begum's wedding was being celebrated in the *haveli*. One day Chunni Begum took a tea tray to Bitya Begum's room and saw the young woman lying on the bed with her head in her bridegroom's lap, talking to him in a coquetish manner. She didn't budge when Chunni Begum came in and that day Chunni Begum felt the longing to find a man to lean on. How weary she was.

Her mother observed her daughter from the corners of her eyes and surmised that Chunni Begum's heart was no longer in her work. She made inquiries for a few days and in no time at all Chunni Begum was married.

Chunni Begum's heart was broken when she set foot in her husband's house. The desire to place her head in her husband's lap was one thing, she didn't even get to put her head down on a straw-filled pillow. Her husband, a worthless, good-for-nothing man, fancied cheap liquor and spent all day dozing.

Chunni Begum was forced to listen to taunts about her husband's idleness and lethargy. She worked herself to the bone from morning to night and served everyone, but the moment she sat down to place a morsel of food in her mouth her mother-in-law and her sisters-in-law would start grumbling.

'Look what big morsels she's gulping down, as if the food was purchased with her husband's earnings.'

Chunni Begum quietly listened to everything and continued to swallow her food painfully with her head hung low between her knees. Every vice the forty-year-old man exhibited was deemed her responsibility; no one felt sorry for her.

Her parents had lovingly named her Chunni Begum, but her mother-in-law and her sisters-in-law succeeded in distorting 'Chunni' to 'Chunnia.' Her husband's older brother's wife, who nursed her well-fed three-year-old the entire day, ordered Chunni Begum about, calling her even when she wanted a glass of water. She was the wife of a man who was earning money and so was the favourite of her in-laws. How hard Chunni Begum tried to get her husband to stop drinking and also start working like his older brother. But talk along those lines only made her husband yawn uninterestedly.

However, following Chunni Begum's persistent pleading, he did take two days off from the liquor-house, but he would spend his time moping all day with his eyes shut as if he were lamenting the loss of his beloved. Tears flowed from his eyes. On seeing her son's condition Chunni Begum's mother-in-law scolded her. '*Arri*, the wretch will devour my beloved son, she won't let him live.' Taking out a *chawanni* from her waistband she handed it to him and pushed him out of the house with the injunction that he should go out and have some refreshments.

That day Chunni Begum lost her cool. She uttered such expletives that people placed their hands over their ears, such were her anguished pleas that all those who heard her were shaken.

When the mother-in-law and the sisters-in-law realized that Chunni Begum was no longer under their control, they threw her out of the house. Chunni Begum forced her way back, retrieved the *lota* and *katora* she had brought with her dowry, picked up her small valise and left the house. Weeping and wailing she started walking and before long her feet automatically took her in the direction of the *haveli* where her mother had been a cook for eight years.

Arriving at the *haveli* and still weeping and wailing, she plunked herself down at the doorstep. When Begum sahiba saw her in this condition she felt obliged to leave her place on the settee and run toward her.

'Why, it's Shabrattan's daughter! What happened?' *Begum sahiba* asked agitatedly and Chunni Begum recounted the whole story from beginning to end.

And then, from that very moment, Chunni Begum took over her mother's place. She put away the *lota* and *katora* she had brought with her dowry in the kitchen cupboard and set to work immediately.

When, after finishing her work, Chunni Begum came and sat in the veranda, the cool breeze and the expansive moonlight made her think of her husband. At that moment she also felt a tiny life move inside her.

'I say, set out a cot for yourself and lie down, and if you're hungry eat first, one gets very hungry in this condition.' Chunni Begum was overwhelmed by happiness when she heard these words of comfort coming from *Begum sahiba*. For the first time she realized what joy there was in satisfying one's needs by working hard. She tried to push away thoughts of her husband. 'So, what's there in this relationship—this kind of love exists only by virtue of seeing someone's face.'

Chunni Begum spent ten years in the *haveli*. Her son was now ten years old. She had taught him to read ten *paras* from the Quran. Chunni Begum's mother had been dead for a while and her husband had remarried. She also received news that her mother-in-law had become extremely fat. Just once she caught a glimpse of her husband on the roadside. Swaying, he went on his way without seeing her as Chunni Begum stood nearby, buying vegetables. Her heart convulsed for a moment, but she quickly got a grip on herself. When she came home, she clasped her son to her breast and cried for hours. *Begum sahiba* calmed her with great difficulty.

Time moved with great speed. Begum sahiba's teeth began to fall. Chunni Begum's son grew into a young man and *Bare Sarkar* employed him as an assistant in his shop. *Begum sahiba* also found a nice-looking girl for him to marry and Chunni Begum's face darkened. For some reason Chunni Begum lost all her zeal when *Bahu* arrived; she hated *Bahu*. Whenever *Begum sahiba* wanted anything done she called out to *Bahu* and *Bahu* didn't waste a moment in taking over her mother-in-law's chores. And this was why Chunni Begum hated her; *Bahu* was usurping her privileges and *Begum sahiba* was providing her with endless encouragement. Chunni Begum was tormented by the thought that because *Bahu* was helping with her chores she would soon assume that it was she who was supporting her mother-in-law.

In the beginning she scolded her and then she came down to calling her names. *Bahu* would look at her, her big eyes wide-open in amazement and, hiding her face in corners, she would weep. *Begum sahiba*, in the meantime, lavished all her attention on *Bahu* who had the knack of completing her work in minutes. It was as if *Begum sahiba* had forgotten Chunni Begum was around any more. If by chance she called her name she would immediately correct herself and say, 'No, not you, send *Bahu*.' Chunni Begum tossed on live coals.

Around that time Chunni Begum heard that her husband had died. She took a mortar and shattered the two heavy bangles she had always worn on her wrist. That day she didn't do any work and stayed shut in her room all day. Who knows what sad memories tormented her. When *Bahu* brought her food, Chunni Begum blasted her with all the pent-up anguish of her unfulfilled longings. She cursed her so severely that *Bahu* had to seek refuge with *Begum sahiba*.

*Begum sahiba* realized that Chunni Begum had lost her reason. Using great care and discernment she advised Chunni Begum to spend her time in worship from now on and allow *Bahu* to serve.

Chunni Begum was crushed, but she thought well, at least everything is in the open now.

'May God not make anyone beholden to anyone *Begum sahiba*,' she began frankly. 'I'll eat only that which I have earned or else I'll starve. If I'm not good enough to work for you, you may certainly have *Bahu* serve you. I'll seek work elsewhere, there's enough life left in these bones to sustain ten others. Please give me leave now, Chunni Begum will always be grateful to you.'

Chunni Begum got to her feet. Ignoring *Begum sahiba*'s protestations, Chunni Begum picked up the *lota* and *katora* she had brought with her dowry, got her small valise, and walked out.

*Bahu* ran after her in her bare feet. Her son pursued her all the way to the railway station. But Chunni Begum's heart did not melt. She now hated this city. She got a ticket and boarded the train bound for Lahore. Her son begged and pleaded, but

Chunni Begum turned a deaf ear to all his pleas. Taking out a ten-rupee bill from her waistband she handed it to her son.

'Go away I say, what care can you provide me? In four days your wife will taunt me, saying I'm dependent on her, and then she will mistreat me. Here, take this money and have some clothes made for yourself, look at the rags you have on—you can't make proper clothes with what you earn.' She saw her son's neat and tidy clothes as rags, but he was in no mood to look at or think about anything except getting his mother off the train. He ran along with the train when it began rolling and for a brief moment Chunni Begum felt as if her chest had been trammelled by the wheels of the train.

As the train departed from the station she saw her son standing on the platform, wiping perspiration from his forehead with a handkerchief. Chunni Begum stuck her head out of the window and continued looking back for a long time afterward.

Upon her arrival in Lahore she roamed around in the inner city for many days, inquiring about work in people's homes. When she went into the houses she saw the mistresses of the houses busy working. Chunni Begum's heart was burnt to a cinder. 'Why, if the mistresses begin to do the work of servants then what's left in this world. The *begums* here have the temperaments of beggars. Ah, what a place our *Dilli* was!' For days memories of her *Dilli* tormented Chunni Begum and finally, as she was wandering, she suddenly found herself in a place where peace and quiet reigned and where she saw some *ayahs* strolling about with children in their care. Chunni Begum stepped into the front yard of a bungalow and struck up a friendly conversation with an *ayah*. In a short while she had all the necessary information. The salaries were good, the work was light, there was money to be skimmed off the top, and if you made friends with the cook then you could enjoy the dietary comforts of home.

Chunni Begum begged her Maker to forgive her sins as she heard all this, but kept her mouth shut. It would be difficult to obtain a position without knowing anyone well. The *ayah* promised to find her work in a nice bungalow soon. While she was promising her this the *ayah* happened to slap the baby in her lap and the baby began to cry noisily. Chunni Begum snatched the baby from the *ayah*'s arms.

'*Arri,* you're an *ayah* and you raise your hands to the *begum's* child? What disloyalty is this?'

Clutching the child to her breast, Chunni Begum ran inside the house. *Begum sahiba* was sitting before a dressing table, beautifying herself. Chunni Begum deposited the baby in her lap.

'So hard she slapped the child, I'm still shivering with shock. Does this barren creature have no offspring of her own?' Chunni Begum was trembling with rage. *Begum sahiba* asked Chunni Begum to sit down and inquired after her well-being. The *ayah* was immediately discharged and Chunni Begum was hired on the spot. Chunni Begum protested vehemently, saying that she would not take this job, that she would not steal someone else's livelihood, but *Begum sahiba* turned a deaf ear to all her objections.

In a few days Chunni Begum was like the mistress of the house. *Begum sahiba* consulted her on every little matter, the children were so fond of her they wouldn't leave her alone for a minute, she kept an eye on the kitchen and a new cook was hired every other week. Stealing and dishonesty Chunni Begum could not tolerate. If a person could make a living by working hard, then why steal?

'When a dishonest person is dying his face is transformed into the face of a pig, yes, that's what's written in the big books.' This was one of Chunni Begum's lofty pronouncements which were always written in big books.

Every month Chunni Begum sent her son five rupees by money-order along with a letter in which she admonished him, saying, 'You wretch, don't roam around dressed in rags—you don't make much, write me when you need anything.' In response her son would repeatedly say, 'Come back please, I'll serve you, take care of you.' Chunni Begum would have the letter read and she would laugh.

'Never did he send me a penny, he wants me there so he can make me helpless and put me away in a corner—what a wretch he is!'

Chunni Begum was very happy here. She had no difficulty taking care of the house, although in the beginning she had to work hard to take care of the lawn. The thing was the city had made no arrangements for water supply in these areas, and as for the families living in the bungalows, they had installed their own hand pumps or had private tube-wells. In the quiet afternoons people from everywhere crowded to these hand pumps. When Chunni Begum shut the gate and stood guard, people with buckets gathered outside the gate and pleaded. Once or twice she was forced into a scuffle with some of the people who were taking water.

'Why, is it a sale or something? *Begum sahiba* has prohibited anyone to touch the hand pump.'

The people who previously drew water without any problems now had to wander off to distant areas to fill their buckets. They couldn't stand Chunni Begum. As they went past the house they swore heavily at her.

'*Hunh*!' Chunni Begum would turn her face away. 'They're only remembering their mothers and sisters. What does it have to do with me?'

*Begum sahiba* was extremely happy with her. She constantly praised her honesty. Before Chunni Begum's arrival people crowded at the water pump as soon as it was afternoon. The servants took a few annas from them and watched the spectacle from a distance. Children wandered all over the lawn, broke off all the flowers and trampled the flower beds. When *Begum sahiba* came to the lawn in the evening she would scream her head off and the servants would behave as if they didn't know anything.

For some time now Chunni Begum had been experiencing small aches and pains in her legs. She didn't feel like doing any work. If she sat down to wash a load of laundry, her knees gave out and if she picked up the baby and got to her feet, she felt like sitting down. But she continued to walk with the baby. She did all her work as energetically as before. Getting paid without doing her work was like eating pig as far as she was concerned. When the pain became unbearable she would grumble angrily and curse the pain, wishing death upon it.

She continued to curse, but the pain didn't die, although the pain did kill her knees. The work was there to be done, but Chunni Begum couldn't do a thing, the children cried to be held, but she could no longer pick them up. When *Begum sahiba* saw all this she was devastated. She was sure that the period of idleness had started; now Chunni Begum wants to eat without working. She didn't say anything, but she began to treat Chunni Begum with indifference.

When Chunni Begum continued to avoid work, *Begum sahiba* was forced to speak. In answer to her complaint, Chunni Begum said, '*Begum sahiba*, this pain in my knees won't let me do any work, but please don't think that Chunni Begum is happy to eat without paying for her food, she has always eaten what she has earned from hard work.' Chunni Begum's eyes filled with tears. 'It was the children who had stopped me until now, please give me leave now. I'll make arrangements for another woman.'

*Begum sahiba* protested. She was ready to provide medical help for a servant like her, but Chunni Begum paid no attention to her protestations. She made arrangements for another woman, showed her around, explained what had to be done, gave her strict instructions. 'Now make sure you don't let the vagabonds come in for water, I'm warning you, be vigilant. During my time this garden has been filled with flowers, and during my reign not a cup of water was drawn from here.'

Chunni Begum picked up the *lota* and *katora* she had brought with her dowry and, wiping her tears, left the house.

For a short while she sat under a shady tree and sighed deeply. Then she went to the owner of the compound nearby and, paying him five rupees in advance, got the keys for a small room, opened the lock, and put all her things there. She had saved about two-hundred and fifty rupees. She was quite sure that after treatment from someone reliable she would be well again. The people living in that compound were the ones who used to come to the bungalow for water. When they saw her they turned away their faces, but Chunni Begum went around asking after everyone's well-being and soon they all put their resentment aside. 'She was a servant after all, it wasn't her fault,' they said.

Chunni Begum began treatment with a *hakim* who also lived in the compound. She spent twenty or thirty rupees, but there was no improvement in her condition. She didn't have enough money to go to a doctor in the city and she didn't know anyone there either. The pain meanwhile seemed bent on crushing Chunni Begum. Every once in a while she was tempted to ask her son to come for her, but then she immediately pushed that thought away. *Bahu* would treat her badly. May God save one from a life of dependence.

When she was feeling really down she would come out of her room and sit under a shady tree. The women of the compound gathered around her and nodded their heads at her wise sayings. Chunni Begum had a hand in all the affairs of the world.

Time passed but Chunni Begum's ailments worsened. Her knees were swollen and now she couldn't even cook her own food. Shabrattan, a widow, had become her good friend. For five or six annas she cooked her meal and also brought Chunni Begum a bucket of water which lasted her several days.

Lack of work had put a dent in her savings, but Chunni Begum was certain that as soon as she regained her health she would make more than what she had. She would definitely get well. In order to warm her swollen joints, she rested in the sun all day, she said every prayer she knew to get rid of her illness.

That was when she heard that Pakistan had been founded. Hindu-Muslim riots had started, the Muslims were coming to Pakistan, *Dilli* was ravaged. Four or five people who lived there arrived in the compound straight from a camp. They claimed ignorance about her son when she made inquiries about him. Chunni Begum's heart broke. She was sure that *Bahu* had deterred her son from coming to Pakistan—she must have realized that she might have to give her mother-in-law a piece of bread. The moment Chunni Begum entertained this thought she started cursing *Bahu* and cried for hours afterwards. A vague kind of a connection that had existed all this time was also broken. Assuming different shapes, the ogre of helplessness danced before her eyes and feeling distraught and defenceless, Chunni Begum refused to look at this bloody dance. She also abandoned all treatment. She roamed around the compound with the purse containing her last remaining rupees clutched to her breast.

Around that time the population in the compound suddenly increased. Not a single room remained vacant. People wandered about in search of water. They travelled long distances for just one bucket of water. One day Chunni Begum had no drinking water for a whole day. It was May. People were hankering after water. That was when Chunni Begum hit upon this idea. She handed thirty rupees to a reliable person who was a *Dilli-wallah* and asked him to buy a second-hand pump and have it installed in the compound. After this she fell down in prayer in gratitude and, tears streaming from her eyes, she begged God that He take her from this world with honour.

Early in the morning the sound of the bugle could be heard coming from the cantonment and in a mosque nearby the *muezzin* was reciting the *azaan*. Chunni Begum rose from her cot with a feeling of exhilaration and turned the handle of the hand pump. A foamy stream of water poured out from the spout and spread on the cemented floor. Chunni Begum ceremoniously swished water in her mouth and gargled, washed her face and then gulped down some water on an empty stomach.

'Even the water from Begum's hand pump was not so cool,' she began thinking. 'And the water that Shabrattan brought me used to be boiling hot. This is what you call water.' Chunni Begum cast a proud look around her. Stretched out on cots in front of their rooms, people were still asleep.

'That's why the wretches can't make a proper living. It's the time of the *azaan* and they're sleeping as if they're dead.' Chunni Begum returned to her cot. The morning was no different than any other, but today she felt God's radiance raining down from the skies.

Soon the inhabitants of the compound woke up. The first thing they did was to pick up buckets and pitchers and run toward the hand pump. The men were in a hurry because they wanted to bathe today before they went off to work and the women were anxious to get the stoves and meals going; both were trying to get ahead of each other.

'Now just wait.' Chunni Begum grabbed the first bucket. 'I've lived this long and never have I eaten without paying first nor have I ever fed anyone without charge. A rupee a month each and you can have unlimited use of the hand pump. But remember, the boys are not allowed to bathe here, the platform will break, all right?'

The buckets striving to get ahead of the line stopped where they were.

'What did you say Chunni Begum? *Arre*, have some fear of God, where do you think we labourers will get a rupee to give you? Why, does anyone sell water?'

'What do you mean? Even the government sells water. Doesn't everyone pay for water in the city? You won't have free water I tell you. Why didn't you have your own pump installed, *hunh*? Now deposit one rupee in advance everyone.'

After paying the brickmason, Chunni Begum had cleaned out her small purse. The water she had gulped down this morning was giving her stomach cramps, but she didn't feel anything. As a matter of fact, this morning she couldn't even feel the pain in her joints.

Only four rupees fell on Chunni Begum's cot and four buckets began receiving water from the pump. The rest of the people left the compound and walked away in the direction of the road. Chunni Begum placed the four rupees in her purse.

'Yes, yes, go and get a lot of water, may God grant you strength, go for miles for water. I'm not going to beg that you draw water from the hand pump—look here, I'll place the bucket under the pump, you're not careful and the cement will break, Chunni Begum is also not going to eat unless she works.'

'No one is an angel in today's world, everyone is a devil— what does she think she is, a *begum*?' When the women were returning to the compound with water, they talked loudly amongst themselves so Chunni Begum could hear what they were saying.

All day long the children swarmed around the hand pump. Scratching their sweaty bodies, united in their purpose, they gazed longingly at it. But Chunni Begum guarded it fiercely.

The whole day Chunni Begum sat by the hand pump, ate there, and placing a cot nearby, she slept there. But despite all this she was still afraid that someone might take water without paying for it, or the boys might start bathing. Luckily the hand pump was in a shady spot otherwise the May sun would have caused Chunni Begum to melt and pour like the water from the hand pump.

The four rupees had proven to be a disappointment for Chunni Begum. What could she eat and what could she buy with this amount, how was she to treat her troublesome disease with this paltry sum? The *hakim* had been tempting her with the promise of a special cure for arthritis, just for fifteen rupees, he said.

It had been nearly twenty days since the hand pump was installed. The four rupees had been spent. There was no flour to make bread with. But Chunni Begum was still not disheartened. She thought that the people were just being stubborn and in a few days more they would come to their senses. How much longer will they tire themselves out going from one house to another for water?

Today Chunni Begum had not eaten anything since morning. When hunger pangs created a havoc in her intestines, she filled her aluminum *katora* with fresh, cool water and drank it down.

'Ah, what nice water.' She burped noisily. 'And these ungrateful wretches think they'll die if they pay a rupee a month for it.'

By the time it was evening Chunni Begum was weak with hunger. However, she still continued to fill the buckets that remained from the four rupee accounts.

She struggled through the night somehow. In the morning when the people came to draw water, she didn't even open her eyes and when she tried to get up she realized she couldn't move.

'Today you fill the bucket yourself, I'll make up for today another time,' she said feebly.

Only Shabrattan knew that Chunni Begum was in this state because she had had nothing to eat. She tried her best to force Chunni Begum to eat food that she had made, but how could Chunni Begum accept this act of charity?

In a short while everyone in the compound knew that Chunni Begum was hungry. Attempting to satisfy their needs, but under the guise of proffering sympathy, two families arrived with payment. The moment Chunni Begum received the two rupees, her energy returned. Quickly she got up and started filling the buckets.

In the evening, after she had finished drawing water, she gave Shabrattan the money and asked her to buy rations for her.

The payments didn't move after she had seven rupees. Chunni Begum's knees were shiny from the swelling now. God knows how long it had been since she had got any treatment. She could barely move about now and operated the handle of the pump sitting down.

June was coming to a close. The young boys, tormented by the intense heat, were forever poised to attack the hand pump, but Chunni Begum kept a close watch at all times. It seemed as if the brickmason had installed her in that spot too along with the hand pump.

'You wretches, tell your mothers to give me a rupee a month and then I'll fill bucketfuls of water for you to bathe—it's such cool, delicious water. Look how dirty your bodies are.' Chunni Begum tempted the boys, but they were unmoved and continued to hover around the pump.

Today the boys seemed to be in a ferocious mood. They were all wearing loincloths. It was the mid-afternoon, the mothers were dozing. The boys attacked the hand pump.

Chunni Begum soon tired of pushing and pummelling them and a sort of wrestling match ensued. Chunni Begum's outbursts brought the mothers out. They scolded the boys, but in a manner that seemed more like encouragement. The boys were bathing with brazen abandonment. One would operate the handle while three or four would jump together into the gushing stream of water.

'Come on, give me an anna each! Why are you just standing there watching the spectacle.' Chunni Begum screamed her lungs out at the women.

'Where are we going to get the annas, get it from the bathers, why didn't you stop them?'

As the layers of dust were washed off from the bodies of the boys, the mothers felt as if clouds of dust were being dusted off from their own chests as well. They hadn't bathed the wretches in such a long time.

After this Chunni Begum's surveillance weakened. The boys had found a solution and the others had also discovered a way. The boys heedlessly took baths in the afternoons and the women forcibly drew water without payment. Chunni Begum protested, shrieked, and cursed, but she couldn't stop them. She hated them all. If she could help it she would bury all of these water-abusers alive. The seven families that had been giving her a rupee each also began to show signs of rebellion. They too took away water without paying. When Chunni Begum's curses rose to a frenzied pitch everyone laughed as if she had gone mad.

Finally Chunni Begum moved away from the vicinity of the hand pump and went and sat in her room. Her sore joints were now so badly swollen that she could no longer continue guarding the hand pump. All she could do was to issue a barrage of expletives and curses at people from her room. Ahh, how mercilessly they bathed, wasting tons of water, and in the meantime the area around the pump was beginning to look like a quagmire. Unable to watch any more, she would shut the door of her room. After all, how could she bear to see what was going on. But this wouldn't last long. Soon she would open the door and start cursing everyone again.

She hadn't eaten anything since yesterday. There was a ringing in her ears due to weakness and she couldn't even hear the working of the hand pump's handle. Shabrattan stopped by frequently and offered to bring her food, but Chunni Begum did not give in.

'*Arri* Shabrattan, I won't live a life of dependence, get the people in the compound to pay me.'

When Shabrattan had left, Chunni Begum crawled to the hand pump and filling her *katora* with water, she gulped it down. Then, overcome by dizziness, she fell right there. When she came to she found herself on the cot in her room.

At night two of the women in the compound brought her a *roti* each with some *daal*. No sooner did she see the food than Chunni Begum found the strength to quarrel anew.

'Go and give charity to your mothers and sisters, do you think I'm helpless? Come on now, give me payment for the water and by God's grace, you will be rewarded in this life.'

Quietly the women deposited the food on the plate on the trunk and left. Chunni Begum proceeded to scream and shout.

'Why you wretches! Throw these *rotis* before your mothers and sisters!'

Night fell. Mosquitoes buzzed in the room. Unable to move, Chunni Begum stayed inside. The melancholy sound of retreat being played on the bugle in the cantonment wafted in. The '*Khata-khat!*' of the hand pump's handle could also be heard. It seemed as if the whole world had descended on the hand pump. Who knows where she suddenly got the strength, but suddenly Chunni Begum got up and ran toward the hand pump.

'Give me the payment for the water! If anyone touches the water without paying, I'll break his hands.' It was the men drawing water this time and Chunni Begum couldn't even break one little finger.

'*Arre* Chunni Begum, what are you worried about? We'll serve you as long as you live.'

"Go and serve your mothers and sisters," Chunni Begum swore at them in her characteristic way.

Everyone broke into laughter. Feeling herself shaking, she returned to her room. It was dark in here. She lighted an oil lamp with great difficulty, lifted the plate with the *rotis* and looked at it, and then put it aside. She somehow managed to pull out her narrow cot and then, panting and out of breath, she lay down on it.

All night she was tormented by hunger. Early in the morning she crawled to her room. The mice, God take them, had made off with the *rotis*. She leaned against the trunk, motionless.

A short while later Allah Rakha's wife came in with steaming hot tea in a brass container along with a *roti*. Chunni Begum quickly extended her *katora*.

'What? So little milk you've put in the tea and you didn't butter the *roti* either, you wretch. And so much water you draw too. Now remember to be more careful, do you hear?'

# Springtime of Life

The whirling smoke from the smoldering, soggy kindling was moving toward the small skylight in the kitchen and she was sitting on a stool nearby, trying to blow life into the flames with hot, hurried breath. Finally, youth's simmering breath succeeded in fanning the flames. The *khichri* on the stove began to bubble and she leaned back against the stained, dirty wall. She was wet with perspiration. The smoke had made large tears quiver on the points of her lashes. In the tightness of the pajama across her thigh were wrinkles caused by the effort of constantly bending to blow into the fire. She let out a long sigh of satisfaction and slowly shut her eyes. '*Khadar badar, khadar badar*'—the rice and the lentils were wrestling with each other. Outside, a young boy walking down on the street was singing 'Come to me, my beloved.' She got up and, striking a match to light the lamp on the ledge, started humming the words of the song. Then, pausing over the word 'beloved,' she smiled, her whole body throbbing at the thought of the beloved's image. The *khichri* bubbled ferociously. Ignoring it, she continued to sing in a voice choked with smoke: 'Come to me, my beloved.'

A gentle gust of wind came from the skylight and the smoke that had been escaping from the skylight turned inward like an undulating snake and swirled about as if it were an echo of her song. The bubbling in the *khichri* soon ceased and because the water had evaporated the *khichri* began to burn. But she was so absorbed in pleasant thoughts of the beloved that she failed to notice it.

'*Hai* Bittan! Did you burn all the *khichri*?' her mother roared as she got a whiff of the burnt food. Her parted lips clamped together and the words, 'Come meet me, my beloved' were caught in her throat. Hastily she pulled out the kindling and removed the pot from the stove. Then she left the kitchen, walked out to the courtyard and lay down on a loosely-knit cot there. Her sister-in-law, her shirt removed from her fat, flabby body, was nursing her baby and *Amma* was still grumbling about the burnt *khichri*.

Bittan also began muttering under her breath. 'So what can anyone do if the *khichri* is burnt. One has to listen to a hundred things when there's the slightest bit of trouble. I cook twice a day, stuff everyone's stomach and still no one has a nice word to say. If I sat down and decided to do nothing, everyone would starve in a day. Yes, that will teach them a lesson. Too much resting has addled their brains.'

'Are you not going to eat?' *Amma* asked.

'No, I'm not eating.' She covered her face with her *dupatta* and turned away from *Amma*.

'Don't eat then, you wretch.'

Her mother sat down with her sister-in-law and began eating. With each morsel she swallowed she thundered at her daughter. Bittan never used to talk back to her mother, but now that she was constantly talking back to her, the old woman would grumble for hours. It wasn't too long ago that she was straddling her sister-in-law's whining baby on her hip all day long, preparing her father's *hookah* regularly and mending her mother's and sister-in-law's old clothes. The entire day would be spent in this fashion and she wouldn't utter a word of protest. But now it was if her life had changed. Even the tiniest bit of work irritated her. *Bhabi*'s baby cried because he wanted to be picked up and she wouldn't even look at him; while filling her father's *chilam* she would get annoyed and break it; *Amma* and *Bhabi*'s clothes were in tatters, but it was as if she had sworn never to pick up a needle again. And if her mother complained she would start muttering as well. She had begun to hate *Amma*, her brother, *Bhabi*, and the baby. She stayed awake until two or three, tossing and turning in bed. Her body was racked with aches and pains and her heart beat violently. She wondered what was happening to her. Her mother knew, but feigned ignorance.

Her brother was home from Calcutta after being away for two years. The poor man had a very short leave. *Amma* was so happy she had several dishes made for her son, *Abba* had the *hookah* prepared over and over again, and *Bhabi* sneaked coy glances at her husband, her eyes red and her look sugary. Sitting next to their son *Amma* and *Abba* talked of this and that while *Bhabi* put in a word occasionally from a distance. And when her brother stealthily caught *Bhabi*'s eye and laughed, she wondered when her own hands would be decorated with henna. It was as if no one in the house was worried about her marriage. She had been hearing for a long time now that her brother was making arrangements for her marriage. The wedding will be the following year, she'd hear. But the following year would quietly come and go and the matter would be shelved for yet another year.

All the time her brother was away, a three-paisa postcard mailed to him would also contain a few words about her wedding as a reminder, but now that he was here no one had mentioned the word to him. Everyone was busy chattering about other things.

In the evening she lay down on her bed, tired from the day's work. Her mother sat next to her son, talking to him, while her father also sat nearby, gurgling his *hookah*. *Bhabi* was strolling with her whimpering son in her lap, trying to quiet him.

'Why Bittan, is your back broken? All you ever do is lie in bed. Why don't you get up and hang a curtain up in the courtyard for your brother—that's where he will sleep. Everyone sleeps in the open when it's hot, and yes, give him some food as well so he may eat and go to bed.' Obviously *Amma* didn't like the idea of her taking time out to rest so she was immediately given more chores to tackle. She rose from her bed and grumbled, 'Where should I get the rope from?'

'Oh girl, pull the rope out from the foot of my cot and hang it up,' *Amma* said.

'You'll be uncomfortable all night, but the love of a son justifies everything,' she muttered, and pulling out the rope from the cot she hung up a curtain for her brother. This done, she served him his dinner. *Amma* and *Abba* also ate with their son while she gulped down a few morsels with *Bhabi*. *Bhabi* made her husband's bed and lay down on the cot next to Bittan. The baby was constantly crying. Irritated, *Bhabi* stuck her nipple into his mouth and started patting him to sleep. Bittan's father carried his cot out into the street since there wasn't enough space to hold everyone's bed in the courtyard. Bhayya also retired and began tossing and turning on his bed. *Bhabi* was still muttering. It was her habit to keep muttering under her breath until she fell asleep. 'Unh…unh…' *Bhabi* breathed heavily.

'Every day you talk until late at night and today you're already sleepy?'

'You should sleep as well,' *Bhabi* mumbled drowsily.

'You should sleep as well,' she repeated *Bhabi*'s remark irately. 'A total silence has fallen early in the evening. Why? Because everyone's so content. And *Amma*, who babbles until twelve in the night, well, her lips are sewn today.' Bittan turned on her side and the bed creaked.

'You wretch, why don't you sleep now. What's this bad habit of staying awake late into the night? If people see you like this they'll spit on you, slut.' *Amma* grumbled noisily, snapping out of her sleep.

Bittan held her breath and lay still.

'If *Bhayya* hadn't been here I'd have shown you what it means to call me 'slut'.' Why do people start muttering and grumbling when they get older. Allah! When will she be rid of all of them? Her life has become a hardship. But how could she be rid of them? Her brother mentions the matter of her wedding in a three-paisa postcard and is rid of his obligation; her mother has prepared two suits for her dowry and has put them away with the thought that everything's taken care of. Those two suits won't go with her dowry, they'll go with her funeral.

*Uffoh*! If her brother could help it he'd have ten more wives and as for *Amma*, why, even in her old age all she can think of is lying close to her husband. But no one is concerned about her. Lost in thought, she turned on her side and, her aching body curled up, she tried to fall asleep. In a short while a sweet drowsiness overcame her, but the sound of someone quietly trying to slip into slippers startled her. She saw *Bhabi* standing over her bed, peering at her and at *Amma* as if she were a thief. She wanted to call out to her, but she remained silent because she was afraid *Bhabi* might ask her why she was still awake.

*Bhabi* had told her a hundred times that it was considered highly improper for young women to remain awake at night, and if *Amma* heard her voice she would start with her foul expletives and wake up the whole neighbourhood. Lying still, she gazed at *Bhabi* through the corners of her eyes while *Bhabi* too continued to stare closely at the two women. Then, suddenly, she tip-toed to where *Bhayya* was sleeping.

'*Hunh*!' She pulled her feet in. She could hear *Bhabi* and *Bhayya* whispering amongst themselves. She tried to listen. But she couldn't make out a word of what they were saying. She understood now why everyone was sleepy so early today and why she had been instructed to fall asleep quickly. She felt as if there were ants crawling over her body. Her eyes were glued to the curtain.

'Oh my God,' her lips moved slowly. *Amma* turned over and scared, she quickly hid her face in her *dupatta*. *Uffoh*! A muffled 'Oh God,' had made *Amma* turn on her back, but the sounds of slippers going *sat, pat* and those other noises like the buzzing of bees that broke the silence of the night didn't make her stand up from her bed, did they? She sobbed at her own helplessness. The night travelled on tip-toe.

The meat cooking on the stove was bubbling furiously. She sat on a stool nearby, her eyes closed. A delightful mist hovered over her heart and her mind. What she had observed last night had created a tumult in her emotions. Forgetful of everything, she became completely lost in her thoughts. Thoughts that were fanciful, thoughts that she had never contemplated before.

Meanwhile the fire had dried the water in the pot and was now making the meat burn.

'Oh my God! Have you burnt the meat?' Smelling burnt meat *Amma* leapt toward the kitchen with a roar, starting Bittan from her reverie.

'You misbegotten creature! You slut! I know exactly what all this means. Always sitting quietly, unconcerned, even if the house is on fire. Ah, such a pain this twenty-sixth year has been for us. You'll not be so quiet if I push you out this very minute with someone.' *Amma* recounted the entire story in one breath. Hearing the sound of screaming and yelling, *Bhabi* also arrived on the scene, her baby set on her hip.

'Is all of the meat burnt?' *Bhabi* said, pushing the baby up on her hip.

'What else? Nothing is left. This creature just sat there like she didn't know anything.'

'That's just great. Now when he leaves at twelve there won't be anything for him to eat.' *Bhabi* gave her a sour look.

Ignoring the curses, she sat quietly, as if in a daze.

'I say *Amma*, why have you kept Bittan at home until now. Her behaviour clearly shows she won't continue like this any more. Why, is this any way for young unmarried virgins to behave?'

'Why have you kept me at home like this? Why don't you marry me off then, who's stopping you?' The pleasurable feeling that had carried over from last night acted like scissors on the lips which had been sewed together with modesty all this time.

'*Hai!*' *Amma* beat her chest.

'The day of judgement is at hand. An unmarried girl asks for a husband with her own mouth.' *Bhabi* placed a finger on her nose in amazement and then she led her chest-beating mother-in-law out of there. Bittan put aside the burnt meat and started scrubbing the pot. Out in the courtyard her mother and her brother spoke conspiratorially in whispers and not too far from them, *Bhabi* sat with her baby, nodding her *dupatta*-covered head in agreement. She saw them all and felt satisfied, as if a large stone had been lifted from her chest.

# The Heart's Thirst

Her flared, filthy *burqa* rustling noisily, she walked hurriedly in order to keep pace with her mother. She stumbled repeatedly, stubbing her toe. She wouldn't have stubbed her toe if she had kept her gaze pinned to the ground; like a kite cut off from its string, her gaze swam in all directions. The bazaar was filled with crowds. She didn't even realize how dreadful it would be if she were jostled by a man. All she could think of greedily were the beautiful clothes. There were rich women and there were poor women, all going in and out of the bazaar; she didn't tire of looking at everyone and nearly broke her miserable toe. She didn't complain, *Amma* would have scolded her, saying, 'Why, hasn't God given you eyes on your face?' Who was going to tell her mother that actually Allah had caused these problems by putting eyes on one's face.

It was these very eyes that had made her so greedy. When she had just learned to walk she would go and sit under the *peepal* tree and stare at the women of the landlord's family who, dressed in saris, a long veil drawn over their faces, strode past her with their anklets jangling. On *Holi*, *Dewali*, and *Eid*, children dressed in bright new clothes strutted around her. She too would get a new suit of clothes, but it was always the same thick *soosie shalwar* and *kameez* with a narrow strip of muslin for a *dupatta*. When she was about seven she began obstinately making demands for a suit stitched from the fabric known as the 'heart's thirst.' *Amma* tried her best to dissuade her, but when she persisted she was given a thrashing. Here was her father, who made only a rupee after a whole day's of labour and all she could do she was make demands to slake her heart's thirst. So much had to be done with that one rupee. A portion of it had to be set aside for her dowry and her wedding. Allah had given her parents offspring, but it was a girl. Sometimes *Amma* wept uncontrollably, but she paid no heed to any of this. After a week or ten days had passed she would start making requests again; she wanted to wear a shirt of 'rapture of the eye,' she'd say. She wouldn't get the shirt, but for a few days the rapture of the eye would pour out with her tears.

When she lowered her head she saw that her toe was bleeding. She felt a twinge of pain and wanted to sit down right there on the ground. She had left the crowded bazaar behind her and her own house was only a few yards away. Two women dressed in beautiful clothes appeared from the front and walked past her in the direction of the bazaar. She lifted her veil to look at them. The women were gone in a minute, but the *paanwala* across the street caught her eye and, clearing his throat, winked at her.

*Amma* turned around quickly in alarm, but she had already lowered her veil.

'*Arri*, walk carefully on the road. Can't you see through the netting? Why do you have to lift your veil?' *Amma* muttered angrily under her breath. 'The bastard doesn't have a mother or sisters to leer at?'

'I was just looking at the clothes of those women there—what do I know? May he die, the wretch!' Feeling flustered, she quickened her pace. Her senses were in turmoil. Leaving her mother behind, she quickly undid the chain on the door and came in. A little clearing of the throat had thrown her in a tizzy and as for her eye, it seemed as though a thorn was lodged in it.

Taking off her *burqa* she threw it on the bed. 'What will *Amma* think—why, I shouldn't have lifted my veil in our own neighbourhood.' Her shame made her forget the pain in her toe and, seating herself next to the wood-stove, she started crumbling up some cow dung cakes. *Amma* arrived soon thereafter. She was still muttering. 'They have no shame, these women, strutting about in the streets like this. Don't they have men in their homes to do the shopping for them? They are spoiling the daughters of decent people.'

*Amma*'s couldn't stop talking. 'When will those people come? There are all these letters saying they're coming soon, that they'll be here tomorrow. If only they would come so I could have a simple wedding ceremony and be done. What does a poor widow like me have? I've worked hard and saved a hundred rupees which *Begum Sahib* is keeping for me. Two suits is all I will be able to make with that sum and then, whatever the girl is fated to eat and wear in her own house, is not for me to worry about.' *Amma* pulled a stool close to the fire and sat down with her head held between her hands.

It was her turn to get angry now. She started to fume inside. So what if she had lifted her veil for a few seconds? The feeling of remorse she had experienced earlier now silently rebelled. *If I can't wear nice clothes should I also not look? Once a year I get a suit of clothing and that too of coarse cotton and in the winter it is infested with lice—all that scratching raises welts on my skin. Yes, indeed, who do they think they are, those people? They can't find a girl in Hindustan that they should come all the way to Pakistan to present me with a shroud?.*

'Now will you heat the food or will you sit forever with your head flung down?' *Amma*'s anger had ebbed.

'Do you see even a drop of *ghee* with which I can heat the food before we eat it?' She spoke sarcastically. 'There's tons of *ghee* lying around in the house, isn't there?' She picked up the pot from the shelf and threw it down. Then, emptying the food from the bowl into it, she placed it on the stove.

'All right! Your mother has been killing herself working hard and you're still complaining. Where should I bring the money for the *ghee*?' *Amma* broke into sobs. A mere winking of an eye had created such a commotion.

'Come come now, don't start crying again.' Softening, she moved toward her mother. 'You get tired working at *Begum Sahib*'s and then you come home and you're exhausted and you vent your anger on me. All I say is you should rest at home, I'll work instead.'

'Oh yes, of course! I'll send you to work. Haven't you seen what this world is like? Today you insisted stubbornly on coming along with me, but if you say a word about going out again I'll jump into a well.'

'All right, come, eat now,' she said and started laughing.

*Amma* let out a long sigh. Ah, how good were those days when her husband was alive. He used to say he would wed his daughter when she was fifteen. How troubled his soul must now be.

She too remembered her father. How he loved her. He beat her only once and that too because she had stolen something. If she hadn't stolen *Thakur Sahib's* daughter's *dupatta*, would he ever have raised his hand to her? Ahh, how soft that *dupatta* was, like an infant's cheek. She was having such fun wearing it over her head, the front pulled down in a long veil. How cruelly *Amma* had snatched the *dupatta* from her head.

She ladled the heated curry in an aluminum plate and placed it before her mother. Both mother and daughter began eating in silence. *Amma* sighed constantly. Perhaps she was thinking of the past when times were good for them. Before Partition, when her husband was alive, they owned a small house. She wore heavy silver bangles then, with every movement of her foot her anklets jangled, and long, gold earrings dangled from her ears and caressed her cheeks. True, all the jewellery was a part of her dowry, but at least it was hers. She was happy to have simple things. She was obligated to no one. Every evening her husband placed some money in her palm. Her only worries were that she didn't have a son and that her daughter had to be married some day. Her daughter was already engaged to a boy from a well-to-do family and ever since her birth she had been putting away two or four annas in an earthen jar for her dowry. She had been able to accumulate quite a sum by the time her daughter grew up. The wedding was only a year away when the country was divided. People got up and left without too much thought to where they were headed and she and her family also fell in with a caravan. Their hands and arms became numb from carrying the heavy earthen jar and the bundle of jewellery. Along the way they suffered terrible hardships and by the time they arrived at a refugee camp, they had been devastated by cholera. Expenses incurred at her husband's burial and their own medical treatment depleted the sum in the earthen jar. In a few days the jewellery was gone as well. Since that time she had been labouring hard to make ends meet. In addition to that her daughter's youth was like a heavy stone on her chest, a burden that made her keel over.

*Amma* donned her *burqa* and left for work after they had eaten while she proceeded to gather the soiled plates to wash them. Soon it was teatime. Today *Amma* had come home in the afternoon because she had to bring her back, but normally she left early in the morning and returned home after dark and so the whole day she sat around by herself, bored and restless. This was when the lice bothered her even more and, feeling fidgety, she would come and sit next to the door. Pulling aside the sackcloth curtain just a bit, she would peer at the street outside. She could see all kinds of women going to and from the bazaar. She would admire their beautiful clothes and guess at the prices. She didn't even know the names of all the fabrics. God knows what these slippery, fluttering fabrics were called. Curiosity overwhelmed her. She knew of two names only: 'rapture of the eye' and 'the heart's thirst.'

After *Amma* had left she went and sat by the sackcloth curtain. Then she stuck her head out a little. The *paanwallah* across the road was alone in his shop, reading something. 'Bastard.' She quickly drew back her head. Soon she was lost in the clothes again. Leaping forward, she draped all the clothes on her own body and, drawing a long veil, she smiled. What a riot the lice make at such moments. Her eyes filled with tears of remorse.

Today *Amma* returned earlier than usual. She hung up her *burqa* on the peg in the wall, and placing the *daal* and the bundle of *roti* near the stove, she turned to scrutinize her with a strange look. She got up and kindled the fire. *Amma* lighted the oil lamp, and placing it on the shelf, came and sat down beside her.

'Why were you sitting in the dark? You should keep the chain fastened from the inside.'

'Who can dare to come in?' The smoke made her eyes water. She looked at her mother with a fierce expression on her face.

'I'm just saying that because times are very bad.'

'*Hmn.* So *Begum Sahib* let you go very early today.'

'I wasn't feeling too well.' *Amma* began rubbing her legs with both hands. 'The clay coating on the floor is flaking everywhere. You have nothing to do all day, why don't you apply a new coating?'

'I will.' Her tone was harsh. Her mother's look had burned her to the core.

They both ate after the food had been heated. There was a chilly wind outside. A few clouds drifted here and there on the sky. Faint puffs of breeze wafted in through the sky-light making the flame in the oil lamp flutter.

*Amma* settled into her bed after eating. She sat next to the stove for a long time afterward, poking at the fire.

'I wonder if it will rain,' she said without looking at *Amma* directly.

'Hmm.' *Amma* quickly wiped off her tears and hid her face in the quilt. 'Go to sleep now.'

She got up and before going to her bed, opened the window and looked outside.

'What clouds!' Her gaze wandered to the *paanwallah's* shop. All the other shops were closed, but he was sitting smugly in his shop, singing loudly. '*Awaz de kahan hai, dunia meri jawan hai.*' (Call out to me, where are you/ My world is young). The clouds were rumbling. She quickly shut the window and as soon as she settled into bed the itching started. Who knows when she fell asleep and in her dream the *paanwallah* jumped on her with a loud thud. She awoke with a start and recited *lahol* for a long time afterward.

*Amma* had tea early in the morning and left for work. She made the beds, swept the room, hurriedly cooked two *rotis* for herself and then went to sit by the sackcloth curtain. As she observed the colourful attire of the women, her eyes frequently strayed to the *paanwallah's* shop. She remembered his winking and the manner in which he had cleared his throat. Her entire being quivered at the memory of that incident. The bastard! Has he not seen his face in a mirror? She started thinking. There's a cow tethered at her fiance's house, he has a better shop than this, if Allah has made them suffer rough times it doesn't mean things will never change for the better, if she gazes at the clothes other women wear today, tomorrow she too will have clothes like these. *Amma* is right. Being unmarried doesn't mean you should go out of your mind. *How wrong it was to lift your veil in the middle of a crowded bazaar.* The very remarks made by *Amma* earlier that had bothered her so much now seemed to make sense.

She shut the door and went to lie down on her bed. She had debased herself just for these clothes. She hadn't been able to look her mother in the eye since yesterday. May she be cursed if she goes to the door now.

For a long time she silently scratched herself, now her back, now her calves. When you are idle these accursed lice itch all the more. She got up and started dusting the walls of the room. When she approached the door she opened it just a chink and peered out. A throng of women and girls was walking by, laughing and talking noisily. Her eyes open wide, she stared at their clothes. The *jharu* fell from her hands.

When she moved away from the door she was sighing. Her life had been spent in longing and yearning. Is this any kind of living? Who knows when things will get better? She suddenly remembered a childhood incident. She had persuaded Khan *Sahib*'s daughter to let her put on her shirt. How big were the flowers on it. Just then Khan *Sahib*, the wretch, appeared and seeing his daughter strolling on the road naked he slapped her face until it was red. Then *Abba* had wiped her tears and had a muslin shirt made for her. Muslin. As if there's no difference between a horse and a donkey. Her eyes filled with tears. *It's all right, even a horse's fate changes after twelve years; why, is she even worse than a horse?*

She reassured herself and, picking up the *jharu*, resumed dusting the walls vigorously. She told herself that tomorrow she would ask *Amma* to bring some cow dung. The floor was flaking in so many places.

After a long period of lies *Amma* finally capitulated tonight. A new prop would have to be sought.

'They have married him off to someone there. They let me hope for nothing all this time.' *Amma* wiped her tears with her *dupatta*. 'By now we could have made arrangements elsewhere—is there a dearth of boys?'

She stoked the fire silently. Her heart was beating violently. The house came crashing over her.

'Every now and then they used to write and say they were coming for the wedding. Six years we waited for them. For what? *Begum Sahib* was admonishing me for having waited this long. Well, I will have a wedding so quickly, it will be a slap in the face for them.'

*Amma* was looking at her from the corner of her eye and she was buried under the rubble, sobbing. The food in the pot was sizzling.

'*Begum Sahib* has offered to help, and if she's involved then what's there to worry about?'

She stole a glance at her mother and slowly dragged herself out from under the debris. The fresh bruise hurt. She quickly soothed it with the balm of new hopes.

She ladled the food in plates and forced herself to eat. She didn't want *Amma* to think she was upset. What a shameful thing that would be.

When she went to bed that night she felt as if someone was clawing at her heart. Heavy sighs beat upon her chest and the lice were biting again. She was seized with a desire to scratch her whole body until her skin was raw. There was a strong wind blowing outside. The curtains in the small veranda on the other side of the room fluttered noisily in the wind. She wanted to cry in anguish but she couldn't shed even a single tear. The new hopes were determined to raze the shrine of dead desires. *Begum Sahib* was bound to do something right, after all. She'll live right here near her mother, and isn't it true that people who live in cities make more money? She will dress up and come out to stroll with her husband. She'll have a nice black *burqa* made. So, whatever has happened is all for the best then. She shut her eyes in peace.

Days passed. The sackcloth curtain became tattered from the force of wind-storms and rains and developed large holes. She could now peer through the holes at the street outside without having to pull the curtain aside. If her gaze happened to fall on the *paanwallah's* shop, she quickly looked away. After every eight or ten days *Amma* dropped some spicy remark about her match, and that too as if she were talking to herself. 'This is the limit, *Begum Sahib* is very strict about her choice, she insists that no match is worth considering until it's someone who will offer the girl a good life, and we also have to find someone among our own people, she says—these Panjabis, they don't understand what anyone is saying, they say they approve but they actually disapprove, what kind of a relationship can we have with them? That's why we're stuck with *Begum Sahib*, because she's one of us and worries as if you were her own daughter. I keep saying, don't worry about financial status, let us just have a quick wedding, but she won't listen.'

She would continue with her chores as if she hadn't heard a word of what *Amma* had said, hiding her face from her because she didn't want her to see her smiling. Then one day she saw *Amma* looking somewhat dejected. She didn't have any spicy chit chat for her either. She realized that *Amma* was sad at the thought of her leaving. After *Amma* had gone to work she sat by the sackcloth curtain the whole day. As she scrutinized different kinds of clothes she thought, 'Well, this suit I'll definitely make for myself.'

Today she found out that she had been stupid and she had been drawing the wrong conclusions at every step. *Amma* looked fearful.

'What a strange place the world has become. Everyone wants to know what they will get. Will there be a cycle given to the boy for the wedding ceremony? And these people from our own side, they've become extremely greedy too. They want to receive three-times over the little they left behind in Hindustan. Compassion has ceased to exist in this world.' Holding her head in her hands, she began sighing deeply. It was true she had attempted to check this household and that, had tried to get cooks and stewards to come around as prospective husbands for her daughter, but to no avail. And poor *Begum Sahib*, she didn't really have the time to look for a boy. She had been turned into a column of support just to provide assurance that there was hope.

*Amma*'s talk shook her to the core of her being. She knew that nothing was going to happen, oh yes, she did. Why would *Begum Sahib* take time out from her pleasure-filled life to think of her? Had she ever let her wear even one of her silken suits?

That night she didn't eat with *Amma* and came and fell on her bed. All night the clouds poured thunderously while her heart smouldered.

The rain last night caused the sackcloth curtain to dangle from one side. Today, while sadly observing the excitement of the world, she stuck her whole head out carelessly. Then, rising to her feet, she stepped outside the curtain. The *paanwallah*, having dealt with customers, was now humming. The passers by were oblivious to her presence. They did not know that a restless soul was yearning to sing.

She had just shifted behind the curtain at the door when suddenly the *paanwallah*, his *dhoti* fluttering in the breeze, went past her. Stopping to peer down at her through the holes in the sackcloth curtain, he gave her an adoring look, and was on his way. She was rooted to the ground. Her breath burst through her lungs. With great difficulty she moved forward, shut the door and put up the chain.

The next day the door opened only when *Amma* returned from work. She was observing her with a strange expression these days. How much pleading there was in her eyes, how the eyes begged that she guard her honour. A muted inability to do anything simmered in her eyes. She shook her head with great pride when she saw her mother in this condition. She could never do anything wrong.

After remaining closed for two or three days, the door opened again and she stood next to the sackcloth. '*Hunh*! Who can dare come in.' She drew the curtain slightly and looked out. Crowds sped past her with heads turned away from her. 'What are you looking at, my dearest, why do you torment us so.' The *paanwallah* was standing nearby, looking down at her. Flustered, she hastily stumbled to her feet.

'I wasn't looking at you, I was looking at the clothes,' she said with great difficulty.

'You should wear these beautiful clothes too, I'll bring them for my nightingale.' The *paanwallah* twirled his thin mustache. She quickly shut the door and fell on her bed, her breathing rapid and uncontrollable. She could no longer think. When *Amma* returned in the evening, she could not meet her gaze.

The door remained shut the next day. She started applying a wet clay wash to the flaking floor to keep herself occupied. In the afternoon when she heard a knock on the door she felt happy at the thought that her mother was home early. She unhooked the chain. The *paanwallah* jumped into the room.

'My love, I have no peace, I can't keep my mind on the business any more.' He moved toward her. She felt as if she could not move from her place. The *paanwallah* grabbed her in an embrace.

'I've had a very nice suit of 'the heart's thirst' made for you. I've told the tailor to stitch it as soon as possible.' He was squeezing her. She suddenly found the strength to free herself.

'Get out or I will scream.'

'This is no way to treat a lover,' he laughed. 'I'll bring the suit tomorrow, you'll be happy then, won't you?' He quickly left.

She shut the door and collapsed on her bed as if she were about to faint. She felt as if a thousand furnaces had started heating up in her body. Her throat became so dry it seemed there were thorns in it.

That night the *paanwallah* kept whispering in her ear, the suit stitched of 'the heart's thirst' kept sliding over her body, and she kept waking up with a start.

The next morning she closed the doors with great care after *Amma* left for work. The dirty dishes were lying about waiting to be washed, the beds were unmade. She didn't feel like taking care of any chores today. She washed her face and after a long time today she applied *kajal* in her eyes and thought how nice it would be if she could wear a suit of 'the heart's thirst' that very instant. The longing that had consumed her all her life took garish form on her face today. She sat on the stool and cast down her head. The lice were again very restless this morning.

Suddenly she rose to her feet and undid the chain on the door. Her head out just a bit, she threw a glance at the street. There were a lot of customers at the *paanwallah's* shop. Shutting the door without fastening the chain, she came in and sat down again. Her eyes returned again and again to the door. Her heart beat in irregular rhythms, her mind was numb.

A strange kind of silence fell in the afternoon. The door which had been shut but not chained slowly opened. The *paanwallah* came in and latched the chain. He had a small bundle in his hands. Breaking into a laugh, he sat down beside her and, opening the bundle, placed an orange suit of 'the heart's thirst' in her lap. For a brief moment she stared at the *paanwallah* and then she grabbed the suit with both hands and hid her face in it.

'Put it on, my dearest, so I can see how you look.' He inched closer to her. 'I'll be your slave for the rest of my life.'

'Talk to *Amma*, then.'

'I will, but don't torment me now.' He wanted payment for the suit on the spot. She tried to extricate herself from his grasp.

'You don't love me. Here, give me the suit and I'll leave.' The *paanwallah* muttered angrily. Who is going to provide favours and ask nothing in return? He extended a hand toward the clothes.

'I'll get money from *Amma* and have it sent to you.' She clasped the clothes to her breast.

The *paanwallah* smiled triumphantly. 'All that will come later.' He lunged toward her. The suit slipped from her lap and fell on the floor.

After the *paanwallah* had left she shed tears of humiliation for a while. Then, wiping her tears, she examined the suit. The silk was soft like a baby's cheek and shimmered like the rays of the moon. Forgetting everything she put on the suit. Once she was fully dressed, she looked in the mirror. The veil of the *dupatta* in front of her face was so long it hid the mirror from her.

Evening approached. She quickly got out of the suit. She wondered anxiously where she could hide the suit. What if *Amma* saw it? Shame leapt toward her heart. After a great deal of thought she folded the suit carefully and placed it snugly under the mattress. Then she sat down to wash the dirty dishes.

When she was eating, her mother looked at her closely.

'Have you been crying?' *Amma* asked, and putting down the morsel of food in her hand, she sighed.

'No, no, of course not.'

'*Hunh.*' Without finishing her meal, *Amma* retired to her bed and tossed and turned for a long time.

This silken suit was like her heart beat. She was afraid that someone might discover it, afraid that someone might turn her mattress over. She was constantly beset with anxiety. The beautiful suit was concealed like a thing of beauty. When she put the suit on in the afternoon, feelings of remorse also clutched at her throat. For many days now she had not sat next to the sackcloth curtain. This mode of entertainment was now also lost to her. She shuddered at the very thought that she might catch the *paanwallah's* eye.

The days slowly dragged. Autumn had bared the small tree in the courtyard. When she had no more work to do, she would steal a glance at the door and put on the suit. For a while spring would grace the room. But then she would find remorse standing before her like the small, bare tree in the courtyard. The suit was now dirty.

That morning *Amma* had a slight fever when she left for work. She said she might get a half day off and come home early. She was worried about *Amma*; what if the fever rose? It was after many days that she was again looking through a chink in the sackcloth curtain. It was late afternoon. She anxiously surveyed the street to see if Amma might be approaching. Her eyes strayed to the *paanwallah's* shop while she was peering through the curtain. He said something to his customers and then looked at her. The customers turned to look at her as well. Distressed, she let go of the curtain and shut the door.

When *Amma* came home after dark, she clung to her and began weeping. Soon she was sobbing. 'Take me with you when you go to work,' she said repeatedly.

'Why you silly girl, how can I take you there now? *Sahib*'s orderly is there and *Begum Sahib* is arranging a match with him. He makes fifty rupees and when he speaks, I swear it seems there are flowers falling from his mouth.' Her face turned away, *Amma* was speaking as if to herself. 'He is so nice, may God bless us this time, I'll give an offering.'

She gazed at *Amma* with vapid eyes and sat down to start a fire in the stove.

Now that she had seen the *paanwallah* laugh and his customers point in her direction, she didn't wear the suit again. When she had finished her chores she would take it out and look at it, but even the act of looking at it was extremely painful for her. The wretched *paanwallah,* his teeth bared, would come and stand before her.

Today when quiet prevailed in the afternoon, she retrieved the suit from under the mattress and for a few minutes she stroked the fabric with her fingers. Then she hastily put it on, watched herself in the mirror as she pulled the veil of the *dupatta* and finally she sat down with her head lowered. A few minutes later she quickly changed back into her own clothes. Her hands trembled as she wrapped the suit in paper. Taking the *burqa* off from the peg she threw it over her head and, the bundle secure under her arm, she came out and quickly crossed the road.

She was standing silently at the *paanwallah's* shop. He was sitting by himself reading through a pamphlet of film songs.

'You want another suit? You had better scoot from here.' He made a face.

'I've come to return your suit.' She placed the bundle on his counter.

'*Arri*, what will I do with the suit, I don't have a wife who can wear it. Take it.' The *paanwallah* looked bewildered.

'Then slap your face with it. I don't like this suit any more.' Anger and grief brought tears to her eyes. 'You were making fun of me in front of other people.' She turned around in haste and walked away toward her house.

How dreary the room looked. The only sign of life that had existed was now at the *paanwallah's* shop. She shut the doors and went back into the courtyard where she lay down on a cot and began looking at the tree swaying in the breeze. She looked dejected, as if she had lost everything.

The suit she had flung down so mercilessly on the *paanwallah's* counter had become a groan that gripped her heart. The lice readied themselves for renewed assault. Ever since she had become the owner of the suit she had forgotten that these shabby clothes of hers were infested with lice. Now she lay on her cot all day long, scratching. No sooner did she fall asleep than she would feel the suit wiggling under the mattress. She would wake up startled and hearing *Amma* clear her throat, she would quietly hide her face.

Several days passed in this fashion. She would roam about looking and feeling lost. In the evening *Amma* would peer at her with lowered eyes and sigh deeply. She hadn't mentioned *Sahib*'s orderly whom she had regarded as a prospective groom for her daughter. She glanced inquiringly at *Amma* often, as though asking, 'What happened to the orderly? Did he too make a demand for a cycle?' *Amma*, conscious of her gaze, would avoid talking to her. How could she say that the orderly was also lost, that he too was dreaming of a girl from a well-to-do family?

Today, just as *Amma* had gone to bed after eating, someone knocked loudly on the door. She paused in her cleaning. *Amma* scrambled to get up, hastily opened the door, and unlatching the chain, waited by the sackcloth curtain.

She heard the *paanwallah's* voice. She wanted to scream.

'*Amma*, take this note and these clothes. If you approve of the match send me word tomorrow.'

In the yellowed light of the oil lamp, *Amma* was bent over the orange suit of 'the heart's thirst' while she, her head lowered, was busy scrubbing the pots.

# In Stealth

He must be around fourteen when he began a life of debauchery. His father had died when he was two and as for the poor mother, well what control could she exercise over her sons? She continued to suffer and finally succumbing to her anguish, died. But Babu was not about to mend his ways nor did he. It was as important for him to indulge in some filthy act or the other every day as it was to eat and drink. The girls in the neighbourhood shuddered at the mention of his name, the boys begged for a safe haven. The people in the neighbourhood had tried every ploy at their disposal to make him give up his vile, decadent ways, but how can a drop of water stay put on a smooth-surfaced earthen pot? He did whatever he wanted to until he was thirty. And then he changed his ways in the most amazing manner. He had already squandered his father's wealth on dancing girls so now he began worrying about a job. Fortunately, Babuji was intelligent enough to have completed high school at his mother's bidding, otherwise he would have had to pay an exorbitant sum for becoming a virtuous person.

After two months of running ragged looking for a job, he found employment in an office as a clerk with a salary of thirty rupees a month and was satisfied that now he need not worry about food and shelter. He would go to the office and spend the rest of his time in the company of the elders in the neighbourhood, listening to their advice and good counsel. His neighbours, meanwhile, began to worry about other things; in other words, they were anxious to keep him within the bounds of decency by arranging his marriage. Babuji made every effort to ward off their efforts, but these neighbours were a real problem; if someone treated them with the slightest bit of respect they would suddenly feel very powerful. In the end they succeeded in shackling Babuji in the chains of matrimony, and this despite the fact that they all knew that a man who resisted matrimony could never have a happy marriage. But the opposite occurred. The very same Babuji who protested that marriage was not for him, fell madly in love with his wife. Everyone who knew them envied him. When the women in the neighbourhood fought with their husbands they cried and lamented that their husbands could not love them the way Babuji loved his wife, and when mothers prayed for appropriate husbands for their daughters, each entreated that God bless her daughter with a husband like Babuji. And why should such prayers not be offered? How grandly Babuji's wife was treated. Babuji might go without, but he provided the best food and clothing for his wife. If she was unwell he would offer special prayers for her recovery, and immediately send for the *hakim* or the doctor. She would be made to lie down, and Babuji would proceed not only to massage her head, but also rub her feet. He would feed her a special diet with his own hands, and run for the medicines she needed, and he fainted from shock if ever her condition worsened. But in spite of all this love and care his wife always looked disgruntled. She always wore a sour expression on her face, cried secretly and cursed Babuji for no reason at all. But Babuji's love was such that none of this made any difference to him.

This was the same Babuji who had once lifted a wooden stick to strike his mother. The entire neighbourhood had condemned him; this kind of behaviour was not proper for upstanding, decent families. May she have a place in heaven, the poor widow, she did not have the good fortune to see her son change his ways or make a single penny. And how could she have any good fortune? Good fortune was meant for Babuji's wife only. But Babuji received his reward for causing his mother such anguish. He got a wife who was so ungrateful that after each prayer she cursed the people who had arranged this match for her. She never had a kind word for her husband and she never thanked God for her good fortune.

She had been penniless. Her parents passed away when she was a child and she was raised by an aunt who treated her badly. She, whose face was like the moon, would always be in shabby, dirty clothes. And now all her problems were over. But she didn't understand any of this. When she was blessed with a loving husband, she lost her mind. As for Babuji, there was nothing that could stop him for waiting hand and foot on his wife. Not only did he take very good care of her when she was sick, he was also extremely attentive otherwise. When he came back from the office he would ask her to put aside the housework and sit with him. Sometimes he massaged her fair-skinned hands, stroked her arms, or just played with the locks of hair on her forehead. While she reclined calmly, he would be seated next to her, talking to her, smiling. But on such occasions too, his wife would sigh, show displeasure, and shake off his hands. He would plead with her to eat more, fanning her with one hand as he placed morsels of food in her mouth. What husband will love his wife like this? There have been extremely loving husbands who have been known to have their wives polish their shoes for them, who will stubbornly impose their will on their wives so that the poor women cannot open their mouths to protest. But Babuji's wife—*uff!* Whatever she uttered was like a commandment from God. And if the wife's demeanour is one of extreme displeasure despite all this, well, that's her misfortune then.

Several of the people in the neighbourhood suspected that Babuji's wife had a secret lover which was why she wasn't at all happy with Babuji, while others felt that she was unhappy because she didn't have children. Some went so far as to suggest that she was barren, because it only takes nine months for a child to appear and this wretch had been married for two years and she had not produced anything.

This was the opinion held by people. Babuji's wife, on the other hand, entertained no regret about not having had a child, and what else was in her heart only God knew. She was so secretive she never shared with anyone else what was in her heart. She was unsociable toward the women in the neighbourhood. They came often to see her, but they spent all their time praising Babuji. Now wasn't that something that would upset just about anyone? For this reason she didn't speak amiably to any of the women.

Babuji's neighbour hated Babuji's wife. She was waiting for Babuji to leave his wife so she could hand him her daughter who was as comely as a star. So what if he had once indulged in excess? All men do a bit of it when they're young. Youth is a time of madness, anyway. The only thing that went wrong was that Babuji began committing during boyhood those excesses that one reserves for adulthood; to be sure, if he had committed these acts in moderation during adulthood who would have pointed a finger at him today? And in truth, since Babuji had changed his ways, everyone had grown to love him and showed him consideration. Never would he cast a dishonourable glance at any girl or boy in the neighbourhood, and he always took part in sorting out any problem that his neighbours were beset with. It was no crime, therefore, for his neighbours to have sympathy for him.

The women in the neighbourhood were so impressed with the splendour that they saw in the lives of Babuji and his wife that for hours after their return from the couple's house they talked of nothing else.

'Babuji's wife was wearing a suit of 'the heart's thirst.'

'Look, even the very rich can't have the kind of high living that they have.'

'And this time she was wearing solid gold bracelets. I wonder where Babuji gets the money for all this. It's said he is heavily in debt.'

'That may be, but just look at the way he loves his wife. If it had been me I would have washed his feet in gratitude for my entire life.'

And hundreds of other comments like this were exchanged.

As for Babuji's friends, they wouldn't leave him alone either. They made sarcastic remarks about his passionate love for his wife and complained that he had neglected his friends.

'Look my friend,' a friend would say, 'You've become your wife's slave. Why don't you show us your face sometimes?'

'You know, there's just no time after I get back from the office,' Babuji would say in his defence.

Another friend would not hesitate to make a cynical reference to Babuji's childlessness. 'And why hasn't *Bhabi* produced anything? We have been waiting for sweets for such a long time.'

'Yes, yes, you'll have sweets of course, whenever it's God's will.' Lowering his head, Babuji would smile sheepishly.

Babuji was married now for four years but there had been no offspring yet. There was no limit to the dismay felt by the people in the neighbourhood because of this. The women now openly proclaimed that his wife was barren, she wasn't going to have a baby. 'Ah, who would be the head of Babuji's house after he was gone? What a misfortune, his line would end.' All this talk finally reached Babuji's wife and she became extremely agitated and cried until her eyes were swollen. She prayed that the people who had arranged this match be cursed, for herself too she prayed for a dog's death, and for three days she continued to quarrel violently with Babuji. But what a man he was. In her presence he behaved like a thief who had been caught red-handed and as soon as she was somewhat calm he ran out and bought her a delicate gold ring, believing as he did that now he had enslaved her. But contrary to Babuji's expectations, the situation worsened. Her dissatisfaction grew until her anger and her melancholy took the form of illness. *Hakims* and doctors were ushered in. Babuji began to dash to the drugstore. But her condition deteriorated. The poor man had already lost weight due to anxiety and concern for his wife's condition; he even began to have fainting spells. He wanted to hire some help at this time to ease the situation somewhat, but when one needs something it is often impossible to find it. Despite the assistance of neighbours, no woman could be found and finally Babuji arranged to obtain the services of a boy called Rahim.

Rahim was almost a young man and at first Babuji hesitated to have him work in the women's quarters. But his beautiful, ailing wife was tossing and turning on her bed and Babuji couldn't sit at her bedside and cook and clean at the same time. So he was forced to hire Rahim.

Although Rahim was an outsider, yet who knows what great sympathy had overwhelmed his heart because he happily and energetically tackled all the work in the house. Not once did anyone hear him complain. The moment Babuji left the house to get medication for his wife, Rahim would stop whatever he was doing to come and take his master's place. He would massage his mistresses' head for hours and would not move until she forced his hands away from her head. In fact, Rahim looked after her more diligently than any relative could have.

Gradually, with God's help, Babuji's wife's condition improved and Babuji felt as if he had suddenly acquired all the treasures in the universe. But, no one knows why, the more she recovered and the greater her happiness, the more Babuji was overcome by despondency. He should have been happy that the wife, whose face always wore a sullen expression, was now budding with joy. There was a spring in her step, which had once been sluggish, her eyes shone, and instead of constantly griping about housework, she was now always seen giving Rahim a helping hand. So what was the cause of his despondency?

When Babuji returned from the office and saw his wife working alongside Rahim, his sadness would grow. After changing his clothes he would fall on his bed and gaze longingly in the direction of the kitchen. But she, oblivious of everything else, assisted Rahim spiritedly, ate *paan* from the *paandan* every now and then, and also offered *paan* to Rahim who chewed the *paan* slowly, deliberately. If she remembered to, she would send Babuji a *paan* as well. Babuji took the *paan*, but how could he enjoy it? *Uffoh*! He tossed on live coals when he saw Rahim's reddened lips.

But in the kitchen the conversation continued on its lively course.

'If I could help it I wouldn't let you do any work,' she said, her eyes roving lovingly on Rahim's face which was ruddy from the heat of the fire.

'Babuji will turn me out in one day,' Rahim pointed in the direction of Babuji's prostrate form.

'*Hunh*! I don't care. I can't do all the work by myself, I've been so sick.' She tossed her head arrogantly and made a surly face.

'I'm your slave.'

'That's what I expect of you.' Her face glowed with happiness.

'Come here, I say.' Babuji, agitated by the sound of their murmuring, called out.

'What do you want?' She came to him reluctantly.

'Sit here, it's cooler here. You'll get sick sitting in front of the fire.'

'I don't need to be cool. In the kitchen I can keep my mind occupied.' She spoke in an irate tone.

'Your mind is occupied when you're at the stove and not when you are listening to me?' he retorted sharply.

'Listening to you?' She became enraged. 'What kind of talk do you have to offer? The same old things — I'll get you this when I get my salary, I'll get you that when I get my next pay. For four years I have been hearing all this. Will I never get tired of it all?'

'I'm not saying you shouldn't cheer yourself,' he said in a subdued tone. 'But look, all I'm trying to say is that you shouldn't let Rahim feel too important, he's a servant after all.'

'So what's wrong with that? If you speak two kind words to the servants you'll get more work out of them.' She broke into a laugh and returned to the smoky kitchen.

'Oh God, let Rahim die,' Babuji prayed in anguish. Quietly. Just as helpless women do.

The wife's happiness grew and Babuji began drowning in sorrow. Finally the neighbours began worrying about him and they were sure that he was like this because he did not have children and on top of that he had to tolerate the continuous presence of a sullen-looking, disgruntled wife.

'Son, why don't you get treatment for your wife? Your hearts will be pacified if you have a child.' An elder in the neighbourhood offered serious advice.

'Yes, I now plan to have her receive treatment.' Babuji lowered his head in absolute deference. The elder proceeded to give him the name and address of a holy man who would give him an amulet to tie around his wife's arm. But Babuji did not go to the holy man, nor did he take his wife to be treated for her barrenness. Instead, he pored over magazines and newspaper advertisements and began sending away for mail-order drugs. Parcel after parcel arrived. The neighbours were astounded when they discovered the cost of these parcels. '*Uffoh!*' they exclaimed. 'Only Babuji, besotted by his love for this barren woman, could be spending money like water.' But who could guess that Babuji was so selfish that he did not allow his wife to touch a drop of the drugs that arrived daily. He emptied all of the bottles himself, gulping down the syrups as if they were a sweet drink.

Another year passed and the neighbours' desire to have sweets and their hope that the mail-order drugs would do Babuji good, remained unfulfilled. But one day Babuji jumped in amazement. Perhaps it was the effect of all those drugs. His yellowed face turned red and glistened. His lean frame shook like a bamboo stick.

'What is this?' He pulled himself up like a wrestler.

His wife recoiled fearfully and the *dupatta* across her chest slipped down to her stomach.

'Speak! What is this?' He pointed to her stomach as if he were about to lunge at her with his fist.

'It's what you think it is,' she said, picking up courage, and for some reason Babuji's face fell.

'Didn't you think I would have become pregnant after you treated me with all those drugs for so many days?' Seeing Babuji slacken, she assumed a brazen tone.

'May you die,' Babuji cursed her as if he were a helpless woman.

'It's difficult to die like this. Yes, first I'll make you the father of a little boy and then we'll see. I say, let's hope that while people are accusing me they don't discover the truth about you.' She laughed in derision.

Babuji's flushed face became pale again and his eyes filled with tears.

'Listen...' Her heart melted at the sight of his tears. After all they had been together for four years. If nothing else she did have the love for him that one may have for someone living in the same house.

'We should both die... I was helpless... and...' Overcome by emotion and compassion for Babuji she couldn't continue and fell on her bed, sobbing.

A few months later...

The entire neighbourhood was buzzing because of the newcomer's noisy arrival.

'Congratulation on your son's birth, this is all due to our prayers.' The elders of the neighbourhood were the first to surround Babuji and he lowered his head bashfully.

# Bhooray

Something had happened to Bhooray's wits. Everyone agreed on that score. But Miss Lall Khan, House Surgeon, believed that nothing was the matter with him because he performed all his duties well and that if he became restless at the sound of the bell at the front gate then that was due to some emotional factor.

Nearly everyone had questioned Muhammad Bhooray about his condition, but he would merely grin broadly in response and laugh as if he were mocking his interrogators. Miss Lall Khan attempted to gain information from Bhooray in a confidential manner, but he carelessly brushed off her sympathy and sincerity, thus isolating himself. Finally Miss Lall Khan also came to the conclusion that he did experience some sort of mental imbalance which was brought on by the sound of the bell but the condition was temporary and therefore he was harmless and should be allowed to remain at his job.

Muhammad Bhooray remained at his job, but no one could ever discover what the story was that Bhooray didn't want anyone to know, nor did anyone guess that he lived in anticipation of a very happy ending to that story. The story goes like this:

A *mohajir* from Sitapur, Muhammad Bhooray had been working at the Hospital for Women's Diseases for nearly eight years. His duties included keeping an eye on the telephone used by house surgeons and members of the training staff. Another telephone, which was located on the other side, was reserved for use by patients and their families. Since anyone could deposit two annas in the box and make a call, there was always a commotion at this telephone. The *chaprasi* at this phone often delivered phone messages to the private patients and received tips from them, making quite a bit of money this way. Bhooray, however, stayed away both from this type of income and this telephone and had never wished to be transferred here. Screams from the delivery room nearby could be heard very clearly and the people in that area seemed to be constantly agitated. On his side, in the veranda with the high arches, peace reigned. Perched in the branches of the trees in the expansive lawn across from him, birds chirped. In summer the hot breezes cooled by the time they travelled to the veranda. In winter the crisp, bright sunshine lolled about for an hour or two in the veranda, and during the rainy season when rain fell in torrents, sometimes the spray crossed over through the arches and wet Bhooray's feet. The silence that prevailed here had other uses as well. Here he could freely flirt with the young *ayahs* and daughters of old *ayahs*. Having seen Sunday film matinees with regularity, he was now adept at the ways in which flirtations could be conducted.

Even though Bhooray spent half his salary on gifts, he was still able to live a comfortable, happy life. The only thing missing was that like the heroines in films, his lovers did not love him nor were they faithful to him; instead, like the shrews in films, they were disloyal and heartless. He knew that these women accepted gifts from others as well and there was no doubt in his mind that they were rotten to the core. For this reason he had not married until now nor had he experienced any need to do so. After he became a *mohajir,* the idea of marriage became a blur in his mind. It is said that when a monkey gets wet it decides to build itself a home, but Bhooray was a human being and could save himself from getting wet. Why then would he think of building a home? Actually, Bhooray wasn't averse to the thought of marriage, but the kind of pure and loving woman who is needed for a wife, hadn't crossed his path as yet. And so, he was happy and satisfied with his life. He had all the comforts that someone in his position could ask for and his job was going well too. All day long he sat in the old, soiled chair and received phone calls or sang songs. When he was in Sitapur he and his friends used to sing folk songs to the accompaniment of a brass plate. His friends praised his flat voice and it was this very praise that pursued him to this day. He hated new film songs because he couldn't imitate their complicated tunes and his voice failed him when he tried to sing these difficult compositions, so he stayed with the old songs that he loved so much. It was ten years since he had left Sitapur, but he had not forgotten those songs.

He was completely alone in Lahore. His parents had died when he was in Sitapur. Only an aunt remained who had raised him and who had stayed behind in Sitapur. She had replied to only one of his letters. He wrote repeatedly afterward, but never got another reply from her which led him to believe that the old woman had died. If you nurse sorrows they grow and bother you later, but if you stifle them as soon as they are created you are free. Bhooray was the type of person who had similar notions, but since he had been attacked by love his world had changed and the daughter of the dark-complexioned nurse endlessly swayed her hips before him, but Bhooray didn't bring her a gift. He was so disheartened that he didn't throw a single amorous glance at her or at any of the others and when they tempted him with the idea of a nightly visit, he pretended to be deaf. Who will run after you forever for a measly sum? Finally the women, regarding him as crazy, left him alone.

When he rejected Zahooran the first time he didn't feel anything on the surface, but when she walked away from him dejectedly Bhooray felt as if a thorn had lodged itself close to his heart.

He began singing to elevate his spirits:

'If I hadn't fallen in love I wouldn't be a stranger
Sitting among flowers, I would be enjoying the breezes—
Hmmm...hmmm...hmmm...*arre*,
I have gained notoriety because of you.'

Sighing heavily, he stretched out on the dirty old chair. Where the hell were all those women who usually came to use the phone? He glanced at his second-hand watch. It was ten o'clock. Why, the classes were still in progress. 'You're always in such a hurry, Mr. Bhooray—it's still early.' He smiled rakishly. It wasn't possible for Bhooray to aim high while sitting so low, but who can command a person's gaze? He found pleasure merely in looking at the women who came to make calls.

Many of the faces he had seen floated before his eyes. He stretched out his legs happily and closed his eyes, but feelings of sadness and tedium gripped his heart again. The old images failed to provide the satisfaction they always did. He started singing once more:

'Breezes come from your neighbourhood,
A thousand punishments for love are meted out,
Hunn...haaa...hmm...
I have gained notoriety because of you..'.

Time had forced the third line from his memory.

'So what if she's gone? There are many more like her. Mr Bhooray, there's no shortage of women for you.' He tried to wave the flag of joy on a day marked by melancholy. How quiet it was on this side today. Bhooray didn't like his spot today. He thought he would be so happy if he were on the other side; there would be the constant noise of people coming and going in all directions, the constant screaming of women in labour. There, all these silly thoughts vanish in an instant, one's brain becomes addled and one begins to hate humankind. And how stubborn a woman is. How she screams when she is delivering a child, how deafening her screams are, how she avows she'll never have another child, and then, within a year, she appears in this hospital again with her bloated stomach. How strange all this is.

And a thought sneaked into Bhooray's mind from somewhere. 'If I had married Zahooran she too would be here one day and I would be at the door of the labour room listening to her screams all night. I wonder if I would have run away or listened—

screams tear the heart.' Bhooray heaved a long sigh. 'Who knows where she is. What a heart she had, such a big world and no one to respect her—how you spurned her, Bhooray!'

The bell went off with a loud noise. He realized that another female patient had come in. The *chowkidar* from the gate at the far end was walking toward him through the lawn. Bhooray sprang from his chair.

'Where are you coming from *badshaho*,' he said with a laugh as he extended his hand. He had learned a few Punjabi expressions which he mixed in with his own lingo from time to time. 'Let's have a couple of puffs together.' Bhooray took out a carton of Bagla cigarettes and extended it toward the *chowkidar*.

'*Yar*, you're in a fine position, sitting on a chair all day long,' the *chowkidar* said, exhaling smoke. 'A woman's body was taken past my gate just now. I felt really bad. The moment one woman left another one came in to deliver a baby.'

'Yes,' Bhooray said dully. He suddenly remembered that his mother had also died immediately after giving birth to him. His aunt had told him this. '*Yar*, these women are something else, aren't they?' Bhooray sighed. 'Sometimes men thoughtlessly get a woman pregnant. How she suffers.' Bhooray's heart was full. He was thinking of Zahooran again.

The whole world is crashing on her. She does it willingly I tell you, and a woman's so filthy.' the *chowkidar* shrugged in disgust and got up to leave. Then he spoke in a whisper, 'I've got a whole bottle of beer. If you like you can come over to my quarter tonight and I'll show you the moon and stars.'

Bhooray laughed and said nothing. He didn't like anything the *chowkidar* was saying at this moment. He kept thinking of his mother. How can his mother be filthy? And this business of drinking, well, he had too much one night and Miss Zaidi came in just then and he didn't even rise from his chair and continued singing, 'What kind of a shot are you, straighten your arrow first.' Miss Zaidi had given him a thorough scolding. 'What's the matter with you? I'll have to report you,' she had said.

'My friend made me drink Miss Sahib, please forgive.' Forgetting Urdu and the smattering of Punjabi and English words he knew, he slipped into his native tongue. Miss Zaidi started laughing and he burst into tears.

'Don't ever do this again, you're such a nice person Bhooray.' She made her phone call and left, but, afraid that she might report him, Bhooray remained tangled in a web of anxiety. However, instead of reporting him, Miss Zaidi made jokes at his expense and told everyone that Bhooray was trying to straighten her arrows.

His thoughts wandering, Bhooray turned his gaze to the scene in front of him. He heard the sound of steps on the stairs and he pulled himself up. This sound was a signal that someone was coming down to make a phone call. There were a lot of young female medical students and house surgeons on the top floor. He knew all their names and histories, he knew who was friends with whom, who called whom, who had been successful in love and who hadn't, who was crying the night before, whose eyes were swollen, who slept peacefully, whose lover was visiting, what films had been seen, and who was getting married when.

When Miss Lall Khan approached the phone with a smile on her face, Bhooray immediately got up from his chair.

'Hallo, is this Nasir? Hun, hun...no, no, oh, what kind of talk is this? All right, you must come tomorrow, *Khuda hafiz*.' Miss Lall Khan's face was red and a dreamy look floated in her eyes.

After Miss Lall Khan left Bhooray, closed his eyes again. 'Everyone is the same Bhooray, but when will Zahooran come?' When she came he would clasp her to his breast. Oh! Where did this thought come from? Why was he thinking of her?

Rakhi *ayah*'s daughter was walking toward him with a special air. Bhooray looked at her with interest. She came and stood next to him with a bashful expression on her face. Bhooray looked around him and then slipped his arm around her waist.

'You haven't gone shopping yet—when will you get the fabric for me?' She spoke coquettishly.

Bhooray pinched her solid flesh. 'I'll bring it soon dear.'

Someone was approaching from the direction of the veranda. The girl moved on as if she had some important task to take care of and Bhooray suddenly felt invigorated. He sighed in satisfaction and sprawled in his chair again. He decided that tomorrow he would get something for the *ayah*'s daughter. The memory of the girl's body produced a pleasurable sensation in his fingers.

Once again the loud echo of the bell rose in the air and instantly dissipated the feelings of pleasure he had cultivated with such difficulty. His spirits fell. He thought again of Zahooran. His eyes travelled to the pillar which stood some distance from his telephone. It seemed to him that Zahooran was still lying down next to it.

It was a rainy afternoon. The air was still and the humidity was stifling. Half-asleep, Bhooray was languishing in his chair. Suddenly he felt someone walking past him on tip toe. He opened his eyes. Dressed in a striped blue shirt and mannish pajamas, a patient from the general ward was arranging a small mat next to the pillar. Bhooray had hoped it would be one of his girls, someone who would help him pass the time pleasurably. He turned his face away with indifference and shut his eyes again. Sometimes, distressed by the oppressive heat, the pregnant women from the general ward came out in the veranda and slept restfully in the airy, quiet atmosphere for a little while.

There were small pieces of clouds floating in the sky like swirls of dust on a roadway. On the lawn a pewit was pecking at the grass and far away an eagle flew off, its wings spread wide. This was when, unable to take the heat any more, Bhooray opened his eyes. His entire shirt was soaked in sweat. The woman was now sitting, her head resting against the pillar, her gaze pinned to the space in front of her. A few black clouds, travelling from afar, arrived on the sky. The woman started singing softly:

'Put down my palanquin under the tree, O traveller,
'The rainy season is come.'

Startled, Bhooray turned toward her; he felt she was singing for his benefit.

'I played with dolls in my father's house,
My beloved has sent the palanquin bearers.'

The woman's voice became louder but her head was still resting against the pillar. As a matter of principle Bhooray did not show any interest in the women who came to the hospital to deliver babies, but for some reason this woman had aroused his curiosity. Perhaps she would be fun, he thought. He lifted himself on his chair repeatedly, but because she was behind the pillar, he couldn't see her face. Bhooray cleared his throat so she could hear him. He forgot that his actions could be reported. He was certain that the woman was singing to attract his attention. After all, there had been other women in the veranda as well, all of whom would come groaning and sighing and immediately fall asleep. No one ever sang.

When she heard him clear his throat, the woman became so quiet that one would think she had indeed climbed into the palanquin and left for her beloved's house. For a few minutes she sat in the same position, her head resting against the pillar. Then, picking up her mat, she rose to her feet.

When she went by Bhooray she cast a disdainful glance at him. But instead of continuing on her way, she came to a sudden stop.

'*Arre*, are you the Bhooray from Sitapur?'

'And you are Zahooran, aren't you?'

Their eyes met restlessly. The woman pulled her *dupatta* down to her forehead bashfully and lowered her gaze. Bhooray jumped up from his chair and sat down again. He felt a blow to his heart.

Time rolled back. Bhooray's aunt had given a token gift to Zahooran's mother at Zahooran's birth to ensure Bhooray and Zahooran's engagement when they were older. When Zahooran was twelve she started smiling bashfully whenever she saw Bhooray. He, in turn, would swipe his hands across the downy stubble on his chin and laugh like an idiot. And when Zahooran was fifteen she would send missives through her friends telling Bhooray she was waiting for him, asking him when he would come to wed her. Bhooray was working hard and saving every penny so he could get married and bring home a wife who would help his aunt with housework. He was also attracted to Zahooran now. Around this time the country gained independence. Bhooray came to Lahore so he could earn millions and after many years of misfortune he found employment at this hospital. The colorful life of Lahore and a man with no one to think of but himself—Zahooran became a dream. And Sitapur? Well, what was left in Sitapur now? All day long clouds of dust hung over the streets, travellers slept in the shade of trees with their bundles under their heads as pillows while monkeys perched in the trees, rolling their eyes as they waited for the opportunity to snatch up the bundles. A few well-kept bungalows, one or two old-fashioned temples, a girls' college where one could hear spiritual songs late into the night. Who could remember this Sitapur?

But now that Zahooran was standing before him his heart suffered a blow. Zahooran belonged to someone else. He was shaken with sorrow at discovering she had been disloyal, she, whom his aunt had bought for him with a gift of an anna. What did it mean to be here at this hospital? Either that a baby had to be delivered or there was some other related problem that had to be taken care of.

'Why are you here?' Bhooray asked, desirous of confirming his suspicions.

But Zahooran did not speak. Her head lowered, she stood still. Then she lifted her eyes and after giving Bhooray a pained look, she turned her gaze toward the lawn where a sandpiper chirped noisily before flying off into the sky.

'It's going to rain, the sandpiper is making such a noise,' Zahooran said softly.

'*Hunh*.' Bhooray wasn't feeling that sorry any more. What did his aunt say? So what if one loses a little to learn who is to be trusted and who is not.

'Where is *Chachaji*, how is everyone?' Bhooray turned to everyday matters. Zahooran's scummy, yellowed eyes immediately filled with tears and she plopped herself down at his feet. She looked so tired and drained, as if she had been walking for miles, hungry, thirsty, with boils festering on the soles of her feet.

'*Amma* died from cholera as soon as we got here, two years later *Babuji* was run over by a truck and passed away. He was in the other big hospital for three days before he died.' She wiped her eyes with a corner of her *dupatta*.

Bhooray lowered his eyes. Despite everything he was sorry to see Zahooran in this condition. He wanted to say something, but no words would come. Centuries had passed but no single word had been invented that could lessen the pain of permanent separation.

The sound of high heels approached. Miss Razia was coming to make a phone call. He got up from his chair. Zahooran did not move.

'Who is this?' Miss Razia asked him as she picked up the receiver.

'She's from Sitapur, my village, Miss Sahib.'

Zahooran lowered her gaze. *Life in the city is nothing, in our Sitapur everyone knew what Zahooran meant to Bhooray*, Zahooran thought wistfully.

Bhooray sat down again after Miss Razia had left. He glanced at Zahooran who, her face lifted innocently, was looking at him in a strange sort of way. Then she started speaking slowly. 'When *Khala* got your third letter I started telling *Babu* he should leave for Lahore immediately. Without you Sitapur was like a wilderness, I missed you terribly. To this day I've kept the clothes *Amma* had made for my wedding, I never put them on. Babu looked everywhere for you in Lahore, but he couldn't find you. The city is teeming with people, but *Amma* used to say that if you look diligently you can even find God. *Amma* was right.' A smile hovered on Zahooran's lips.

'Don't talk like that now, you belong to someone else.' Bhooray felt irritated. *What* wiles *women have*, he thought, *what airs she's putting on.*

'You're saying this?' Zahooran shut her eyes in bliss. 'I'm yours Bhooray, body and soul.' She was trembling. A faint blush appeared on her pale face and Bhooray saw a young, flowery-complexioned girl in Sitapur, draped in a red *dupatta*, peering at him from behind a door. All at once he felt like drawing her into his arms.

Then he examined her closely. What's the use of taking this body and this soul, he thought. What's the use of remembering the past. 'Why are you in the hospital?' he suddenly asked.

Zahooran opened her eyes and began looking around her. 'Look, the sky is becoming overcast,' she said.

'Why do you hide the truth? Why don't you just admit that when I couldn't be found, your father gave you in marriage to someone else. Don't give me this *filmi* drama.' Bhooray spoke angrily.

'What do you mean?' She arched her neck arrogantly. 'Zahooran is not the sort of woman who would marry a second time. I've been married to you. It was for you that I left my village and lost my parents. If *Maa* hadn't come here she wouldn't have died of cholera and *Babu* wouldn't have been run over by a truck.' She started weeping. 'This has been forced upon me. After *Babu* died who was going to feed me? I had to work in the bungalows to keep myself alive, but these city *babu sahibs* are very bad. Every year I come here to this hospital and have abortions. Each time I die to live again. The *babu sahib* puts down the name of the cook or the steward with mine when I'm admitted. This time the cook said, "How long can this go on Zahooran, why don't you marry me, I'll take you far away from here." But how could I do it?' Sobs racked her body. She spoke between sobs. Now I've found you Bhooray, now I won't go anywhere. Look how raw my hands are from scrubbing pots and pans.' She extended her hands helplessly. Her palms were pitted with callouses formed by endless toil and labour. She placed her head down on her knees and sobbed violently.

Silently, as if she were a stranger, Bhooray watched her weeping. All the love and jealousy he had experienced earlier were dissipated. What connection could he now have with this Zahooran, he wondered. There were so many others who were in constant pursuit of him, his every wish had been fulfilled. He had never imagined that a woman like this could ever be his wife and now Zahooran, who had borne God knows how many bastard children, had returned to torment him with past memories.

Finally Zahooran stopped weeping and dried her tears. Perhaps she was thinking that Bhooray would tell her to stop crying, wipe her tears with his silk handkerchief, would comfort her.

After she had wiped her tears she pinned her gaze on him. Bhooray tried to avoid looking at her. How could Zahooran possibly become Bhooray's wife? Bhooray, who reigned over the veranda and the telephone. If only Zahooran could see how grandly he picked up the receiver and said 'Hello,' and how so many women pursued him all the time.

'Then you should marry that cook Zahooran,' Bhooray offered sympathetically. 'What will people say if I marry you?' He looked about him cautiously.

'What? You're saying this?' Her eyes widening, she stared at him in astonishment. Then she got up. '*Hunh*! I'm not like you. I swear that I will never marry again.' She shook her head haughtily. 'Zahooran will be yours for the rest of her life and she'll deliver other men's babies in this very hospital. This is all a game of fate, Bhooray.'

Tears welled up in her eyes again and once more she wept bitterly. But then she wiped her tears and stood straight. Her frail body was trembling. '*Maa*, may she rest in peace, used to say "Zahooran you can even find God if you search carefully." I wonder why people say such things.' She lowered her head despondently. For a few moments she stood still. Then she gave Bhooray such a look that he felt as if his heart was being crushed in his chest. But by the time he decided to say something,

Zahooran had already walked away from him, her slight frame flailing the air as she left.

Bhooray gazed for a long time at the corner of the veranda around which Zahooran's form had disappeared. The ringing of the telephone startled him.

'Miss Zaidi is on leave, she's not here,' he said, lying for the first time while on duty.

The day marking Zahooran's rejection passed slowly and without event. He tried to sing:

> If I hadn't loved you, I would not be a stranger to you
> I would be seated among flowers, roam in the garden.

But his spirits were dampened. In the evening, after work, his steps led him to the general ward. The *ayah* told him that the woman he was inquiring after had already been released and had left the hospital.

So what if she had left? Why had he come enquiring about her? Bhooray asked himself, and while he was returning from the ward he again tried to sing spiritedly, but couldn't. A wave of despair engulfed him and instead of roaming about he came to his room and flung himself on his bed.

When darkness spread, the Zahooran of Sitapur with her red *dupatta* peered at him from behind a half-open door. Bhooray was shaken to the core. He rose and, putting up the chain on his door, he spurned Zahooran once again.

It was raining heavily outside. Someone was knocking furtively on the door. Bhooray thought he was imagining the sound. He swore heavily at himself, and, turning on his side, pulled the covers over his face. He had completely forgotten that a few days ago he had invited the *jamadarni's* seventh daughter to his room and now, standing outside his door, she was wringing her soiled and only suit of clothing while knocking impatiently on his door. Every cruel drop of rain fell with a tinkle like a rupee, taunting her.

Tired of getting soaked, the seventh daughter broke into tears in pain and as she was leaving, she cursed Bhooray. 'May he die, may his corpse be carried away—he had promised to give me a rupee and now he's acting like he doesn't know anything about it.'

And then this is what happened: the impressions of that day and that night became permanently etched in Bhooray's consciousness. Again and again he shrugged Zahooran's thought from his mind, he gave the *jamadarni's* seventh daughter three rupees instead of one, he also bought the dark-skinned nurse's daughter fabric for a blouse, and whenever he wasn't doing anything he sang spiritedly, but it is said that what is carved in stone cannot be erased. Zahooran's love was slowly transformed into writing on a stone. *Bhooray, I'm yours, I swear I will never marry someone else, I'll live for you and continue to deliver other men's babies in this hospital—*

Then the rains came and were gone. Winter ran its course. Spring turned its face away and when summer returned Bhooray counted nine months on his fingers.

That day when the *chowkidar* at the gate rang the bell to announce the entry of a pregnant woman, Bhooray jumped excitedly to his feet. Taking a short cut through the veranda he arrived at the spot where the *ayahs* brought stretchers out to carry the women inside. The bell rang several times during the day. Women came and went. But there was no sign of Zahooran. He thought that these things do take time after all and, returning to his room, he sang cheerfully:

By God's grace those who have been separated will meet again.

May and June also came to an end, but Bhooray waited without respite. Miss Lall Khan jilted her lover to marry someone else and left the hospital. Miss Zaidi had found a better position in another hospital. Many of the young women in the hospital had departed and many new ones had come in their place. The seventh daughter of the *jamadarni* in the general ward ran off with somebody. But Bhooray did not concern himself with any of this. He had collected all kinds of things for Zahooran in his quarter. Among them was also a red bridal suit.

It was cloudy today. The thirsty sandpiper screamed as it flew off. A small mat tucked under her arm, Zahooran was making her way toward the veranda. Bhooray rubbed his eyes. When will Zahooran come? When will she come? He counted on his fingers again. It was exactly twelve months now.

How was Bhooray to know that the woman who had arrived on a tonga last month with her face covered by a red *chaddar* of rough cotton, and whom the *ayahs* had transferred onto the stretcher with great difficulty, was Zahooran, Zahooran who had given 'Tameezan' as her name and who had died from excessive loss of blood, and how was he to know that the husband appointed by the *sahib* who was with her had left her corpse for the medical students.

It was exactly twelve months. Bhooray told himself that she would be along any day now, tomorrow if not today. He calmly stretched his legs and began singing cheerfully:

By God's grace those who are separated will meet again.

# Lost and Found

If it were just a question of his own life he would strike his head against a stone and free himself of all his woes or get rid of life as if it were garbage. But he had to consider the three other lives that were strung around his neck like a necklace. And Rafique avowed that he wouldn't let a single bead from the necklace fall off.

When they were young, he and his wife had pleaded for a child to illuminate the darkness of their house, but their prayers were not answered. And when youth was about to disappear as if it had been a momentary catastrophe, they began to lose faith in prayers and their effect. When the neighbours saw Rafique so despondent, they explained that prayers had the power to melt even a stone and when he heard them talk like that, he thought, irately, that it would be better to strike his head against a stone than to pray any longer. Sometimes when he saw children playing in his neighbourhood, he would lift them up in his lap, kiss them and then suddenly drop them from his lap as if he were throwing them down. The all-consuming desire for a child had caused him to lose interest in the world around him and just then, when he was feeling dejected and the sight of children playing in the street had begun to irritate him, his wife bashfully stuffed a corner of her *dupatta* in her mouth and told him that their prayers had been answered. Having been blessed once with the outcome of prayers he was quite satisfied, but when the following year his prayers bore fruit again he was beside himself with joy and jumped up and down like a child. He fell before God and thanked Him. Because the children were such a great source of happiness for him, he didn't even think about his monetary troubles. He didn't even give consideration to the fact that with age his body was also becoming slack—a lifetime was needed to raise these young lives and bags full of money were needed to live that lifetime.

When he was young he had worked hard and he and his wife had saved a goodly sum of money which was now being used up because work was so scarce. The savings could have taken them through a whole year if they spent it generously, but his wife, who had foresight, had stretched it to last them until now by eating less grandly and spending more wisely. She suffered all kinds of hardship, but never breathed a word to her husband. She knew how Rafique had toiled in his search for a good job and how his body was racked by arthritis. Perhaps that was why she didn't say a word to him. But what could she do now? They were drowning. She couldn't very well cook her good behaviour and feed it to the family. Finally she told her husband that the stove would remain cold tonight. Darkness assaulted his eyes the moment Rafique heard this and in the darkness he thought he saw witches dancing.

When he left his quarter and came outside, he saw swirls of smoke rising from the chimneys of adjoining quarters. He felt his heart constrict. What could he do? If he couldn't provide a meal for his children today he would never again put a morsel of food in his mouth. He ran his gaze helplessly all around him. Several of the people living in this compound knew him, but none of them was his friend. Then again, he had never asked for a handout which was why he couldn't go and beg a shopkeeper for flour or lentils on credit. The only person he knew well was Molla, the general merchant, and that too because every morning he would sit at Molla's shop and read the newspaper to him in broken Urdu. Molla couldn't read, but he never failed to buy the paper. He was very interested in abductions, burglaries, assaults, and the market's rates. He would beg someone or the other to read these news to him. Sometimes he would have to face disappointment because he wouldn't find anyone to read to him the newspaper he had just bought. Rafique enjoyed reading the paper and that was how the two had become friends. But, as chance would have it, Molla's shop was closed today. Rafique was sure that Molla would advance him something on credit. True, the shop was a very small one, but he wouldn't refuse altogether. Not only did Rafique read the newspaper to him, he also occasionally ran errands for him. So, filled with hope, he decided to wait for Molla.

Around ten o'clock Molla appeared to open his shop and handed Rafique the newspaper he had rolled under his arm. Rafique took the paper and sat down on the chair whose uneven legs had made it shaky and unstable. He started reading, but today he was distracted. He frequently stumbled over words and had to spell them out and after he was finished with the reading he flung his head down; a heavy silence followed, but Molla seemed not to notice anything. He finished dusting the small interior of his shop and then started examining his accounts notebook. After some time had elapsed, Rafique voiced his need. At first Molla was flustered by his request, but when Rafique convinced him that he would pay him by the end of the day, Molla weighed two *seers* of flour and one *pao* of *chana daal*, and as he put everything in a bag, he explained emphatically that his was a small business and he could not afford to extend credit for three or four days. Hearing him say this made Rafique recoil with shame, but what could he do? How could he bear to see his children starve? Who had the courage to deliberately rub off the shine from real pearls? He went home and, giving the bundle to his wife, he left the house to search for work.

After he had roamed about tormented by hunger and had looked desperately for work for three or four hours, he realized that it was no longer possible for him to feed his children. A proper means of livelihood would entice him, like a sweets shop, from afar. But, after great difficulty, he finally managed to find some work in the vegetable market, a job which involved transporting four baskets of vegetables to a shop half a mile from the market. He earned twelve annas. When he was transporting the last basket he felt as if his head was the horn of the buffalo which carries the whole universe on its tip; when the buffalo gets tired and shifts the weight to the other horn, the world suffers an earthquake somewhere and Rafique felt that if he took the basket off from his shoulders an earthquake of tears and hunger would ensue. The buffalo has at least two horns, while he had only one horn and he had no choice but to continue carrying his burden.

He gave Molla all of the twelve annas he had earned and returned home, his heart sick with grief. He had worked so hard and he couldn't even bring some sweets for his children. The moment he came home he fell down dejectedly on a loose-bottomed rope cot from which parts of the rope dangled like wisps of straw. This was the first time ever that his children had not seen him for an entire day. The moment they set eyes on him they began screaming with delight, climbed over him, jumped on his legs and his stomach, and making galloping noises, they demanded that he play horseback with him. But he was in no condition to carry them on his back and trot about the courtyard on his hands and knees. He just made some noises with his mouth to satisfy them and when they got upset he tried to explain to them that the horse had become old and old horses needed rest. Disappointed and angry, the children left him. He lay on the cot alone, staring at the sky where birds, spreading their dark wings, were flying off to their nests.

His wife probably knew what he was going through. She fired the stove with kindling without saying a word to him. He quietly squeezed his toes. The work he had done today had reactivated the pain in his joints.

At night he patted his children on the head as they lay sleeping beside him, and began talking to himself: 'I'll bring delicious candy for my sons tomorrow, I'll bring milk and cream—no, no, not milk and cream.' He grimaced and shut his eyes. His arthritis gave him no respite. But when his wife slowly started rubbing his feet, he finally fell asleep.

The next morning he purchased more flour and *daal* on credit from Molla. Today Molla didn't hesitate to extend him credit. Perhaps he was now sure that he would be paid back promptly. And that is exactly what happened. Rafique brought back a rupee this time from a day's work at the vegetable market. He handed twelve annas to Molla, bought candy for one anna, and then came home. Because he had carried an extra basket today, his joints ached, but still, he experienced a strange kind of exhilaration when he saw his sons sucking on the candy and his wife tucking away the remaining three annas in a corner of her *dupatta*. With no thought to his tired body, he tried to play horseback with his sons, but despite their prompting noises, he couldn't move and soon had to get them off his back. The boys were disappointed. Rafique tried very hard to explain that the horse was now very old and hence stubborn. 'You should sit on the horse,' he said, 'but you shouldn't expect the horse to trot because all old horses need rest.'

This was now his daily routine. Every morning he went to Molla's shop, read aloud all the news about abduction, theft, assault and strikes, dropped off at his house the flour and *daal* he had purchased from Molla that morning, and finally went off to the vegetable market. Unmindful of his physical limitations, he transported six baskets every day. Only after the burning, sun-filled day had come to a close did he get to set eyes on his home again.

But this situation didn't stretch beyond fifteen to twenty days. He suffered heatstroke one day, his knees swelled and he couldn't get up from his bed. In the delirium of his fever he kept talking about vegetable baskets and the money he earned. His wife, who had stepped out of the house until now only to socialize, was forced to wear her long *burqa* and make trips to Molla's shop and to the *hakim*'s clinic. The rest of the time she pleaded with God and lamented the appearance of this sudden catastrophe by shedding tears of woe. The children roamed about dolefully, distressed at the thought that no one was playing horseback with them any more. Gradually, in about fifteen days, Rafique's health improved.

During his illness Molla regularly gave them flour, *daal* and sago on credit. The medicines were purchased from the *hakim* with the money he had so painstakingly given his wife to tie up in a corner of her *dupatta*. The *hakim* would not extend credit.

If the patient died he would lose his fee. His motto was, 'Bring money if you need treatment.' And because Rafique had money, he was able to get better. But his debt toward Molla grew and the very thought of it sent shivers down his spine. When he was well again all he could think of was how he would pay Molla. There was still some swelling on his knees and he was so weak there was no question of leaving his bed right away. Nevertheless, he was quite sure than in a week to ten days he would be well enough to start his work at the vegetable market again.

A young man returns to good health in no time, but Rafique's sliding years and poor diet soon made him realize that his life was rapidly becoming worthless. A trip to Molla's shop to read the newspaper made him dizzy and the pain in his knees would become unbearable. On his return home he would lie down alone, with his face covered, and then, when he glanced at his children, the thought of their impending ruin made him break into uncontrollable sobs.

It was essential that he show up daily at Molla's shop. For one thing he had to assure Molla that his debt would be paid. If he sent his son instead even once, Molla would get quite upset. Rafique was now like the merchant's oil for Molla: whether you use it or not, at least keep it in front of you in a cupboard with a glass door. Actually Molla did not seem to be perturbed by the fact that Rafique owed him so much money. Rafique attributed this attitude to Molla's inherent decency and feelings of friendship. One day when he made a reference to Molla's integrity and the steepness of his own debt, Molla informed him that he was not in the least bit concerned about the sum that was owed him. When he was in trouble, Rafique would simply hand him his cottage; that's what friendship is all about—one must be forthcoming at the time of need.

Ever since Molla had shed his cloak of decency, Rafique felt as if his own clothes were about to be reduced to tatters, he imagined his wife sitting on the roadside, leered at by onlookers and he saw his children, frightened by the barking of dogs, seeking refuge in their mother's lap.

Today when he forced himself to go to Molla's shop for flour and *daal*, his gaze happened to stray to the 'Lost and Found' column and became fixed there. There was a reward of five-hundred rupees for anyone who found the lost child. He started to think that if he could find a lost child all his problems would be solved. He would save his cottage, which held the memories of better days, he would regain his lost strength, and for a while at least he would be able to provide well for his children. And soon he would be able to stand on his own feet. At this time his meagre diet prevented him from getting well. If only he could find a rich child. The report in the paper said that the father was not a very rich man and couldn't afford a reward of more than five-hundred rupees. What if the child he found belonged to a rich man? A man could give up anything for the sake of his offspring.

On his return home he presented the idea of the reward confidentially to his wife and also directed her to pray diligently.

It was not possible to find a lost child by staying at home all day so Rafique began roaming the streets and roads of the city. When he felt dizzy or the pain in his joints acted up, he would sit down somewhere for a while and rest. He looked closely at each child he saw, trying to gauge whether the child was frightened and apprehensive on account of being lost. He often did see a child alone and weeping, but before he could ask questions the child would go into a house or a shop, or the child's chaperon would appear suddenly and, hoisting the child on his shoulders, would walk away from there. Rafique would look at the child helplessly and sigh deeply in disappointment. Still, he knew that children are very naughty and sooner or later he would stumble on a child who, having run off from home and away from a chaperon, would be roaming the streets, lost.

Today when he was walking along a wide-open, clean road in search of a child, his steps led him to a house where a wedding seemed to be in progress. Tents had been set up in the garden and tables and chairs were being arranged under them. The band played and children, dressed in expensive-looking clothes, dashed about playfully. He stood at the gate and started thinking.

When his children were getting married he would have the musicians play the *shehnai*, he would feed the guests *pulao* and *zarda*, and have beautiful, expensive clothes made for the bride—yes, he would certainly have a jingling anklet made for the bride. He was lost deep in his reverie when suddenly Molla jumped into his thoughts like a ghoul. His knee-joints crackled and a storm of tears flooded his eyes.

He hadn't quite dried his tears when two young children ran out the gate in pursuit of one another. The boy, who was somewhat older, caught up with the girl and began beating her. Rafique rushed forward hastily and pulled them apart, but the boy, who seemed to have been overly pampered, succeeded in boxing the girl's ears even while Rafique was trying to push him away, after which he ran back in. Rafique lifted the sobbing girl and patted her. Gradually her sobbing ceased and she became quiet.

'What is your name, my child?' Rafique asked her gently.

'Tatti,' she said. She lisped so much Rafique couldn't understand what she was saying. He was still patting her head lovingly when suddenly the thought of abduction sneaked into his mind. What if he abducts this girl—but that would be wrong, his conscience berated him. The ghoul, Molla, lunged toward him, threatening to destroy him. Frightened, Rafique looked around him apprehensively. He felt as if everyone was staring at him, everyone was aware of his intentions. But when people continued on their way without paying attention to him, he held the girl close and dove into a *gulley*. Making his way through dark back streets, he arrived at his home. Her head resting on his shoulder, the little girl was soon asleep. The moment Rafique's wife saw him she ran toward him eagerly like a child.

'She was lost, wasn't she—where did you find her—it looks like she's from a rich family.'

'Yes, she was lost, she's from a very rich family.' He didn't want to tell his wife the real story. 'Come on, bring a clean pillow for the girl, make her comfortable and fan her, she's used to living in a house with electric fans.' Overwhelmed by happiness, he spoke in a loud, excited voice.

His wife ran into the storage room and got a pillow for the girl. Taking the girl from her husband, she held her for a few moments and then, setting her down on the bed, she began fanning her. Her two children were looking greedily at the girl's glittering dress.

'I'll get you clothes that are even prettier than this and I'll also buy you nice shoes,' Rafique said to his children as he hugged them both closely. Then he said to his wife, 'Stay with the child now, she might be scared when she wakes up. I'll go and get something for her to eat, we can't offer her the meagre food we have here.' With that he left the house in haste.

When he asked Molla for five rupees, Molla looked in the direction of Rafique's cottage and immediately handed him the money. For a long time Molla had been living with his wife in a rented house; the longing to have his own house discouraged him from refusing Rafique the money.

Rafique bought sugar, rice and milk for *kheer* and his wife fired the stove and began cooking the *kheer*. While the *kheer* was bubbling on the stove, Rafique dashed off to the bazaar again and purchased some sweets. The little girl woke up and began weeping. She would stop when he put a sugary-sweet morsel in her mouth, but soon, staring at everyone with a frightened look, she would burst into tears again. When the sweets were finished, he picked her up and proceeded to make strange noises to keep her still.

'Clap, both of you,' he told his children who complied by clapping hard. The girl became quiet, but started whimpering when the noise and the excitement ceased. The *kheer,* now ready, was placed before her and, forgetting her tears, she began eating contentedly while Rafique sat next to her, observing her lovingly. All at once he saw his own children standing nearby quietly and he got to his feet angrily.

'Why haven't you given my children any *kheer*? It's for them that ...' Suddenly silenced, he turned his gaze toward the sky. Smiling, his wife bought a plateful for the children.

'My poor girl was hungry, look how quiet she is now,' Rafique told his wife cheerfully.

'Yes, but I wonder if the dear girl even liked the *kheer*.'

'*Munee*, did you like the *kheer*?'

The girl nodded.

'What's your father's name?' Rafique's wife asked her.

'*Abba*,' the girl said, her lips quivering.

Both Rafique and his wife broke into a laugh.

'What does your father do?' Rafique said, trying to distract the child.

'He eats food,' the girl said, lisping.

Rafique laughed and lisped jokingly, 'Oh, so he eats, and drinks ice-water, and listens to the radio and gives his little girl sweets.' He put her down. 'Well, that's what important people do, eat when they get up, eat when they sit down, just eat all the time.' He looked at his wife as he spoke and burst into a laugh of merriment. Today even the pain in his joints was bearable. He was very happy. He didn't possess the riches as yet, but he would have them soon.

'Will my little girl play?' he asked her and she responded with a broad smile. He tucked in his *dhoti* and then, carrying the girl on his back, trotted all over the courtyard on his hands and knees. When, finally overcome by fatigue, he put her down, his knees were bleeding.

'It's all right, it didn't hurt me a bit,' he said to his wife when he observed the look of concern on her face and then, lifting a corner of his *dhoti*, he wiped the blood with it.

All day long the girl played with them, but the moment evening fell she wept again. His wife fed her sweet rice and then, taking her to the small room in the back, tried to sing her to sleep, but she wasn't going to stop crying nor did she, until, tired from the effort of weeping, she finally drifted into sleep.

The moment she was asleep silence invaded the house. The two boys were instructed to stay quiet and Rafique's wife sat by her bedside fanning her so she wouldn't feel hot. After all, she must have such comforts in her own home. As for Rafique, he circled the girl's bed all night. Tonight there was no peace for him.

If he received a reward of a thousand rupees all his problems would be solved. Rafique conversed with his wife in hushed whispers.

'How long do you think a thousand rupees will last?'

'We could spend five years eating just chutney and bread,' his wife said after some thought and then continued in a low voice. 'The children are now eight and nine and by then they will be old enough to take care of themselves, and your health will improve, you'll be able to maintain a good diet.'

'Yes, yes, that's true.' He edged closer to his wife. 'The monsoons are about to start, we should have the roof repaired otherwise both the rooms will collapse, and if the reward money is more than a thousand, we can have a new roof put in.'

'Yes, yes, the house will last a long time, our daughters-in-law will come to live here one day.'

'So I should tell the repairman that he can start work tomorrow. God is keeping watch over our house, how envious the bastard Molla will be.'

'Yes, you should tell him, but wait until tomorrow morning.'

'No, I'll tell him now, if I could help it I would have the repairs started this very instant. Molla, that bastard...' He got up and tip-toed out of the room.

After giving the repairman the word he returned home and quietly slipped into bed. But there was no sign of sleep. All night he tossed and turned and early in the morning he was stationed in front of Molla's shop. The shop was still closed so he waited.

As soon as Molla appeared with the newspaper tucked under his arm, Rafique came forward hastily and snatched the paper from him. Quickly he scanned all the headlines and then on the last page he found the report about the lost girl. There was a complete description, the address of the bungalow, and the report also said that the person who found her and brought her back would be rewarded. Rafique trembled as happiness overtook him.

After returning the newspaper to Molla, he made a demand for fifteen rupees. Molla made a face at first, but then handed him the money without saying anything. Money in hand, Rafique rushed home and whispered to his wife that the report about the missing girl was in the paper.

'How much is the reward?' his wife asked breathlessly.

'It just says that the person who finds her will be rewarded.' Looking up at the sky Rafique extended his hands and prayed. 'May Allah keep them happy.' After the prayer he shut his eyes and, a strange expression floating over his face, tears escaped from his eyes and slipped over his cheeks.

Rafique's wife quickly made breakfast for the little girl, bathed her, combed her hair and fed her.

Rafique put her in a *tonga*, told the *tongawallah* where to go and also instructed him to drive past a toy shop. At the toy shop he paid ten rupees for toys. The little girl was ecstatic when she saw so many toys and, collecting them all in her lap, she huddled over them protectively as if she was scared someone might snatch them from her.

When the tonga came to a halt in front of the bungalow, Rafique was awestruck. The bungalow was like a ship. Filled with a sense of joyful expectation, Rafique became unsteady on his feet. He got the girl out of the tonga and tried to hold her securely because, finding herself amidst familiar surroundings, she had begun to squirm in his lap. He hadn't gone half way across the garden when she slipped out of his grasp and ran toward the house, making strange noises as she got away from him. Rafique was about to run after her when a grand-looking car entered the compound and he stopped where he was. The girl disappeared into the house somewhere. Rafique was very disappointed that he would not be able to personally take the girl laden with toys to *Sahib bahadur*. Finally he sat down on the steps leading up to the house and waited.

He hadn't been waiting long when a man dressed in white clothes appeared.

'Are you the person who brought Tehmina?'

'Yes *Sahib*.' Rafique lowered his head deferentially.

The man broke into a laugh. '*Sahib bahadur* is inside and he has sent for you, I'm just his servant.'

'All right, brother, all right.'

'Move fast brother,' the man said impatiently when he saw Rafique dawdling. Rafique felt euphoric.

Rafique now found himself in *Sahib bahadur's* presence in a lavishly decorated room, such a room as he had never heard of or read about even in fairy tales. When *Sahib bahadur* glanced up and down at him, he felt his clothes were very dirty and he wished he had asked his wife to wash his clothes before he wore them this morning. It's not proper to appear before people of high standing dressed like this.

'Did you bring the girl?'

'Yes sir. I found her crying on the street and...'

'We're very happy with you, you have done us a great favour. The girl went to a wedding with our wife and there she wandered out of the house and—'

Rafique interrupted *Sahib bahadur*. 'Sir, I...I...' A sense of exhilaration caused his voice to flutter.

'The girl's father has been unconscious since yesterday from the shock of his daughter's disappearance. He's our cook. We were having problems in the kitchen because of that. You've been very kind. Here, take your reward.' Slipping a five rupee note in Rafique's hand, he disappeared behind the curtain.